10772428

CHRISTINE TELLACH

Beyond the Gallows

A Gothic Western Tale of Redemption and Love

First published by Mrs. Speech LLC 2024

First edition

ISBN: 979-8-9906153-7-3

This book was professionally typeset on Reedsy.
Find out more at reedsy.com

Contents

Playlist

It was hard to narrow down to a smaller list (I had over 200) but here are my favorites:

"God's Gonna Cut You Down" Johnny Cash

"Ain't No Grave" Johnny Cash

"Grave Digger" Blues Saraceno

"Evil Ways" (Justice Mix) Blues Saraceno

"Blood On My Name" The Brothers Bright

"Me and Mine" The Brothers Bright

"Just Won't Let Him Go" Robin Loxely

"Life of Sin" Nick Nolan

"Better Than Dying" ITG Studios, Dough Otto

"Go to the Light" Murder by Death

"Blaze of Glory" Jon Bon Jovi

"When It Rains, It Pours" Shawn James

"The Burnin'" Nik Ammar

"Fuga A Cavallo" Ennio Morricone

"The Gallows" Poor Man's Poison

"Walk with the Devil" Karliene

"My Wicked Bones" Var., Nick Nolan

"Symmetry of the Cemetery" Tombstone Three

"Ticking Bomb" Aloe Blacc

"The Wicked" Blues Saraceno

"Snake at the Window" Stomper, Lucy Tops

"Shot Down Like Jesse James" Ghost of Johnny Cash, Philip Bowen

"Death Don't Have No Mercy" Delaney Davidson, Marlon Williams

Full Playlist on Spotify: https://open.spotify.com/playlist/3qGPJ0HWEJLR
H5w2pfTNnB?si=657e88598dbe464c
   User: Love My Dog
   Playlist: Dark Country

Content Advisory

This is a Gothic Western novel and contains dark themes associated with this genre. This sensitive material may be triggering for some readers. To assist readers in making informed choices, please be aware of the following:

- **Violence and Death:** The book features violence and death with brief descriptions of moderate gore, mostly blood. There are two deaths of minor characters.
- **Attempted Suicide:** A character attempts suicide.
- **Animal & Child Endangerment:** Animals & children are placed in dangerous and possibly deadly situations. There are cases of mistaken deaths. There is a brief story of a past animal death.
- **Child Abuse:** The narrative discusses and includes memories of child abuse, both emotional and physical. It also alludes to past sexual abuse of a child.
- **Racism & Discrimination:** The book portrays mild/subtle depictions of racism and discrimination consisting of brief comments, labels, and mild differences in treatment, reflecting the attitudes of the historical setting.
- **Threat of Sexual Assault**: A main character is threatened with sexual assault but it does not move beyond verbal threats.
- **Kidnapping:** Adult characters are kidnapped in the course of the story.
- **Spice level:** Kissing only (and some poetry).

Our main characters go through a lot, but rest assured, there is a bright HEA!

1

The Itch

The itch was a rattler coiled tight in my gut, its rattle near to shakin' loose as my hands trembled from the need. Sweat ran down my face like a preacher's tears, stingin' my eyes, the strong breeze carryin' dust to settle on top.

Every body that shuffled past me on this dusty main street was a target, a potential poke at the darkness gnawin' at my insides. None of 'em, though, none of these hopeful rubes with their pockets full of dreams and spit, could offer the kinda relief I craved.

I needed a special victim. One that relieved that need to see Death once more. Just anybody wouldn't do. It had to be someone full of life, to watch Death take over.

Then my eyes caught on 'em. A young couple, all smiles and sunshine, loadin' their wagon with supplies like they planned on hunkerin' down and outwaitin' the devil himself. The woman, hair the color of bleached bone in this unforgivin' sun, laughed like a silver bell. Here were the perfect prey. I melted into the shadows like a coyote in tall grass, waitin' for its moment to pounce.

This town was a sorry sight, just a handful of shacks clingin' on for dear life under the relentless sky. The wind howled a lonesome tune through the skeletal branches of the cottonwoods, a mournful echo of the emptiness gnawin' at my own soul.

A long drag from my cigarette sifted deep into my lungs before I exhaled, sent a plume of smoke spiralin' skyward, a wraith dancin' with the desert wind. Soon. Every muscle in my body thrummed with a dark anticipation.

I kept track from the corner of my eye, waited until they were a goodly distance out of town, a cloud of dust followin' behind their wagon like a hungry ghost. Then, I tipped my hat and nudged my horse into a slow lope. Didn't need to rush this. Patience was a virtue, they say. In my life, though, patience was just another tool, just as sharp and deadly as the big knife strapped low on my thigh.

The aroma of horse and leather wafted up to me as the sun warmed us. It was familiar, somethin' I hardly gave a thought to most of the time. My senses always sharpened when I was on the hunt, the shakes and the gut burn of the itch fadin' as I narrowed my sights on my target.

Half a day's ride north, that's where they headed. Nice little place, well-kept. The kinda place a family might settle down, plant roots. But bad things happen, tend to follow like wolves after herd of deer.

I knew all too well about bad things. The world was a predator's playground, but I was no longer prey. I preferred to be the hunter, striking before the prey knew I'd been watchin'.

I rode a wide circle around the place, far enough they couldn't see me. Had to make sure no neighbors were close by. Women, they tend to get real loud when it all goes down. Early mistake, that was. First time, I misjudged things.

Still got the memory of Martha etched on my brain. I only knew her name 'cause I'd heard someone call her before I'd gone home with her, a shadow on her tail. She'd screamed, a skin-crawlin' wail that could've rattled the stars loose.

Messy. Real messy. Her blood, that unique metallic smell that drowned the itch with relief like a Baptist drownin' sins at the river, stainin' the floorboards like a spilled bottle of ink.

Nearly ended me right there. Too close to neighbors, I'd underestimated the power of a woman's scream. That fool farmer went for the sheriff instead of handling it himself. Lucky for me, I got her quiet and vanished before the posse rode in.

Took a week to lose them in the canyons. Came close to starvin', gnawin' on jerky that tasted like boot, sleep nothin' but snatches in the saddle, one ear twitchin' for the sound of pursuit.

Now, I knew better. An' I had to be on the lookout, rumors of a bounty hunter in these parts addin' to the threat of a posse. Didn't like the tables turnin' on me, so I did my best to lay low, slip under folks' notice.

These folks, though, they wouldn't know what hit 'em. Peaceful folks, they're like chickens in a coop at night. Just waitin' for the coyote to come stealin'.

I waited in the questionable shade of a mesquite, the lacy leaves no match for the Texas sun. Mid-October, I was still sweatin' despite the breeze, a lone buzzard circlin' overhead, as they arrived home, began unloadin' all them necessities they'd got from town, the woman chirpin' in oblivious bliss. I waited for just the right moment before I made my move.

I rode in as the man was bent double, hefting that shiny washer outta the back, blind to the danger. One shot, got him clean through the head. The fella never saw it comin'.

Shootin' ain't the same as the blade, though. Doesn't quite quell the itch. Still, gets the job done quicker most times. The scent of blood and somethin' darker, somethin' raw and fatal, filled the air as I hopped off my nag.

The woman screamed, of course. High-pitched, like a rabbit caught by a hawks talons. Didn't surprise me none. They all scream. Pointless, really. Nothin' but wasted air out here. I'd made sure there weren't no close neighbors to hear. Wouldn't want no interruptions.

She turned on me then, eyes wild like a cornered mustang. Tried to slam the door shut, but I was there quicker. Boot wedged in the crack, I pushed it open with ease. Ain't no lightweight, me.

And she, well, she was a wisp of a thing. Petite, pale, despite the sun that was always burnin' overhead, her blue eyes wide and watery. She smelled clean, laundered clothin' and woman.

She backed up against the wall, breath hitchin' in her throat. Fumbled for somethin', anything, I reckon. But there was nothin' but fear in those blue eyes, a fear so raw it almost made me look away. Almost. Seen that look a hundred times before. Freezes a body like a deer in a lantern beam.

This one, though… she was different. No tearful pleas, no cowering, even with the waterworks. She stood there, jaw clenched like a vise, and spat right at my boots. "How can you do this?" she rasped, her voice laced with a fury that burned brighter than the desert sun. "Don't you feel even a twinge of conscience? Doesn't the thought of judgment keep you awake at night?"

I stared at her, the smirk on my face faltering for a moment. Pity and regret? Useless notions I'd discarded a long time ago. Didn't understand why folks clung to such foolishness. Logic, that's what mattered. Cold, hard logic. Seems I was built different, born different. No room for those messy emotions clouding my purpose.

"Why would it bother my sleep?" I drawled, my voice flat as the desert plains. "It ain't like I lose any sleep over puttin' down a sick dog." My gaze drifted back to the man sprawled in the dirt, blood staining the ground a deep crimson.

Life one minute, gone the next. Blink of an eye, that's all it takes. Always fascinated me, that moment between livin' and dyin'. Like a door slammin' shut. All to nothin'. Black or white. Nothin' in between.

Then I looked back at the woman. Tears streamed down her face now, but her eyes held a spark that refused to die. Hated the cryin'. Made my head throb somethin' fierce. "Give me your valuables," I gritted out, the words like gravel, hard and sharp.

She spat again, defiance spittin' out with the spittle. "Not a chance in hell!"

I sighed. Always somethin'. Wouldn't they learn? Their little tantrums wouldn't change a thing. Just wasted time. Made a mess of things. Some folks begged. Begged for their lives like a whipped cur. Didn't make no difference in the end.

"Hope you burn in hellfire!" she snarled, her voice shaking with a righteous fury.

"Ain't no such thing," I scoffed. Didn't believe in no pearly gates or fiery pits. Just life and then… nothin'.

The glint of my blade caught the sunlight as I drew it slow. A crimson bloom blossomed on her throat, stainin' the pale skin a vibrant red. Beautiful, really. The color of life, drainin' away.

I savored the metallic tang in the air, the way her breath hitched, the slow glaze creepin' over her eyes. Didn't pierce the windpipe, just a nick on the side. Wanted to make it last a spell.

She clawed at her throat, a strangled sound escaping her lips. Slid down the wall, leavin' a crimson streak behind. The blood pooled around her, and I dipped a finger in it, holdin' it up to the light. The warmth seeped into my skin, a temporary balm for the itch gnawin' at my insides. Lifeblood. Fresh, sweet. There was nothin' quite like it.

"Curse you," her voice was a whisper, fadin' like an echo in a lonely canyon.

Somehow the next words came to me like they rode on the wind.

"…haunted by the ghosts of your deeds," I finished in a low murmur, without any conscious thought, like I was some puppet in a show. I studied her eyes, the windows into the soul, some said.

The anger that had her spittin' at me had dimmed, replaced by a dull horror, but a touch of something else remained - a spark of stubbornness, a refusal to completely surrender. It annoyed me.

She was different, that much was clear. Most folks crumpled at the first sight of steel, their bravado melting faster than butter on a hot griddle. This one, though… she clung to that spark like a lifeline.

The woman's gasps went shallow, her fingers slippin' off the wall like a lizard losin' its grip on a hot rock. The world seemed to hold its breath, the only sound that pesky fly buzzin' like a rusty hinge around her head. The crimson stain on her throat bloomed brighter, and the fear in her eyes… well, that was somethin' else entirely.

Not fear, not completely, but a defiance that chilled me to the bone. A morbid curiosity gnawed at me. What made her so different? Was it some God-fearin' faith, a belief in a life beyond this one that fueled that fire in her eyes even as she faced the big sleep? Or somethin' else entirely?

A memory flickered in my mind like a campfire spark in a dusty wind. A younger me, no more than a scrawny kid, staring down at a lifeless rabbit caught in a rusty trap. There was no fear in the creature's vacant eyes, just a stillness, an absence.

Even then, something about that empty look had fascinated me. Maybe… maybe that's what I craved. Not just death, but the complete absence of anything after. The ultimate silence.

The woman's chest gave a final shudder, her body slumping lifelessly to the floor. The spark in her eyes had winked out, replaced by a hollowness that mirrored the emptiness I craved. But for the first time, the kill didn't bring the usual satisfaction. Instead, a disquieting emptiness settled in me, a hollowness that the blood couldn't quite fill.

I knelt beside the body, my finger tracing the crimson stain on her throat. A strange thought slithered into my mind. Maybe… maybe this defiance, this spark of life she clung to, was what I was truly missing. A new and disturbin' notion, one that sent goosebumps pricklin'.

With a snort of disgust, I pushed the thought away. No. Couldn't be. I was a creature of logic, not fancy feelings. This was just the aftermath, the usual melancholy that followed the thrill of the kill, the blood goin' stale. It would pass. It always did.

2

Bounty Hunter

I poked around the house, neat as a pin, lookin' for their stash. Most folks had a hidey-hole, some secret place they thought kept their valuables safe. Usually, findin' it ain't no harder than shootin' fish in a barrel - behind the stove, in the flour tin, under the mattress.

Folks ain't exactly the most creative bunch when it comes to hidin' things. Dunno why they bother, considerin' how easy it is for a fella like me to sniff it out.

I lifted the tick mattress, filled with hay if my nose served me right, and there it was - a flat tin heavy with coins. Yep. Less than five bucks, my guess. Looks like I'd been barkin' up the wrong tree.

I eyed the rings on her finger, cheap things flakin' gold paint. Seems I'd miscalculated. Figured they'd have somethin' more tucked away. Could be I just hadn't found the real stash yet.

Heaved the man onto the porch and dragged him through the door, brought the wagon and horses into the barn, and kicked a pile of dirt over the bloodstain until it looked decent enough from a distance. Gotta keep things lookin' normal, you see. Then I took another look at the house, studyin' every nook and cranny. Plenty of time on my hands, after all.

After I'd gone over most everything, somethin' caught my eye. A floorboard out of place, didn't match the others. Nudged it with my boot, the wood soaked with blood and hard to tell. Pulled out my knife and pried at the edge. Popped right up, easier than a grasshopper jumpin'. An old tin, still bearin' the aroma of the coffee it once held, now filled with silver and paper money.

Grinned from ear to ear. "Celebration tonight," I muttered to myself. A splatter of blood caught my eye, crawlin' up my sleeve. Washed it off at the well, most of it came clean. Left with just a brown smudge, a touch darker than my brown shirt. Could be from anythin', as far as anyone could tell.

Cold water cooled off my face, sweatin' like a stuck pig under the afternoon sun. Pushed back my hair, gettin' a tad too long. I'd even splurge on a fancy trim in town.

Rode back into town, straight for the saloon. A drink or two, that's all I ever needed. Unwind a little. Then I'd be on my way. Gotta be careful, bein' a man like me. Can't stay in one place too long, or folks start gettin' suspicious. There's others like me out there, folks with their own itches to scratch. Don't want to draw their eye.

The saloon was dark and a welcome respite from the sun and wind. The familiar miasma of sweat, wood, tobacco and liquor teased my nose, offerin' a calm borne of sameness. This one was much like any other. The bartender was a scrap of a guy, long handlebar mustache nearly outweighin' the rest of him. He poured drinks quick, though, chatted easily with the fellas who wanted to chat.

A saloon always has its own rhythm - folks talkin', movin' around, the usual hustle and bustle of drinks bein' poured, cards bein' played. Then somethin' changes, like the sound in the wood when a predator walks through. The sound drops, the talkin' dies down like a coyote's howl silenced by the wind, folks go still, rabbits hopin' to escape unnoticed.

This one had a friendly card game goin' on in the corner, men sittin' easy in their chairs bettin' pennies for a way to pass the time. Floorboards creaked with movement, the wind outside a quiet roar under it all.

A hazy cloud of dust and tobacco smoke floated, dancin' around like a ghost stuck at a country dance, ticklin' the nose. Conversation was a low murmur, an occasional shout from the card game, the bartender takin' orders and shootin' the breeze.

Two drinks in, I was savorin' the burnin' comfort of whiskey, when the murmur of voices fell quiet. The bartender froze, face turned white, bottle in one hand, glass in another. The hairs on the back of my neck stood up. They'd caught me with my back to the door, an' I cursed myself for a stupid get.

Determined footsteps cut through the sudden hush, headin' straight for me. I can't really describe the feelin' come over me then, because I knew. Things had caught up to me. Was it fear, that energy that comes on you when danger greets you, or relief? Or some strange mixture of it all?

Turned around slow, not wantin' to spook nobody if it weren't necessary. Three of them, guns drawn and pointed right at my gut. Jaws clenched, the middle one's eyes narrowed like a rattler sizin' up its prey. Always knew this day would come, someone or another comin' for me. Nothin' new.

Hemp rope and a short drop. Been waitin' for it a long time, me and death. Been friends since I was a scrawny kid in that nightmare place they called a home. That first time I'd been choked 'til everything went black, I woke up a tad surprised every mornin' after.

Seems like death and I been playin' a long game of cat and mouse, and this time, the mouse might just be cornered.

Figgered playin' it cool was my best bet. Maybe talk my way outta this mess, one last time. Three against one with those revolvers already drawn and a shotgun aimed at me? Wasn't exactly a fair fight.

'Course, as I looked at them, I thought I recognized the fella in the middle. Thought he mighta been the one after me while back, trailed me into the desert. He had the mean look of a bounty hunter, eyes as black and cold as a snake.

Besides, a morbid curiosity had been gnawin' at me ever since that woman's defiant stare. What was it like, that final step? All these times I'd stared it down as life fled the eyes, never knew for sure. Part of me, a real dark part, kinda craved knowin'. The answer to the question that's haunted mankind since the first sunrise.

They surrounded me, a nervous energy cracklin' off them like static electricity. Two of 'em, inexperienced and twitchy, eyes dartin' around like spooked jackrabbits. Fear clung to them like sweat, and the scrawny fella on the left kept lickin' his lips like a thirsty dog in the desert.

Almost laughable, the way they trembled. More likely to shoot themselves in the foot than hit me. But you had to be extra careful 'round men like them, they got trigger happy.

The one in the middle, though, he held himself steady. Seasoned eyes that had seen the dark side of life, the kind that recognized a rattler like me when they found one. He was the one to worry about. No stars on their chests. Didn't figure them for a local posse, leastways, not the one with the shotgun.

I leaned against the bar, elbows propped up casual like. "Howdy, fellas," I drawled, voice smooth as oiled iron. "Somethin' I can do for ya? Those irons lookin' a tad heavy for a nice fall day."

"I'm takin' ya in, Will Carter," the leader growled, his voice like gravel rolling down a mountainside.

He wore his years well, this bounty hunter. Seen his fair share of trouble, that much was clear by the way he measured me, eyes glintin' with somethin' I recognized, darkness that yearned for violence. Good thing I'd opted for cooperation. Especially considerin' the shotgun aimed right at my chest. Seen up close what buckshot could do to a man, and it wasn't nothin' pretty.

Kept my hands where they were, slow and easy. Didn't want to give them any reason to get jumpy. "Is that so?" I said, grinnin' like a fool. "Got a wanted poster out with my mug on it?"

"Three cold-blooded murders, Carter," spat the scrawniest one, spittle flying with his words. "You're a rotten coyote, that's what you are!"

Three? Surprise tickled my gut. Figured for that last couple, sure, but who else? Just one more? There were so many more I could brag about. If I was gonna hang, at least it'd be for somethin' grand. Somethin' that'd make folks whisper my name for years to come. Evolution, that's what I was, like that fancy professor fella had said. Evolved beyond the simple needs of most folks.

The bounty hunter's face hardened like granite. "Tie him up, boys," he commanded, his voice leaving no room for argument.

Didn't fight it none. Ran the odds, and surrender was the smarter bet right now. I'd have no luck if I fought, would end up with lead in the belly most like. I'd bide my time, watch for a chance, a weakness. I'd slipped out of some tight situations. Maybe I could slip outta this one.

Skinny fella spun me around, faster than a rattler strikes, and tied me up tighter than a bull to market, the rope chafin' against my wrists. The other two kept their irons trained on me, like I was some wild animal ready to pounce.

Funny, really, the fear they had even when they outnumbered me. Almost made me wanna jump at 'em an' say "boo", just to watch them twitch.

"You can stop smilin', you varmint. Ten thousand, I'm gettin' for you," the bounty hunter growled. "You'll be dancin' a jig at the end of a rope before the year's out."

"So who are you, tough guy?" I sneered.

A slow, hateful smile spread across his face, highlightin' his gold tooth. "Montalvo," he grunted. "I always get my man."

They hauled me out of the saloon, past the gawkin' faces, and across the dusty street to the jailhouse. Well, 'twas a storage room, to be honest. Guess the little town didn't have no proper jail.

Montalvo didn't follow them in, stoppin' at the door. The others roughed me up a bit, before shovin' me in a leanto against the general store, with all manner of dry goods. Pushed me against the wall, gave me a couple nice rope burns on the wrists when they untied me.

Just petty revenge, nothin' more. These folks weren't born for violence, that much was clear. Too fancy for the dirty work. Shame, really. Could've taught them a thing or two.

Truth be told, I ain't complainin'. They fed me good enough here, the grub better than anything I'd scrounged on the trail lately. They even brought in a bed, softer than a feather tick. Stuck in a cage, sure, but at least I had a window. A tiny thing, I might could fit my head through it. No luck crawlin' out of that.

The window was a small mercy, but a mercy all the same. Gazed out at the endless stretch of prairie, the golden light of sunset painting the sky in fiery hues. A free man would see beauty in that, I reckon. All that empty space, the colors pleasin' to the eye.

But the landscape was another prison, another cage, just bigger and prettier. Somethin' to trick the fools into believing they had freedom. A man was always trapped by the things in his mind, the darkness in his soul.

* * *

The silence stretched on, broken only by the rhythmic creak and bang of the store door swinging in the dusty wind. Time, it seemed, had slowed to a crawl. Plenty of time to think, to revisit the yella-haired woman's defiant stare in my mind's eye.

What was it about her? Some deep-seated belief, a faith that burned brighter than the fear of death itself? Or somethin' else entirely?

Suddenly, a memory surfaced, a shard of glass from a broken mirror reflecting a face I barely recognized. A younger me, scrawny and scared, huddled in a corner, the stench of sweat and fear clinging to me like a shroud.

A preacher man stood over me, spittin' fire and brimstone about the wages of sin and the eternal flames of hell. Back then, it scared the bejeebers outta me. But now... now it just sounded like a fairy tale for scared children.

Maybe that was it. Maybe the woman held onto some childish belief in a life beyond this one. A heaven or a hell, some kind of reward or punishment. Me? I didn't believe in nothin' but the cold, hard dirt beneath my feet and the endless sky above. This life, right here, right now, that's all there was.

A cold wind blew through me, despite the heat of the day. What if...the emptiness I'd felt after killin' the woman, it wasn't just the absence of her defiance, but was the absence of somethin' within myself. Something I'd never had, but maybe, just maybe, the woman did. A hint of some unnamed ghost that transcended this mortal coil. A spark of somethin'... human.

3

Judge and Jury

The heat shimmered off the dusty street, hazy and thick as molasses, warmin' the horse dung and makin' the pungent piles swarm with flies. Sweat trickled down my neck, but it wasn't from the sun. It didn't take long, to ride to the next town over, one with a proper cell. Just long enough for the townsfolk to get a good gawk at the monster they had locked away.

Sure, they called me names, most of them. But there was somethin' else in their eyes too, somethin' besides hate. Fear, possibly. A morbid curiosity like flies drawn to a carcass. I liked that. Let them fear me. Let them whisper my name in hushed tones, use me to scare their children to behave.

Back in the cell, a fella showed up – a lawyer, he said he was. Mr. Abernathy. Young, wet behind the ears, with a suit that looked like it belonged on a fancy city slicker, not out here in the dusty frontier. He sat across from me, bars between us, all stiff and proper, with a notepad and a fancy pen. He smelled like some hoity-toity toilet water and ink.

"Mr. Carter," he said, voice all crisp and starched. "I'm here to represent you."

I stared at him, not sayin' a word. Didn't know what a lawyer was supposed to do, exactly, besides pontifyin' on things most men payed no attention to. 'Specially didn't know what he'd do for me, what he meant by "represent."

He cleared his throat, lookin' uncomfortable under my gaze. "The accusations, Mr. Carter. Three murders. James and Helen Cook, and Benjamin Sanders. Did you do it?"

"Don't rightly recall," I said, my voice a low rumble. Truth was, thirty of them was closer to the mark, but I prob'ly shouldn't share that with this fancy fella. 'Sides, I rarely got the names of my prey. Certainly didn't know the names of these last two.

He blinked, like he wasn't sure what I meant. "You don't recall? They have witnesses placing you near the scenes of the crimes."

I shrugged, smirkin'. "Plenty of folks look like me."

He pushed on, pushin' his glasses further up his beak of a nose, his voice tremblin' a little. "Mr. Carter, the evidence is strong. A lighter sentence might be possible with cooperation."

I leaned back, a slow smile creepin' across my face. There was a thrill in this, watchin' this city slicker squirm. Excitement coursed through me, pushin' back the encroaching hollowness. I had naught else to bide my time. "Don't think so, Mr. Fancypants."

A flash of anger sparked in his eyes, then died down just as quick. He sighed, a sound of defeat. "Not guilty, then. What can you tell me that might help your case?"

"Memory's a fickle thing," I drawled. Then, I reached out, calloused fingers brushing against the cold metal bars. "But some things stick."

He shuffled in his chair, eyes flicking away from mine. Then, he reached into his satchel and pulled out somethin' unexpected – photographs. Black and white squares of death, the victims sprawled out in a gory tableau.

Now, somethin' about those pictures... they brought a smile to my lips, a real genuine one. Memories flickered, sharp and vivid. The thrill of the hunt, the hot rush of power as life drained away. The thick, warm crimson, bringin' that metallic tang to the air. It was almost enough to forget the gnawing emptiness inside.

"Yep," I said, my voice a low chuckle, knowin' he saw the darkness in my eyes, lovin' it. "I remember them alright."

He flinched, dropping the pictures like they were hot coals. They fell to the floor between us, a line between dark and light. "What happened?

Self-defense?"

"Nothin' like that." I pointed to the picture of the couple. "Just happened on this cabin. They were hospitable, offered me some grub. Mighty friendly folks." Then, my finger moved to the picture of the man in the alley. "This one here, well…let's just say things got out of hand."

His face drained of color, lookin' like he might faint dead away. "Out of hand?" he rasped quietly, harsh against the thick silence.

"He was a scrapper," I answered with a shrug, my voice gruff, hidin' the pleasure his horror brought me. "Fought harder than I expected."

He licked his lips like a nervous dog. "Why did you do it? Did you need money?"

I leaned back, savoring the fear that rolled off him in waves. A slow smile spread across my face. Yes. This was what I needed. "It's hard to say, city fella." I waited for a beat, letting the number hang in the air. "Truth is, I don't remember much. After a while, the details get blurry. All that blood starts to look the same."

Or maybe it just all fades, a colorless memory, a reflection of the emptiness that filled me. That thought vanished as quickly as it came, replaced by cold satisfaction, the thrill of the hunt.

Abernathy didn't answer, just sat there frozen, his face a mask of horror. His eyes darted down the hall, like a jackrabbit, lookin' to escape, or maybe a rescue, I didn't know which. I whimper escaped his lips, the sound of prey that had my itch risin'. His "toilet water" scent had soured into something that tickled the nose.

A cold laugh escaped my lips, a sound that echoed through the cell. This was better than any whiskey. To see a man like him, so full of life, crumble before me, that was power. Fleetin', but that surge was enough to keep me goin'.

It was a small victory, I suppose, in the scheme of things. I was gonna be dancin' at the end of a rope, but I was gonna enjoy lettin' everyone know what I'd done, feel the twisted pride as they leaned away, all while they waited with bated breath to learn more. It was a pathetic substitute for what I needed, but in that empty cell, it was all I had.

Thing was, I had no idea it would take so long it to get me dancin'. Didn't seem right, leadin' a man on for so long. It got to where I'd wished for a lynch mob, if you want to know the truth of it, just to get things done. And mebbe I'd miscalculated my odds for escape, too.

* * *

Days bled into each other, a monotonous rhythm of flickering lamplight and stale air. The lawyer, Abernathy, hadn't returned. Didn't much matter, I guessed. Those fancy fellas wouldn't understand a thing like me. They hadn't been raised in the hell I was. Thing is, when folks talk about raisin' hell, they forgot the part about livin' in it. I could tell them summat 'bout that.

The deputy brought my meals, more often than not, but he was a skinny thing, young, and slipped in and out like my knife in the soft flesh of the throat. He paid me no nevermind, never responded to anythin' I said, other than a flush in his ears or a tightenin' of his mouth, eyes dartin' like a scared deer.

Weren't no satisfaction from him. Nothin' to note the passin' of time 'cept the coolin' of the days and the length of my beard.

The itch was a wild thing, restless in captivity, burnin' deeper than I'd ever felt it. I had little else to think on, besides that itch and memories of my prey. I stopped noticin' the stink of the cell, the stink of my unwashed skin.

The meals they brought were dry, bland fare, and I took little joy from consumin' them. My denims relied solely on the strained leather of my braces to keep them from poolin' around my ankles. Sleep evaded me, like smoke through my fingers. When I did sleep, it was filled with that woman's curse, haunted just like she'd said, but it was the boredom of that cell that echoed in my mind, empty and cold.

One mornin', though, things stirred, a portent in the air like a lightnin' storm movin' in. They hauled me out, wrists shackled tight in irons, and dragged me down the dusty street. The sun beat down mercilessly, and the jeers of the townsfolk echoed in my ears.

"Murderer!" one spat. "Hang 'im high!" another bellowed.

I met their gazes head-on, a smirk twisting my lips. Let them gawk. Let them fear. There was somethin' else in the crowd too, a morbid fascination that lit my blood on fire. They wanted a show, and me, Will Carter, was gonna give them one.

The church doors creaked open, revealing a scene straight out of a coyote's nightmare. Pews overflowed with townsfolk, their faces a grotesque mix of curiosity and bloodlust. The stench of stale incense mingled with the unwashed masses, turning my stomach.

A judge, a pudgy man with muttonchops that took on a life of their own, sat in a chair behind the altar. I lunged forward just to see him jump before I sat in the chair they had for me, laughin'.

"Mr. Carter, have some decorum or they'll strap you to the chair," he glared at me, his voice booming through the quiet hall.

He slammed his gavel on the altar, gunshots in the cacophony of the crowd. "Order in the court!" he shouted, and the noise died away.

"Prosecution, what are the charges?"

The fancy lawyer lept to his feet. "Three counts of murder, your honor."

Didn't surprise me none, Abernathy'd let me know 'bout those. They had no idea of the whole tally. I chuckled, pleased at the shivers that shot down a few spines, the faces pale.

"Mr. Abernathy," the judge barked, "your defense?"

Abernathy stammered, his voice cracking like a twig under pressure. "We… we maintain Mr. Carter's innocence, your honor!"

The courtroom erupted in scoffs and murmurs. Innocence? Laughable. Sure.

"Call your witnesses, Mr. Lane."

A tall woman, her face lined with grief, took her place in a chair beside the altar, swore to tell the truth. The lawyer set up her story with a series of questions, waitin' with excruciating' patience each time she began to sob. "Who did you see, holding the knife, Mrs. Jackson?"

She looked up at me and pointed, her eyes a mixture of grief, rage, and fear. "I saw him."

I stared back at her until she lowered her gaze, her hands white knuckled as she clutched them to her.

Abernathy rose then, his disgust apparent in his face. He didn't want to be on my side, but he was honorable. "You said it was dark, Mrs. Jackson. How can you be sure it was Mr. Carter, there in the dark?"

"It may have been dark," she said, eyes once more venturing up to mine, "but I'll never forget those empty eyes."

I scoffed, loudly. The judged glared at me, a look he wouldn't have attempted had I not been cuffed and sittin' 10 feet away. "Consider this a warning, Mr. Carter. I'll not have this trial turn into a circus."

I held my laugh in, but couldn't stop the grin. Yes, this was a right fine entertainment.

Then the other lawyer began to bring letters to the judge, statements he called them, sworn testimonies givin' evidence of my crimes.

He droned on and on, about bloodstains and alibis, them sheep in the chairs behind me givin' off a palpable interest. Sure, they pontified and sermonized on my evil, but their souls craved it, just as did mine. Shadows of somethin', maybe regret, most likely the itch, danced inside me, makin' my skin crawl.

Then came the part that surprised me. Another fella came forward, a lawman by the way he was dressed.

"We have evidence of two more murders, your Honor," he growled. "Here in our own nick of the woods."

Ah, at last I could claim the yella-haired lady. Seems like my reputation had preceded me.

The judge smirked at Abernathy, his blood-thirsty eyes glintin'. A murmur of outrage rippled through the crowd. This whole thing was a game, some twisted performance where I was the main attraction. But I wouldn't play by their rules.

"Hold on," I called, my voice cutting through the noise. The whole courtroom went silent, all eyes on me. I paused, stretched my legs in front of me as I leaned back in my chair, relishing the sudden attention. "Just between us folks," I continued, my voice low and dangerous, "those ain't the only ones."

A satisfyin' gasped rippled through the crowd, murmurs of "evil" and "devil" reachin' my ears. Even the judge's eyes bulged. Abernathy looked like he might have an apoplectic fit.

"How many?" the lawman's words shot out, his voice tight with hatred. It only fed my itch.

I grinned, a slow, feral smile, enjoyin' the play of fear and fascination on all those faces. This…this was power.

"Lost count after a while. Maybe twenty, maybe thirty. More sheep than I could count."

A roar of shocked whispers erupted throughout the church room, fillin' up that empty void that lived inside me. My smile widened as the judge slammed his gavel, tryin' to restore order, but the damage was done. I had planted a seed of fear in their hearts, a chilling reminder of the darkness that lurked just beyond the edge of their tidy little town.

This whole trial business wasn't so bad after all. It gave me a chance to play with them, to watch them squirm. They wanted justice? They'd get a little entertainment instead. It all beat sittin' alone in that metal trap of a cell. I even got myself a nickname, "Bloody Bill." I wasn't right fond of Bill, but I accepted it as my due.

After that, things got blurry. More lawyers, more questionin', hours turned to days. Finally, a man in the jury stood, a nervous fella who wouldn't meet my eyes. "We find him guilty, your honor, on all counts." The crowd grew to a deafening buzz, but I was only surprised it took them so long.

The judge stared me down, his eyes flickerin' with a predator's gaze. He just dressed it up as justice. He slammed his gavel until things quieted down a might, then pronounced, "Will Carter, as you are guilty of at least 5 counts of murder, I sentence you to," he paused then, licked his lips with anticipation, enjoyin' the spectacle. "Hung by the neck until dead." He slammed his gavel down.

As they led me back to my cell, I couldn't help but laugh. Death might be comin', but at least I'd left my mark. They wouldn't soon forget "Bloody Bill" Carter, the wolf among the sheep. I'd be talked about for a long time after, immortalized in the papers.

* * *

As the days wore on, a cold certainty replaced the thrill of the performance. Escape was a distant mirage. They had me caged like a cornered wolf, no chance of runnin' free. I understood then, why some animals'd chew their foot off to escape. It got to where I'd have cut off my own hand if it got me out, gave me somethin' new to break up the sameness.

I guess I'd underestimated these folks after all. There was still a game to be played, and the beginnin' of a dangerous plan started to form in my mind. I still had time to turn the tables on them.

They continued writin' about me in the papers, a whole lot. Wouldn't have known myself if folks hadn't come tellin' me, the sheriff, his wife, Abernathy. "Bloody Bill" Carter, layin' all manner of misdoin's at my feet. A strange kind of pride swelled up in me.

Who would've thought that scrawny, scared kid from the Guadalupe Orphanage would become the man everyone in this territory feared? Funny how things turn out. Ma Josie, rot in hell, woulda gotten a kick outta this. She always said I had a fire in my belly, even back then when she used to try and beat it outta me with her wooden rod.

4

Hung

I started clawing at the walls after a while. A man ain't built for sittin', his mind achin' as bad as his muscles. They'd taken me to another prison, shoved me in a room with nothin' but a straw mattress and the stink of despair.

Iron bars, two inches wide, caged me in, leaving only slivers of the outside world. A metal pot was my only company for anything private, and twice a day they dragged me out to the outhouse. Fresh air and sunshine, even that little bit, was a treasure.

The buildings and trees outside might as well been ghosts, just as far away as the lawmen watchin' me. The sun didn't even sneak through the bars 'cept for a couple hours in the late afternoon. Stars? Land sakes, I couldn't even remember the last time the moon had shone on me, felt the cool night breeze on my face.

The sheriff's wife, an empty-headed biddy always lookin' for a good deed, brought the slop. She was maybe 10 years older than me, middle-aged, silver beginnin' at her temples. Always prattlin' on about them spiritualist folks and their seances, talkin' to the dead. Seemed crazy to me. Dead was dead, and I hadn't seen nothin' to change my mind.

I didn't talk much, just let her chirp about what she willed. It was better than the silence that surrounded me otherwise. Sometimes, she'd bring me a newspaper. I didn't let on I only looked at it for my name, just set it aside to puzzle over later.

She came in the second or third day, with a chunk of roast and a piece of pie, pulled out a deck of cards.

"Do you play cards, Mr. Carter?"

I nodded, my mouth full of pie. She began dealin' with the expertise of a fancy saloon gambler, face down, clockwise around the table.

"That ain't Blackjack," I muttered.

She snorted delicately. "I should say not. This is Whist, a respectable game."

It was my turn to snort. "You know Poker? Faro?"

She drew back with an indignant huff. "I'm not a two-bit gambler!" she retorted.

"Alright," I placated. I'd play her ladies game. It beat starin' at the ceilin'. "So, what are we bettin'?"

"My word, Mr. Carter. Gambling is a sin!"

I just looked at her, struck dumb by her foolishness. Did she not realize I'd done busted up the Sixth Commandment and rode over it twenty some odd times?

"We play for points," she added weakly. "Just to while away the time."

"How about pie? If I win, I get two pieces of pie tomorrow."

Her forehead creased as she thought about it, but she nodded. "I suppose that would be all right."

It was a silly game, countin' to twenty-one, bidding on trumps, suits and tricks. But easy enough to learn, as she wasn't a half bad teacher.

I didn't get two pieces of pie the next day. But I got them every day thereafter.

* * *

I was watchin' out my window one afternoon, a brown mutt dog had caught my attention. It sat on the boardwalk, on the other side of the street, just starin' at me. I stared back at it, somethin' odd ticklin' behind my eyes.

I shook my head to get rid of the weird feelin'. I'd spent too long in this cell, left to my own company except that air-headed woman. She was alright enough, I supposed, but I was restless, the itch like ants crawlin' beneath my skin. It'd been months since I'd been free to hunt what I'd craved.

The sheriff's wife come bustlin' in, cloth covered bowl of stew in her hand. "Theodore Freeman is in town!" she crowed. "And I've been invited to meet him in Mrs. Crawford's parlor! She said to bring artifacts to draw the spirits to us."

"Superstition," I snorted, shovelin' the stew in. It wasn't much, simple fare like always, but kept the belly from grumblin'.

"Oh, but it's not!" she chided airily. "Why, they say even Mary Todd Lincoln had a spiritualist call her boy to this plane."

I looked her in the eye. She'd never really seemed afraid of me, simple as she was, a lamb ripe for the slaughter, but then, there were two inch metal straps between me and her. "I seen plenty of dead folks, watched the life leave their eyes. There's no comin' back. That body's just a shell."

Her smile faltered as she avoided my gaze, but the hope in her voice didn't disappear completely. "Maybe. I suppose I'll see what my visit brings."

"Who you want to call back? A child?" I supposed if I was gonna call a blasted spirit up, I'd think I'd want Ma Josie. It'd give me right fine pleasure to do her all over again, push her back down to Hell.

Her eyes took on a faraway, sad look. "My sister. She died in the crossing when I was a girl. Diptheria outbreak."

I shifted, uncomfortable, as I scoffed. "Anythin' you see will be parlor tricks and smoke."

"Oh, you men!" she huffed. "You have no faith! There's more to the world than the physical plane!"

I met her eyes, steady, ignorin' how that idea made my insides roll. "You're wrong, lady. This is all there is. We're all just flies on the dung heap, crawlin' around until we die."

She pursed her lips, cheeks flushed hot. Anger kept her silent as I cleaned the bowl with my finger, scooted it back to her.

There was this bone deep need, then, to twist the knife, to see how she'd squirm. Mebbe it was borne out of boredom, mebbe it sated the itch in some measure. "You let me know what comes of this spiritualist. Cain't talk with the dead," I grunted. "You'll never hear from your sister again."

She took the bowl without another word, glarin' at me all the while, then swept out of the cell room. It wasn't as satisfyin' as I'd wanted it to be, left me feelin' hollow and cold. I needed more.

As the door slammed behind her, I turned to look outside. That brown cur sat across the street, starin' at me again. Its tongue lolled out, dark, like its muzzle. As I watched, its folded down ears pricked, and it stood, all attention on me. It made my insides twist somethin' fierce, and I pulled back, away from the window, heart thuddin' in my chest.

Scoffin' at my silliness, I looked back out the window. There was no sign of the dog. And somehow, that spooked me worse.

The sheriff's wife came back the next day, face pale, 'cept for her red-rimmed eyes. She set down my plate, but didn't speak. I could figger out what'd happened, and I was eager to heap the hurt.

"Talk to yer sister?" I taunted, cravin' the power that came from her hurt. "Bet that seance was a right laugh. Did she come tappin' on the table with a thimble, spellin' out messages? Ghostly whispers and cold breezes? All parlor tricks and smoke, I tell ya, and all to line some magician's pockets."

Hot spots showed on her pale cheeks, her mouth tightened. Yeah, I was gettin' her goat alright. Satisfaction filled me, the itch rejoiced, so I continued. "You're wastin' your time and money on foolishness, lady. There's nothin' beyond this life, nothin' at all."

Eyes waterin', she pushed the plate toward me and stumbled to a stand. I twisted the knife, stickin' it where it would bleed the most. "What, the truth of it hurt? You'll never see her, speak to her, again. She's dead and gone." Putting her hand to her mouth with a sob, she run off.

I never did hear what happened at that there seance. She stopped visitin' me after that, and the sheriff and his deputies were a touch more… enthusiastic when they took me to the outhouse, leavin' me no doubt what they thought 'bout our conversation. My water bucket went dry more frequently, and my soap disappeared. Not to mention the vittles became a bit more…chewy.

Guess I regretted my harsh words after that. Didn't realize how her visits broke up the sameness of each day, the way time stood still in that dank cell. Now the days stretched like an endless, empty trail, dry and barren, nothin' to separate one from the other.

I'd hear folks walkin' by, sometimes watch their blurry shapes through the bars. Jealousy gnawed at me. They were in a different world, bathed in sunlight, livin' life. And me?

It was like I was back in Ma Josie's cellar, a dark, suffocatin' hole reserved for the "bad boys." Her ghost was right there with me, her hateful words slitherin' into my head whenever I closed my eyes, whenever my mind went quiet.

So I filled my head with blood, with the memory of the life drainin' from those eyes, the way I'd filled up somethin' deep in me each time. But even blood goes stale after a while.

The mind craves somethin' fresh, somethin' new. That's when the itch started again, that gnawin' hunger deep down. Like sunburn, but burnin' from the inside. I guess that's why I fooled with the dog.

He came sniffing by my window one day. It was level with the ground, open to the air. Two inch strips of metal barred me from leavin', but my hand fit through the spaces, if I was careful. Nothin' much to look at, just a big mangy yella cur-dog, hair short, ears folded down. I threw a rock at him, wantin' to hit him, chase him off. The bars fouled my aim, I missed, threw it a few feet off.

I'd found me a dog once, in my younger days. Sam was his name, an' I had him for nearly a whole year. We did everythin' together, though I had to hide him from Ma Josie. He took a long time to die. I wasn't so good at killin' then, botched it up good. Didn't know the sweet spots like I do now. That was back when the itch had first started.

But don't you know it, that cur dog came back to my window. Fool dog brought me the rock. Sat pantin' outside my window, actin' all proud of himself, that slobbery rock layin' in front of him, right where I could barely reach it. What was I supposed to do then?

Well, then me and that dog just got us a game goin'. I'd throw that stupid rock, and that feather-brained dog would bring it back. Eventually he lost interest and wandered off, but he came back the next day. And the next.

I came to rely on that dog comin', just like the sun risin'. Until that day they told me it was time to wear that rope necktie. I'm guessin' it was about April, don't know for sure, they ain't seen fit to bring me a calendar, didn't bring me newspapers. The sheriff's wife had done that, and she hadn't returned.

The sun had started comin' back strong those last coupla weeks, grass started growin'. I'd been waitin' for nine months to end it, by my guess. If I'da known 'bout it all when the law come for me in that saloon, I'da taken the shotgun to the gut. Woulda been less painful than sittin' in that dark cell all day, every day.

I wasn't scared. I'd never been scared of Death. That wasn't the feelin' that came over me. I guess I just got to feelin' all melancholy, being shut in and all. I didn't feel regret 'bout the things I'd done, that wasn't it, I didn't think. I was just…done with the world, tired of bein' shut up in that awful hole. Wasn't no more for me, and I was all right 'bout that. You get sometimes where nothingness sounds a might better than the pain of existence.

* * *

The sheriff's wife come back to visit, right before it all came down to a head. She was a touch wary of me now, stiff and pale. "The spirits say they can help the livin'," she confided nervously. "That it shortens their purgatory." I saw the trail she was layin', workin' to give me some twisted sense of hope. I chuckled. Hope was for fools, and I was no fool.

"You think I give a lead nickel about purgatory? Half the folks I sent there deserved worse. The rest? Well, a little extra sizzle on the griddle ain't gonna hurt nobody. Maybe it'll liven things up down there. Gets a mite dull after a while, wouldn't you say?"

I wasn't happy with her lack of a response as she just stared at me sadly, so I had to continue, heap coals on her head, anythin' to make me feel somethin' again, "Maybe your sister down there ain't so happy about you spendin' your time with a monster like me. Maybe it lengthens her stay instead. You ever think of that, sweetheart?"

Her eyes filled with tears, jaw slackened a moment before it firmed right up, the steel inside her surprisin' the both of us. "You want to hurt me with words?" she rasped, voice thick with tears. "That's your last action on this earth? You're powerless, Mr. Carter. All you have left is this cell, your anger, and that emptiness inside you try so desperately to fill with cruelty."

She stood, resolute, not sparing me another glance, slammin' the door shut behind her. Funny, I'd never learned her name. A strange tightness settled in my chest, the itch burnin' with unslaked need.

I scoffed, leaned my head back against the wall. Closed my eyes, only to see that yella-haired lady in my eyes once more, her curse, that I'd given voice to, echoin' in my ears.

"Haunted by the ghosts of your deeds," I mocked the words. I cursed her, the sheriff's wife, women in general. Turned to the window to find that blasted dog layin', tail a flag in a mild wind, nosin' a rock to me.

"You feather-brained mutt," I grumbled, even as I grabbed the egg-sized rock to toss it, glad for a break from my thoughts. He brought the slobbery thing back, again and again, offerin' me the comfort in the rhythm of the game.

I roughed up his ears some as he panted, the feel of the soft fur the only softness I could remember, soothin' the burnin' itch coiling inside. For a moment, with my eyes squeezed shut, I let myself pretend it wasn't the cold stone of the cell floor beneath me, but something…more.

When they finally led me out to the high-jump stage, the sun was shinin' and the birds were singin'. It was a right pretty day, and I breathed it in deep. There was a crowd turned up to see me meet my maker. I figured on that.

Seems like everybody wants to meet Death, just not everybody goes lookin' for it. I always thought I was smarter than most, willin' to take what I needed, rather than waitin' for life to give it to me. Those that wait…well, they wait. And wait some more. And I was pert near famous, to boot. "Bloody Bill" Carter. I heard the whispers of it in the crowd, along with the name-callin'.

I walked right up those stairs, like they asked me to. I didn't figure it was worth givin' them much trouble. I was far outnumbered - it wouldn'ta made a difference. Better a rope than a gut shot, I figured, now that the months wastin' away in that hole of a cell were over. Like I'd always said, no skin off my nose. They asked if I had any last words. I hadn't thought about that. Somethin' niggled at the back of my head a moment, then it was gone.

"Don't guess I do," I said, wonderin' what it was other men had said at these events.

They looked kinda surprised. I guess they were wanting me to give my apologetics or some such. Nah, I wasn't sorry. Learned long ago sorry got a man nowhere. 'Sides, I'd enjoyed every bit of it, reveled in it even. And I was bone-deep tired of that cell, of sittin' with nothin' to do but think.

They led me up the steps then put a black bag on my head, a foul-smellin' thing that made the heat double. Always wondered why they thought to do that. I guess even if folks wanna see Death, they don't want to stare it straight in the face, wanted some separation to protect them from the final threat. Don't rightly know. I'd never really understood the workin's of my fellow man.

I could make out blurry shapes of the crowd, the lawmen, a flicker of sunlight. I'd seen that feather-brained dog slinkin' behind the crowd. He'd find someone else to throw his rocks, I figured.

The murmur of the crowd died down as they tightened my new necktie, yanking it rough. Hurt a bit, made it hard to swallow, which made me chuckle to myself. Swallowin' was gonna be a real chore in a minute. Funny how things strike you when you're about to meet your maker.

Someone droned on about my crimes, the sentence of hangin', as the boards beneath me creaked. I had news for them folks. I'd known that for nigh about three months, maybe longer. Everyone there probably knew it too, else why come gawk at a dead man walkin'?

I just wanted them to get on with it. The black bag was stifling, sweat drippin' into my eyes and stingin' somethin' fierce. Couldn't even wipe it away. Now that was a real bother. Irritation rose, wonderin' how much longer they'd make me wait.

Just as the trapdoor gave way beneath me, a thought flickered, sharp and fleetin': "I coulda done it different." The meaning hung there, a question with no answer, just beyond my reckonin'. A split second of thought, a flash of a vision of buryin' that knife, vanished as quickly as it came.

The next moment, my body jerked, a sharp pain shot through my neck. Blackness, and then I guess I was dead.

5

Alive

I heard the scratching first thing, a persistent noise that urged me to wake. It was so dark I wasn't sure if my eyes were even open. They ached something fierce, gritty like I'd been caught in a sandstorm.

The scratching was heavy, deep, not like the little scritches of rodents. It was close by, too, right in front of my face. With each scrape, a shower of dirt rained down, stinging my eyes and filling my mouth.

I smelled dirt and pine and rot, and the stink of my unwashed body, close, humid in that heavy way it gets right before the storm. My every breath echoed in the space.

My throat sure was sore, throbbed like when I'd had mumps. I could barely swallow. I tried to raise my hand to feel the tender spots, but then, as my elbow hit something solid beside me and in front of me, I realized I was laying in a box, the wood rough hewn and raw. Panic clawed its way up my throat, squeezing the air from my lungs.

I couldn't move, and the air felt thick and stale, suffocatin'. This wasn't right. Not right at all.

I cried out, my voice a hoarse, pitiful thing as I thrashed like a horse caught in a barbed wire fence. I struck out at the boards around me as I flailed, only managin' to bruise and scrape myself. My panic burned itself out quickly enough, leavin' me gaspin' in the small space.

Finally gatherin' my wits, I pushed at the boards nearly restin' on my chest, my arms strugglin' for enough leverage. The lid over me gave a little, there was more scratching, excited at my movement. I pushed again and again, and slowly, dim light broke through, along with more sprinkles falling, filling my eyes and mouth, makin' me blink and sputter.

"Blast this infernal box!" my voice scraped like a metal file as I pushed harder, splinters catchin' on my fingertips. I tensed all my muscles, usin' my legs, at last flipping the lid out and over with a loud thump as dirt fell freely over me.

I sat up, just as that cur dog from my window pounced at me, his big body wigglin' as he snuffled and licked my face. I pushed him away, confused, blinking my waterin' eyes to get the dirt out.

"Whatcha doin' here, Feather-Brain?" I croaked.

Bemused, I looked around, squintin' in the glare of the risin' sun. It took me a moment to gather my thoughts, get myself together after such a strange awakening. I was in a shallow hole in the ground, next to a small cross with my name painted on it. I stared at it, head full of cotton, tryin' to make sense of it all. Slowly, a sickening realization dawned on me.

I scrabbled outta the coffin right quick, my legs those of a newborn foal, all wobbly and weak.

The world seemed off-kilter, blurry around the edges. How long had I been there, beneath the cold embrace of the earth? A day, at least, judgin' from the dried out dirt clods.

The thought made me shiver, a chill that wasn't of this world. I was suddenly reminded of the sheriff's wife, her insistence on spirits returnin'. I looked at my hands. They looked solid enough. I didn't think I was no spirit come back to haunt the livin'.

My body tingled painfully, like when the fingers thaw after freezin'. Even my brain felt numb and prickly, like it was just waking from a long, dark sleep. I turned back to the crude coffin.

Just a plain pine box, cheap and small as they could make it and still fit me in. It was hastily covered with a thin layer of dirt. The name on the small cross, nothin' more than two sticks nailed together, mocked me – a cruel joke considering my predicament.

I sat there, memories flickering back slowly, fragmented like a dream. The trial, the noose, then… nothing. Just a strange emptiness. My mind was a jumbled mess. Waking up from death? Didn't seem likely.

The sunlight, early-weak and veiled by a hazy horizon, was different. It held an odd, coppery hue, unlike anything I remembered. As I sat there, a dry and withered bouquet of wildflowers under my cross caught my eye. Their once vibrant colors were muted and dusty. Surely, they wouldn't have wilted so quickly if I'd only been gone a day. I touched a petal, and it crumpled to dust under my finger.

A strange weakness overcame me. My limbs protested as I tried to stand. My stomach rumbled with a ferocity I'd never known, and I had a cactus in my gullet. A shiver, colder than anything the night air could offer, ran through my limbs.

Memories flickered at the edges of my mind – fragmented and hazy. The trial, that dark cell, the noose… then… nothing. Just a vast emptiness filled with a cold, gnawing loneliness. A steer sat on my chest, keepin' me from gettin' my breath, as my blood whooshed like a freight train, and the dark come closin' in on me.

A soft whine broke through, then a nudge , callin' me back. Feather sat beside me, tail thumping softly against the dusty ground.

"What happened, Feather," I mumbled, the name slipping out before I could stop it. Guess grave digging wasn't the only trick that varmint had up his sleeve. He tilted his head at me, those soulful brown eyes filled with an intelligence that seemed…off somehow. Not like any dog I'd ever seen.

A strange warmth spread through my chest, a feeling I couldn't quite place. Could it be gratitude? For what, I wasn't sure. But the dog appeared to understand, letting out a soft whimper and nudging my hand with his wet nose.

"Let's go," I said, more to myself than to him. Talking to a dog. Now that was a new low, even for me. But somehow, it was right. This whole experience had rattled me more than I cared to admit.

Feather whined again, nosin' at the lid to that box, then pawin' at the dirt. It finally dawned on me. I closed up that box, kicked most of the dirt back over it, hopin' no one would notice I was no longer in the box. I laughed, bitter and crazed. Rubbed my hand over my chest, tryin' to settle the tightness in it, workin' to breathe.

I needed boots, and a hat. Man couldn't go around looking like a scarecrow, not to mention the sun beating down on my head. I'd seen men go heat crazed. And a horse. Needed to get outta here before someone realized they hadn't quite finished the job.

Sooner or later, they'd find this empty grave, and whoever did wouldn't be too happy about it. Maybe they'd done a plumb lazy job of my hangin', or mebbe I wasn't meant to die. Too down low mean for the reaper to take me. I chuckled. That was prob'ly it.

I got my bearings as I stood, castin' my eyes around the cemetery. Couldn't make out much from where I was, though I figured my cell must've been somewhere in the middle of that dusty town. The stable wasn't hard to find, the faint whinnies of the horses a beacon in the stillness. They were all inside, still locked up tight. Sneaking one out wouldn't exactly be a quiet affair.

Followed the dust blowin' through the street, like a driftin' tumbleweed, limpin' along tender footed without my boots. Feather trotted beside me, tongue lollin'. A couple of horses were tied up out front, easy pickings but for the risk of being seen. I glanced up at the sun, just risin' in the bruised sky. It wasn't quite openin' time yet. This time of mornin', anyone rode into town last night would likely be asleep. Fair pickin's.

Feather padded silently beside me, a shadow in eerie light. I didn't pay him any mind, my focus solely on getting away. Just as I was about to reach the hitching post, the saloon doors swung open, and two cowboys emerged, laughter echoing in the night air. Both were packing iron, holstered low on their hips, butts facin' forward like they liked to wear them. Easier to draw from a horse's back.

"Guess you saved me again, Feather," I whispered, a wry smile tugging at the corner of my lips. This whole time was like a twisted dream, one I couldn't seem to wake up from. Beholden to a gravedigging canine? Life sure led a twisted trail.

I looked back toward the stable, a ghost of defiance igniting me. Second chances weren't always easy things, but sometimes, they were the only things you had. Feather whined, a low, urgent sound. He trotted a few steps down a dusty alley, then looked back, his gaze fixed on me, that strange look in his eyes.

Right now, I had more pressing concerns, like getting myself a decent horse and headin' out before I was caught and they did the job proper.

Following Feather deeper into the maze of back alleys, the scent of manure and sweat clinging to the air, a new worry lifted its head. This town wouldn't exactly be hospitable, especially towards the recently deceased. We emerged on the outskirts, the buildings giving way to a vast expanse of scrubland bathed in the pale sunlight.

A lone figure stood silhouetted against the brightenin' horizon, a dark horse saddled and waiting just beyond the town limits. My breath hitched. This wasn't part of the plan. Who would leave a horse out here, especially such a fine one?

It was a big horse, black as night with a coat that shimmered like polished obsidian. Its powerful muscles rippled beneath its sleek hide, and it snorted impatiently, pawing the dusty ground. I almost thought it a specter, a piece of a stampedin' imagination. Or maybe I was the specter. I was so kerfuffled I hardly knew.

Feather whined again, this time a high-pitched, excited bark. He darted towards the black horse, circling it with a joyful energy that seemed impossible for a dog who moments ago had been lethargic. The big black horse itself remained calm, watching the dog with a large, liquid eye on the side of its hammer-shaped head.

Hesitantly, I approached the sturdy creature. It tossed its head, nostrils flaring, but its movements lacked aggression. Curiosity? Reaching out a tentative hand, not wantin' to spook it, I stroked its muzzle. The black lowered its head further, allowing the touch. Its coat warm beneath my fingertips, like living velvet. A low whicker rumbled from its throat, a sound that vibrated through my very core. It almost felt like...friendship.

I checked the saddle bags, relieved to find a top-notch Colt Frontier six-shooter that gleamed even in the dim light. It was a fine piece, pearl handle and engravin' along the muzzle. I belted it on before I hoisted myself onto the horse's back. The saddle, though simple, was comfortable, though bare feet were wrong in the stirrups.

As I settled in, a surge of confidence filled my veins. With a nudge of my heels, the big black surged forward. It moved with an effortless grace that belied its size, its powerful strides eating up the ground beneath us. Feather, no longer lagging behind, kept pace beside us, his form a blur against the dusty road.

The town receded rapidly behind us. Good riddance. I'd had my fill of it.

<h1 style="text-align:center">6</h1>

Failed Attempt

I dreamed that night. One of those dreams where you're almost awake, but ridin' a mustang without a bridle. I was in that blasted jail cell, throwin' rocks at that cur dog, but it was dark as night, the bars crooked and oozin' black tar. The trees outside moaned, seemin' to reach their skeletal fingers toward me.

Outside the cell door, the sheriff's wife was in a white nightgown. She was dancin' in a circle with a little girl, skin as pale as bone. They sung a child's ditty about fallin', over and over, before they collapsed onto the floor, dead, skin sunk in and bones tryin' to push out. Their deathly grimace laughed at me, the sound echoin' off the stone walls.

Then Ma Jose come up to me, my feet glued to the floor, as she wrapped those bat wings around me, pushed me into her chest. I struggled, pushin' against her doughy form. I tried to get my breath while at the same time tryin' not to inhale her scent of death and too sweet perfume, because I knew it would kill me for sure if I did.

"You just love Mama's hugs, don't you, boy?" she cooed, squeezin' me tight enough to crack my ribs, suffocatin' me. Then she turned angry, like she always did. "Well hug me back," she screamed, her face waverin' as it turned blotchy red, shakin' me somethin' fierce. I was just a rag doll in her hands, my head lollin', before me before she pushed me hard.

I fell down into a black pit, hittin' the soggy bottom, the stench of death thick. The darkness was thick, pressin' down on me, full of meanness and spite. I tried to run, but my legs were heavy tree trunks, thick, stiff and heavy.

Boss Rawlin's laugh came from the shadows, a moment before he glided toward me, a tiger stalkin' its prey. His evil grin made me shiver. A snake come out of his mouth, bit me on the cheek, just above the scruff of my beard.

Once again, I was a wooden statue, helpless and small as he came at me with his big knife, the blood drippin' off it like paint on a rail. I squeezed my eyes shut, but I could still see his sneer as he threw me into that coffin.

The rough hewn wood left splinters in my face, hardly missin' my eye, as he pushed me down. I went easy, again that helpless rag doll, weak, soft. He reeked of stale sweat and liquor. I retched. Pain exploded behind me, and I screamed, but no sound come out. The men on the jury laughed and jeered as the blood ran down my sides, my legs, thick, warm, almost ticklin'.

I woke with the sound of the yella-haired lady's curse echoin' in my ears, 'cept it was my own voice repeated it back to me, words comin' out without my foreknowledge or permission. *Haunted by the ghosts of your deeds.*

Something pinched my cheek, a twist bringin' a jolt of pain. I bolted upright, gasping for air, heart thunderin' fit to give out. A monstrous buzzard loomed overhead, its beady black eyes staring me down, its weight heavy on my chest. The smell of carrion turned my stomach. I hollered, a startled yelp that sent the creature hopping off with a squawk.

I pushed myself up, wild-eyed and wobbly, searchin' for signs of the nightmare that lingered. My sweat had soaked through my shirt, and it clung to me like a shroud as my lungs worked like a bellows and my heart near burstin'. I clenched my fists to tame their shakin', swallowin' bile with determination. My head pounded like a blacksmith's hammer.

As the fear left me, anger flowed in to take its place. All them people, Ma Josie, Boss, the jury, all of 'em tryin' to take me down. But I'll show them. I wasn't no pansy boy. The itch rose in me, fierce and relentless, like it was alive under my skin. The urge to kill somethin', someone.

Feather sat, watchin' me, his head cocked in that way dogs do. He opened his mouth, pantin', and a sudden I knew he was laughin' at me. I kicked at him. he dodged my boot easily. I saddled Hammer none too gently, yanked his reins to the left when we come to a crossroads. I was on the hunt.

It was a lonely stretch, not traveled enough to harden the dirt, but the grass was shorter – a sign of infrequent passage. Roads like these were familiar companions.

One of my earliest memories was from before I was even three years old. My mama had taken me down a similar road, tied me to a tree so I wouldn't follow her. Guess she'd gotten tired of me. She left me crying by that tree, thirsty and scared. I didn't even remember her face.

All I could recall was the harsh rope chafing my leg, the knot an unsolvable puzzle. I'd a knowin' that my mama'd come back for me, as the endless tears eventually dried up and my thirst deepened. I'd fought the man that found me, hopin' she was comin' just around the corner. He'd given me somethin' to eat, dropped me off at the orphanage. I'd always wondered if he knew what Hell he'd condemned me to.

Mama Josie soon learned me not to cry for nothing. Not many things were worth the salt in your tears. Cryin' never helped nothin', nohow. The rest of my memories I kept tamped down. Hadn't thought so much on my childhood ever.

Angry again, I kicked Hammer into a trot, trying to outrun the unwelcome memories. Dwelling on the past only fueled a cold anger that did me no good. It must be the weirdness of the past few days messing with my head.

It was high time to find some prey. I needed cash, an' I needed weapons, boots, a hat. My eyes scanned the horizon, searching for any opportunity.

The next day, after another night of hauntin' dreams that left me chilled and shaky, I came across a small house that stood out like a sore thumb. It looked more suited for a bustling town square than a farmer's field. White clapboard with large glass windows and red curtains fluttering in the breeze – it screamed money.

I stopped Hammer by a tree and surveyed the house for a while. I wasn't the type to jump into risky situations. I preferred a well-laid plan. I hid the pistol in my trousers, stuffin' the holster back into the saddlebag for now.

A short, scrawny man emerged from the barn behind the house, clothes hangin' off him like a scarecrow. I judged him mebbe forty years or so. Easy pickings, I thought, my fingers twitchin' with the need to kill. I missed my knife. That's where the satisfaction was at.

He was joined by a young woman, hair dark as night, hanging laundry on the line. No sign of children – good. Kids made people unpredictable, pushing them to desperate measures. I liked a clear path.

I was still hatless and tender footed. That meant I had to play the game nice and easy, bide my time, wait until the sheep had relaxed, laid down in the pasture.

After waiting a bit longer to ensure no one else was around, I walked Hammer up to the porch, metal bits jinglin', his hooves cloppin' on the sun-baked dirt.

Just as I expected, the man met me at the door, shotgun in hand. Living out here, you learned to be cautious. Not everyone passing through was friendly.

I gave him an easy smile, hands raised in surrender. It was a practiced routine by now. Ask for water, a meal, offer to work for it. Most folks were happy to have someone else do the chores. Honest folks always had a never-ending list of tasks.

"Howdy," I cajoled. "I, uh, met with some trouble a ways back. Got waylaid. I just needed to water my horse." I reached down to pat Hammer on the neck. "Do you mind?"

The man squinted at me, undecided. I was as helpless as a babe, sittin' with a shotgun trained on me.

"No matter," I answered his glare with my easy words. "I s'pose I could just mosey on over to the next place." I started to pull Hammer's reins to turn him.

"Oh, John, let him in," the woman appeared at the door, chidin'. "Supper's almost ready. Maybe we can find you somethin' of John's."

"That's mighty kind of you, ma'am," I smiled at her, noddin' politely, as the man scowled. "I wouldn't mind doin' some chores, pay for your kindness."

She glanced at her man, who nodded sullenly, lowered his shotgun, but kept it ready, eyes alert. My itch was pleased. This was goin' to be a fine game, pittin' myself against his suspicion.

"I thank you kindly," I nodded back, slowly slidin' off the horse, keepin' my movements slow and well laid out.

I joined them at the table for dinner, the woman bustlin' about. Ate what they gave me, heapin' compliments on the cookin', even though it tasted like dust. I had to force myself to eat every bite, chewin' like a cow. The Colt dug into my liver as I sat there, pretendin' with those folks.

I'd always thought I had a way with words, especially when it came to charmin' the ladies. But you had to be careful not to flag the bull by paying too much attention to them. It was a delicate dance, one I had mastered over the years. Leastways, that's what I thought.

As the woman started clearing the table, I readied to make my move. A swift draw, gun at the man's temple, while she fetched the cash. The gentler sex always wanted to steer clear of trouble, less likely to get trigger happy. Neither of them, of course, knew my plan was to enjoy watchin' the life drain from their eyes.

Feather set to barkin' outside as I went for the revolver. Except, this time, my hand wouldn't budge. Stuck, glued to my side like feathers on a woman's hat. A cold dread snaked through me as I frantically tried to yank it out of my trousers. My fingers twitched uselessly. I cursed under my breath, a string of colorful words that would have made even Boss Rawlins blush.

"Is everything alright?" the woman asked, her voice laced with concern and some condemnation. The man, however, glared at me with narrowed eyes, suspicion replacing his initial hospitality.

"Just a touch of indigestion, ma'am," I mumbled, forcing a smile through my panic. What was going on?

The man leapt to his feet, heftin' his shotgun again. My easy target had turned into a threat.

"I think it's time for you to head out," he growled, gesturing with the barrel towards the door. There wasn't much room for argument with cold steel and gunpowder. I stomped out the door, frustration boilin' over.

As I stormed toward them, Feather wagged his tail innocently by Hammer's side. The urge to lash out at him lingered, feelin' like he somehow was at the bottom of all this. With a frustrated growl, I mounted my horse and kicked him into a gallop.

Feather effortlessly kept pace, his tongue lolling out in a carefree manner that only deepened my irritation. Years at the orphanage and then under Boss Rawlins' firm hand had honed my vocabulary, and a string of colorful curses left my lips – a talent that apparently lye soap couldn't scrub away.

"Go on, get lost," I growled at the dog, his happy face just spit in my eye.

Then the horse got a mind of its own. When we came to a fork, he ignored my usual left turn and stubbornly took the right one. Left turns had always been my lucky charm. But he took the bit in his teeth and did as he dadgum pleased.

I hopped down and grabbed his reins, trying to steer him left. Hammer dug in his hooves, refusing to budge. Stubborn as a mule, that horse. I whacked him on the rump with the flat of my hand to get him moving.

He lashed out, his ears pinned back, nearly kicking my leg. He took another step in the wrong direction, pulling the reins taut in my hand. A man doesn't stand a chance in a tug-of-war with a three-quarter ton beast set on its own path.

I hollered at the stubborn beast. He flinched at my noise and ended up behind me, nudging me hard with his snout, steering me to the right. I stumbled forward a few steps to keep from getting knocked over. Hammer followed, pushing me along.

"Hold on now!" I yelled, turnin' back to the horse. "You ain't the boss of this here ride!"

Feather reappeared, that infernal grin plastered on his face, barkin' excitedly at me. He grabbed my pant leg and began helpin' the horse, pullin' me to the right. I kicked at him, frustration and rage fillin' me, which just made him bark more.

"You shut your yap, dog!"

Hammer shoved me again. I'd had enough. I drew the Colt, its weight not yet familiar to my hand. Cocked it, the metallic click echoin', and aimed it straight at the dog, who was still barkin'. Shot him dead on the spot, the crack ringin' in my ears.

I'm a good shot. Always have been. Got him right between the eyes, clean as a whistle. He flung back with the force of the bullet, then lay still. His head was a mess of exploded brains drying out already in the harsh sun. It filled me with a twisted satisfaction, silencing that stupid dog for good. No more of him yapping at me, those eyes sendin' me messages no earthly dog had the brains for.

I cocked the six-shooter again, holding it to the horse's head. "You're next if you don't get in line."

The horse snorted, but didn't flinch, too dumb to know the danger. But then that fool horse nodded at me. Like he understood every word. Sure, why not? I thought sarcastically. Wakin' from the grave, that strange hitch in pullin' my sidearm, a dog and a horse conspirin' to make right turns…what else was goin' to happen?

"Just remember who's boss," I muttered, more to myself than the horse. I was losin' my mind, runnin' straight to the madhouse.

Unfamiliar and highly unpleasant, guilt began to tingle. I ignored it, yankin' the reins to the left, uncarin' about the horse's mouth. He whinnied with protest but followed my direction, just like any normal horse. I don't think I'd ever appreciated normal as much as I did in that moment.

We rode for a while, stopping for the night under a blanket of stars. I felt a strange sense of peace, having finally shut up that feather-brained dog. Sleep came easy, despite the lingering questions about my strange situation. I didn't know why I was alive again, but I never was one to dwell on the whys of life. What mattered was the now, and how to make the most of it.

The next morning, after another night of unwelcome dreams, includin' one of Feather's brains glistenin' in the road, I woke before the usual buzzard serenade. I chased them off with a yell and a wave of my hat, feeling foolish all the while. Bullets weren't exactly plentiful, since I didn't have a spare box of 'em, and no money to buy them. I couldn't waste them on pesky birds.

That old urge, the one that had me drawn to the moments of life's transition, started to gnaw at me again. It was like an itch you couldn't scratch, a constant hum in the back of my mind. It had never truly left me, not since that time in the cell. But it wasn't unbearable yet. I still had a few days, or so I hoped.

7

The Old Lady

We rode for hours, the sun climbing higher in the sky, baking the land a dry brown. By afternoon, I pulled up in front of a ramshackle cabin, barely more than a one-room affair.

Carefully, I approached the cabin, senses on high alert, listening for movement inside, scenting for smoke, any sign of an inhabitant. Every rustle of the leaves, every creak of a branch, sent my muscles twitchin'.

I peeked through an open corner of the oiled paper window. Empty. Finding the door unlocked, I slowly swung it open, the creak of the hinges screaming in the silence. I checked the potbellied stove for heat. It was warm, the coals banked, lettin' me know I should get a hurry on, every moment riskin' the occupant's return.

Inside, a table covered with some fancy needle-worked cloth held a newspaper. Curious, I checked the date…seven days after my supposed hanging. My skin crawled. Seven days, and I knew I'd woke up four times.

I wasn't good at sums, but even I could manage this. I'd been in that grave for three days, at least. I wondered how old the paper was. My mind spinnin' its wheels like a locomotive on greased tracks, I folded it up, stuffed it in my shirt for later perusal.

A quick search yielded what I needed, a handful of coins in a small tin by the stove, the rest all nestled in a small, weathered chest. It was as if unseen hands had laid them out specifically for me: a dusty Stetson that seemed

44

molded to my head, boots, worn and soft, that fit my feet as if bespoke, and a Winchester rifle, in near mint condition, usin' the same bullets as the revolver. Two boxes of hefty slugs sat beside them, a promise of firepower.

But the real prize was a long Bowie knife with a handle of deer antler, carved with a depiction of a man and a dog, both tensed toward a common enemy. Its cured leather sheath bore the faint scars of past adventures.

I could almost see the crimson drippin' from the sharp edge of the crucible steel, soothin' that itch that even now chafed under my collar. Even a dark wool riding coat, worn but impeccably tailored, was folded under it all.

It was a mother lode for a man on the run, a gift from the dusty plains themselves. I grinned in excitement as I fit them all to me, relieved to have somethin' more to defend myself. I left the nearly empty chest on the floor, only a few doodads remainin' - a worn pocket bible, a circlet of braided brown hair threaded with black beads, mementos of the previous owner.

As I straightened from the dusty floorboards, something caught my eye – a mirror. The man staring back was the same weathered face I knew, perhaps a touch paler than I'd been, before livin' months in that cell. There were wrinkles around the eyes and the mouth, more prominent than I remembered, sandy hair a bit long, darker beard a bird's nest, blue-gray eyes glinting with a calculating edge.

He looked hungry, a bit crazed 'round the eyes. The reflection mirrored my feelin's, exposed and reelin' from the strangeness of the day. Dead or not, that itch inside dug at my insides, the same as always. Had anything really changed? I shoved the question aside, not willin' to follow that trail.

Stepping outside, a new confidence filled me, with boots on my feet and a knife at my side. That's when she appeared – an old woman peering at me through her spectacles. Her face held surprise, but none of the fear it should have. Plain and open, it was…unusual.

As the hairs on my arms raised, my hand instinctively reached for the gun, years of habit ingrained. But before I could draw, somethin' wet pushed hard to get my fingers away from the handle. I jumped, my head snappin' down, to find Feather, his dark eyes gleaming as he gazed at me.

Surprise speared through me. Did the dog just.... He'd been dead, no doubt about it. I'd seen his brains splatter on the road. But here he was, not a single mark on him. Just like me. My mind skittered away from it all like a wild horse from the lasso, and I tamped it down firmly in to the dark corners of my mind.

Did he just stop me from drawing on a harmless old lady? The thought was laughable, impossible. Feather wagged his tail, seemingly unaware to the tumblin' thoughts in my head. There was no mistaking the intelligence in his gaze, a wisdom that didn't belong in a dog's eyes. The way he stared at me… my mind skittered away from the thought like a horse spooked by a rattler.

"You found Jack's things," the old lady spoke, distractin' me from Feather. Her voice was smooth and mellow, like the fine scotch I'd once bought after a fine take. A warm smile creased her face, but her voice sounded off to me, like it was too kind. "I'm glad someone can use them."

"Jack?" I mumbled, as I took a step back, feelin' alarmed for reasons I daren't consider.

"My son," she sighed. "Been gone a couple of years now. It gets lonely out here."

She herded me back inside, flappin' her hands at me to get me to move, and offered me a seat as she began to stir the coals and lay a fire in the potbellied stove. I sat, bemused to the point of silence, and watched her work.

"You know, my roof's been leakin' a mite," she mused as she turned to butcher a chicken. Had she had that in her hands outside? I hadn't noticed, nor had I seen it when I'd searched the two room cabin. "I've been meanin' to replace the shingles, but haven't got the gumption to get up that ladder."

A memory held me captive for a moment, of my hands grippin' a ladder set against the wall as Ma Josie whaled on me with a stick. I sat awkwardly, tryin' to hide the shakes, wanting to skedaddle but feelin' somethin' gluin' me to that rickety chair.

As if sensing my hesitation, Feather whined softly, his gaze fixed on me. A wave of warmth washed over me, an odd comfort that seemed to emanate from the scruffy dog. It was then I felt a strange urge, a compulsion to help this kind woman. Nope, I was not entertainin' such thoughts.

"I'd be happy to fix your leaky roof, ma'am," the words tumbled out like a runaway stagecoach.

The old lady's smile widened, crinkling the corners of her eyes, eyes that pierced my soul. "That's mighty kind of you, young man. Jack always talked about helping others. Seems like some of that rubbed off on you, even if you are a stranger."

I mumbled something unintelligible, the warmth spreading through me intensifying. It felt... good, satisfying in a way I was unused to, while also unnerving in its strangeness.

Following Feather's lead as he trotted eagerly outside, I grabbed the ladder and the bucket of nails and wooden shingle slabs beside it. Though my hands shook, they were strangely strong and steady as I climbed.

The scent of fresh-cut wood and sun-baked earth filled my senses, calmin' me. Looking down, I saw Feather at the base of the ladder, his tail wagging furiously as he watched me. There was something almost knowing in his gaze.

Sweat beaded on my forehead under the burnin' sun as I hammered shingles into place. It didn't take too long, as the hole was small and easily patched. Despite the discomfort, a strange satisfaction filled me at completing the task. It was a far cry from the mindless violence that had filled my past.

Finally, I scrambled down the ladder, landing with a thud. I took a deep breath as I brushed myself off.

"All done, ma'am," I called out as I entered again, the aroma of chicken and lard heavy in the air. My stomach rumbled, my mouth watered, both forgotten sensations. Yet, the sight of the food filled me with a strange unease.

"Dinner's ready, young man," she turned from the stove with a plate of chicken in her hand. I had a flash of thick crimson stainin' the neck of her blouse before my sight returned to the here and now. "What is your name, by the way?"

Good question. Been a while since I used my orphanage name, had several names since then. They hung me as Will Carter, didn't want that one for sure. Time for a new moniker.

"Eli. Eli Colton." I winced. Stupid name. But I hadn't had time to think on it. Well, I could come up with a new one tomorrow. Names don't really matter much to folk like me.

"Well, Eli, come on in." It looked delicious, as she finished fryin' up chicken and set it on a plate, next to a bowl with golden mashed potatoes and green beans swimming in butter. But the thought of taking a bite…

She'd heaped a plate full of golden, crispy fried chicken, buttered mashed potatoes, and fresh green beans for me. I obediently sat in front of it, uncomfortable, not sure what else to do.

"Thank you, ma'am," I said. Ma'am this, Ma'am that. It brought back memories I didn't much like. Ma Josie hittin' my hand with a wooden spoon for reachin' for a bite to eat.

Taking a bite of the chicken, crisped to perfection and smellin' like bliss, the familiar crunch of the crispy skin should have been followed by a burst of flavor. Instead, a dull sensation filled my mouth. It wasn't bad, exactly, but muted, like the sun-bleached paint on an old house. A faint echo of what it should have been.

Disappointment rattled through me. My shoulders slumped, and a frown etched itself onto my face. The thought of food had seemed so appealing earlier. Now, it sat heavy in my stomach, a reminder of something… different.

Feather, ever perceptive, tilted his head and let out a soft whine. It was a sound laced with concern, a sound that resonated deep within me.

Pushing the plate away, I mumbled, "Not hungry anymore, ma'am. Thank you for the kindness."

I stood up woodenly, anxious to leave this woman, and all the thoughts she stirred, behind. "I gotta get going, ma'am. But thank you again for everything."

"Now, Eli, you at least have a slice of pie before you head out," she insisted, already cutting a generous piece of the apple pie.

I hesitated, then took the fork. The warmth of the pie seeped through the plate, a comforting sensation, its golden crust light and flakey, the apple slices covered in a warm glaze. The aroma hit me – sweet apples, warm spices – a memory from a lifetime ago.

Maybe it was the memory, or maybe something more, but a sliver of hope flickered within me. Taking a bite, I braced myself for the first taste.

The first bite sent a shiver through me. The barest hint of sweetness teased my tongue, a spectrum of flavor that was both warm but darkened and dreary, like old paint on a weathered board.

It should have been familiar, the memory of apple pie a comforting beacon. Yet, it was different, once again muted, distant, like a dream half-remembered. Worse than bad cookin', it was just faint, and I wondered, was the pie a dream, or was I?

Tears welled up in my eyes, a mixture of confusion and a strange yearning. Was this what it meant to be alive? To experience the world through taste and smell, a symphony of sensations I'd forgotten, or perhaps never truly known? And what was I now? What was this strange world I'd woken into?

The old lady studied me with a worried frown, but her eyes dug deep into my heart. A knot formed in my throat, makin' it difficult to swallow. "Are you alright, Eli? You look pale."

I forced a smile as I stuck my hat on my head. "Just a long ride, ma'am. I'll be fine."

The truth was, I wasn't fine. This feeling of disconnect, this muted existence, was unsettling. It wasn't quite like being dead, I didn't suppose, but it wasn't quite being alive either.

The old lady patted my shoulder, her touch surprisingly strong and steady. "Sometimes, son," she said, her voice soft yet firm, as her eyes flickered strangely in the dimming' light, "we're so busy runnin' we forget about the livin'."

Looking at Feather, his eyebrows raised and head cocked inquisitively, I knew she was right. My journey had just begun, and somehow, this scruffy dog with eyes full of ancient wisdom was going to be my guide.

"I appreciate the offer, ma'am," I said, pushing the unfinished pie away. "But I think I better get a move on. Could get a couple hours down the road before dark."

"Oh, you could stay in the barn for the night, Eli. No need to sleep on the ground tonight."

I backed away. "No, ma'am. I gotta get goin'. Could get a couple hours down the road 'fore dark." There was something about this kindness, this feeling of normalcy, that unnerved me. It was somehow…wrong. Like I wasn't supposed to be here.

"Well, thank you again, Eli. I truly appreciate your kindness."

"No trouble, ma'am."

I tried not to look like I was rushing to my hammer-headed horse, but truth be told, I was in a hurry to get away from the unnaturalness that had kicked me in the face there. Mounting, I kicked him into motion, and put that odd little cabin behind me.

"You mind tellin' me why my taste is soured?" I mumbled, the question tumbling out before I could stop it. Consarn it, it was like my mouth had the trots.

And…I was talkin' to the dog again. I grit my teeth. Stupid dog.

I twisted in my saddle to look at that odd little cabin once more. My eyes searched the clearin', unbelieving. There was nothin' there. I clenched my eyes shut, opened them again to the empty meadow.

My stomach lurched, and I leaned over and lost what I'd been able to swallow of that mirage meal.

I looked to Feather, flummoxed and nigh to scared. He whined, standin' on his hind legs with his paws on my boot, there in the stirrup. Was he tellin' me it would be okay? Whether he was, or wasn't, I felt a smidge better as I kicked Hammer into a trail-eatin' canter.

Was I still dead? Dreaming? Or something else entirely? All those times I'd stared death in the face, yet I couldn't tell if it had finally come for me this time.

Frustration and helplessness bubbled up inside me.

I wasn't exactly in a good mood, to put it mildly. The strange happenin's of the grave and the old lady had me ill at ease, and that blasted dog wasn't helping. He looked at me sometimes like he was tryin' to deliver some cryptic message, and I thought back to the sheriff's wife and her obsession with spirits come back to haunt the living.

I narrowed my eyes suspiciously as he darted into a bush, leaving me and Hammer standing there like a couple of fools. Frustration tainted every breath. I looked down at my hands. They looked alive enough to me, rough, calloused, scarred, the hands of a man with years of hard livin' - not like some waxy corpse shell.

An idea struck me, as odd as everythin' else I'd been through. Grittin' my teeth, I took out my new knife, the antler hilt cool in my hand, and sliced open the back of my arm, a morbid test to check my mortality. Pain, sharp, real and immediate, just as one might expect. That was a good sign - at least I could still feel pain. A moment later, bright red blood welled up, starting to trickle down.

So, I was alive enough to bleed normally then. New blood, too, not some old, stagnant stuff. That meant I could probably die again. Mebbe. Death might take next time.

I wanted to know why I was back. How I ended up…not quite dead. That dog knew more than he was letting on, I was sure of it. He returned, like I'd summoned him with my thought, cockin' his head at me. Strangely.

I mounted Hammer. "You got any answers for me, Hammer?" I muttered, frustrated and unsettled.

His ears flicked back, but he offered no enlightenment. Of course not, I told myself. He was a horse. Horses don't talk.

8

The Mission

The saloon reeked of stale sweat, cheap tobacco and spilled liquor, the desperation of men, a familiar stench that, paradoxically, usually soothed my frayed nerves. Today, it did nothing, my gut tight like a rattler before it strikes. All I craved was a soul-scorching swig of whiskey to drown out the constant itch under my skin, ants crawlin' under my skin. My craving for darkness, the calm blood offered me.

It was a small, dark building, with one small window covered over with oiled paper, scarred floorboards and a rough wooden counter, just a dusty hole where weary travelers like me drowned their sorrows for a nickel a shot. My hand tremblin' like some town drunk, I nearly dropped the coins before I slapped them on the counter. Clenchin' my fists against the palsy, I barked out my request, the bored bartender not giving me a second glance as he pushed a glass my way.

Whiskey usually burned a welcome path down my throat, a fiery blanket that numbed the edges of reality, soothed the itch, cooled my mind. This time, it went down like water, no burn, no relief. I slammed the empty glass down, frustration bubbling like cheap beer.

"Same again," I growled, suspecting the bartender had filled the bottle with colored water just to spite me.

Or maybe that cursed dog had tampered with it – like he'd tampered with everything else since I'd crawled out of that strange grave. Why else would the liquor fail me? The second glass went down as easily as the first, just like water, and I beat it out of there before I started a commotion I didn't need, the itch diggin' its claws even deeper.

Days blurred into one another. Hunger, thankfully, wasn't a problem, and the cut on my arm healed to a shiny pink scar despite my lack of tendin' to it. The itch settled deep into my skin, causin' me to tremble like an old coot with the strength of it, my guts sick and twisted.

I didn't speak to Feather, not a word. Was he a demon sent to torment me for my past sins, or a spirit guide leading me on some bizarre journey? Neither explanation sat well with me.

Truth is, I was adrift in a sea of my own making, and Feather and Hammer were just along for the ride. Didn't have much choice, did I?

* * *

I suppose it was about ten days after waking up in that coffin, accordin' to that newspaper, anyhow, we stumbled upon an abandoned Spanish mission. These old relics were usually crumbling husks, testaments to a cast away faith. This one, however, defied expectations. It was mostly intact, with weathered adobe walls and a surprisingly sturdy roof. Smoke curled from a hidden chimney, a beacon in the gathering storm.

The sky looked like a bruised peach, spitting angry gray tendrils that threatened hail or worse. Hammer whinnied, sensing the coming tempest. I figured we might as well seek shelter for the night, and with a sigh, I dismounted near the weathered wooden door. Maybe I'd even get a chance to slake the itch, calm its burnin' under my skin.

A pounding on the floorboards from within made me tense. More than one pair of footsteps. This could spell trouble. A girl's voice, soft and sweet, drifted through a broken pane.

"Just k-k-eep moving, mister."

I peered through the dark, catching a glimpse of dark hair and the unmistakable double voids of a shotgun. A tiny thing, this guard. Doubtful she could even hold the weapon steady. I'd have no trouble with her.

A grin, practiced and easy, stretched across my face. Familiar territory. A sheep to my wolf, I only had to get in the gate. "Now, now, little lady, no need for such hostility. Just looking for a place to rest my weary head before the storm hits."

"This ain't it," she retorted, the sharp sound of the shotgun cocking makin' my muscles freeze.

Then something completely unexpected happened. Feather, who had been silent until now, let out a low, mournful whine, a sound that sent shivers down my spine. It wasn't the playful yips I was accustomed to. The barrels of the shotgun wavered for a moment, the hostility momentarily forgotten.

"Ssscoot!" she scolded the dog, her voice losing its edge. Ah, she had a soft spot for dogs.

Seeing my chance, I took a hesitant step forward, only to draw her attention back to me. I stopped again, hands still up, hunchin' my shoulders to make myself smaller, less of a threat.

"G-get back, mister. You and your mmangy mutt. Two loaded b-barrels aimed right at you, and I ain't afraid to use them."

Bluffing. This girl couldn't be older than twenty, her voice tremoring and catchin' over the howl of the wind. An easy target. I could almost feel the itch quietin'.

"Nasty storm brewing, miss," I said, gesturing at the sky. "Just recovered from a bout of pneumonia. Don't fancy spending the night soaked to the bone. I'll even sleep in the barn."

There wasn't a barn, of course, but desperation has a way of making you creative. Lyin' offers like that put people at ease. I truly did not want to spend the night out in the storm. As if an afterthought, Feather whined again, a silent plea for her to relent.

Silence stretched, thick and heavy. The girl was clearly torn. Her face was young, only a few years past childhood, I reckoned. Her hair'd likely be chestnut in the daylight, but now it was dark and red when the fire hit it. A largish nose, dark eyes that were altogether too seein' for comfort.

"I'll even give you my gun," I offered, reaching for my holster.

The shotgun jerked back up, aimed at my chest. I froze, my smile hardening into a snake oil salesman's grimace.

"Just givin' you my iron. I don't want no trouble, just shelter. Might be lightning, and hail, tonight."

Feather whined pitifully, rising to plop his front feet in the opening right in front of the barrels. Her expression softened at the sight of the dog. Huh, I thought. If I'd had a good dog like that all these years, the things I mighta done!

"J-just the pistol, mister. And no funny business. Shelter only." she agreed unhappily. "We don't have a barn, you'll have to come in."

She didn't lower the gun, but tried to keep one hand on the trigger while reachin' out for my piece. Carefully, I unbuckled the holster and handed it over. "Thank you kindly, ma'am." Appeasing young girls was all about the formalities, I'd learned. A touch of respect goes a long way.

The door creaked wider, just a sliver, and I near about jumped outta my skin. A dozen pairs of dark, frightened eyes stared back at me, huddled together like they was expectin' trouble.

Not adults, but children – Apache children dressed in a mashup of traditional garments and tattered white man's clothes. They ranged from barely walkin' to a boy, maybe 12 years old, his dark eyes watchin', measurin'. A wave of unexpected emotion washed over me – a mixture of surprise and… something else.

The distrust in their eyes called to mind memories I didn't want to inspect further. The young woman, looked to be just older than marryin' age, stood in front of them, a double-barreled shotgun aimed plumb center at my chest.

"Let the man in, children," she said, her voice surprisingly steady for such a skinny thing. "He'll sleep in that corner there." She jerked her chin towards the far side of the room, that shotgun never leavin' my gut. Her arm was shakin' with the weight of it though, a tremor that danced right down to the weapon.

"Sure thing, ma'am," I mumbled, keepin' everythin' calm and easy, movin' slow and predictable, calmin' her suspicions. Didn't want no surprise to tighten her finger on that trigger. "No need for that big shooter. I'm not here to make trouble."

"Forgive my caution, mister, but I can't be too careful of strangers," she replied, lowerin' the shotgun a hair. "What's your name?"

"Colton. Eli Colton." I offered it up, a name a strange social lubricant that seemed to calm folks down more than anything else I could say, as if it wasn't easy as pie to come up with a false moniker.

"Good to meet you, Mr. Colton," she said, a hint of defiance still clinging to her voice, "I learned a hard lesson a long time ago: wolves easily hide in sheep's clothing." There was a flicker in her eyes, somethin' I couldn't quite place.

"Heard that one before myself, ma'am," I said, keepin' my expression neutral, my hands where she could see them. She was still twitchy.

"You can call me Mmiss G-granley." Her voice had a hitch to it, but she paid it no mind, 'cept for an occasional quick blink of her eyes. She uncocked the shotgun with a practiced ease that surprised me, but still held it ready. Feather slunk past me and curled up in the designated corner without a whimper. Smart animal.

I followed Feather, hat clutched in my hand. Hammer would be fine tethered under the overhang outside. Settling into the corner, I kept my eyes on her as she settled the kids, a question gnawed at me.

"What's the story here?" I asked, my voice rough. "You folks hidin' from somethin'?"

Miss Granley scanned the room, her gaze lingerin' on the children, like she was countin' heads, before meetin' mine. She thrust her beak of a nose up in the air, eyes flashin'. "That's none of your concern, Mr. Colton. You're here for shelter, that's all."

"But that fire," I said, gesturin' towards the cracklin' flames, "ain't exactly discreet. Especially with a storm brewin'. The light from the window will be seen for miles."

Her eyes darted to the fire, panic replacin' her earlier defiance. She lunged for a bucket and doused the flames with a hiss and a splatter of sparks. Smoke billowed out, chokin' the air from the room. The schoolteacher coughed, wavin' at the clouds.

"Sand woulda been quicker, with less smoke," I offered, unable to resist a jab despite the situation. Something about Miss Granley rubbed me funny.

I watched her struggle to control her emotions, a flicker of somethin'… surely not sympathy…threatened to spark within me. I shoved it down. No use gettin' tangled up in someone else's problems. I never did, just let things happen like they were s'posed to.

"Look, Miss Granley," I said, my voice flat, "I ain't here for trouble. Just passin' through. If someone's after you and these kids, well, I don't got a dog in that fight." Why'd that feel like a lie? I rubbed at my chest, tryin' to ease the tightness there.

Miss Granley stared at me, her face unreadable. She knelt down beside a little girl who was clutchin' her skirts tightly. The girl's dark hair obscured her features.

"It's alright, Goyan," Miss Granley whispered, her voice tremblin' slightly. "We're safe here."

I couldn't help but ask, "Safe from who?"

"That's none of your concern," she snapped again, her defiance returnin'.

I looked around the room again. These weren't hardened outlaws on the run. They were a young woman and a bunch of scared children. What kind of danger could they possibly be in? I couldn't place it, but somethin' about the whole situation didn't sit right with me.

"Look, lady," I said slowly, not wantin' to rile her, not with that shotgun still in her hands. "I may not know the whole story, but I can tell you're scared. And those kids…" I trailed off, searching for the right words. "What are you hidin' from?"

"Who said we are hiding?" she shot back, hackles up.

I looked around at the room. It had the air of a building long empty, recently occupied. There were no personal effects, no signs of daily livin'. They'd just come to it in the last few hours, by my reckonin'.

"No one. Figured it only made sense. Young white woman, a dozen Indian kids, alone in an abandoned mission. Only logical explanation."

"I'll thank you to keep your nose out of our affairs. As you said yourself, you are here to shelter for the night, that's all."

Fear flashed through me, a moment then gone. It wasn't my own, was it?

I glanced back toward the other side of the room. The teacher had her arm wrapped around the girl and was stroking her hair. Her face had this hopeless look on it, like she knew she couldn't win but she was gonna go down fightin'.

All a sudden, I felt it too. Something I'd give my life for, just to say I stood for it. But I didn't feel that, had never felt any such thing. Did I?

I glared at Feather, my mind scrambled like an egg. He thumped his tail on the floor, head on his paws, eyes looking up at me with a knowledge a normal dog didn't have.

I looked again at the girl. I'd die for these kids, just to give them a chance at a decent life. Wait, no, not me. She would. Those were her feelin's. Feather nudged my leg.

"Stupid dog," I muttered, laying back.

"He is perfectly well-mannered," she said primly, that beak of hers in the air yet again.

"If you only knew the trouble he gets me into, ma'am," I answered, not movin' a muscle.

I was hit by a wave of wishing I wasn't alone in the world, had someone to lean on. I sat bolt upright, lookin' to the girl, then to the dog. Feather thumped his tail again. Not me. Her. It had to be her..

A warm, peaceful sensation hit me. A feeling of intermingling, of wanting the best for another. I shook my head to rid myself of it, started to get to my feet. I'd rather sleep in the rain than feel this mess of emotions.

9

Takin' them On

Feather whuffed at that moment, poppin' up to his feet with ears perked, eyes focused on the window. It was a warnin', pure and clear. I stood, leaned against the edge, and peeked out.

That girl was instantly beside me with her shotgun, barrel down, face pale. Her eyes wide and white, like a spooked horse. At least she had sense enough not to stand in the window, but peered from the side, like me.

"What is it?" she asked in a loud whisper, like she'd never really had to be quiet before.

I put my finger to my lips, wanting her to keep quiet. I looked to Hammer, watchin' his ears. He had his head up, his ears pricked to listen down the road.

I hopped like my pants was on fire, feelin' stupider than all get out. Anybody rode by they'd find the cotton-pickin' horse. I threw open the door, jumped out and grabbed his bridle, and pulled him in. The kids scattered away from his dinner plate sized hooves, their eyes huge. I put him in the room next door, with fewer windows.

As I came back to the window, two riders were approaching from a distance. I put my finger to my lips and waved my hand down, hoping the kids would stay down and quiet. Any luck, the men would just ride on by.

My gaze met with hers, her mouth firmed up, and she gave a curt nod. She

59

had her shotgun ready. She was a little thing full of gumption and spit, like a little kitten fightin' off a bear.

We were out of luck. They were coming closer.

"Hold it right there!" I called, a stronger mimic of her earlier command. "We've got you covered."

The horses drew to a sharp stop. The men raised their hands. "Just looking for shelter from the storm comin'."

"We c-can't let them ssee the children," she hissed beside me, fingers turned to claws in my arm.

I eyed the strangers, my muscles tensin' as I read their plans on their faces, the way they sat their horses. Their eyes gleamed with a predatory light, ice runnin' through my blood, wolf recognizing wolf. "We're full up here," I barked back. "Keep on ridin'."

If it was myself, I'd invite them in. Raise less suspicion, thataway. Folks expected hospitality, and if you didn't give it, they thought you might have somethin' special you didn't want to share.

But couldn't let them see the kids. I'd get all caught up in it…if I wasn't already.

"Sure thing, friend," they called back, easy voice not matchin' the way they straightened in the saddle. "Don't want no trouble."

They reined their horses back toward the road, same steady pace they'd come in with. I watched them go, not trusting a bit. Likely, if my read on them was right, they'd circle around and catch us by surprise. I'd have to keep watch.

The lady studied me, a frown on her face, before she relaxed and gave a little smile.

"Thank you," she said reluctantly. "You were a lot more convincing than I would have been."

I almost smiled at her thanks, surrounding me with warmth. I scowled at the feelin'. Didn't want it, didn't need it.

"They come in here, I'm tied up in whatever you got goin' on whether I like it or not."

Time was, I woulda lied and used her gratitude for my own ends. Didn't feel like it tonight. I was tired, and all this superstitious hootenanny'd got me right turned upside down.

"Tarnation, lady," I cussed again, her wince bringin' me somethin' akin to pleasure. "You stealin' these kids?"

"Absolutely nnot!" She stomped her foot and exhaled furiously. "We are on an ex-excursion."

Here's a tip: don't ever try to lie to a liar. I studied people, their moves that betray their thoughts. I know what they feel and how to use it to get what I want. And I know when someone's hidin' somethin'. How else am I gonna make sure I'm not givin' myself away?

And this peculiar woman, I knew as sure as up was up that she was hidin' somethin'. Somethin' big.

Her pointed little chin rose up in the air but her amber eyes flashed to the side. She didn't even lie good - a baby could see through her.

"Try again." I crossed my arms, glarin' at her.

Granley looked up at me, eyes narrow as she tried to cotton on to what I was after. She was a little thing, foot or more shorter than me. She had shadows behind her eyes, her fear runnin' through me. Unheard of, for me, before this strange week, to feel things like this. Unwelcome, for sure.

There was enough moonlight I could count the freckles in her face. She was pretty, the random thought flickered through my mind. I stomped it down good.

"I teach them, at the orphanage. The cavalry was coming. To take them to a boarding school, in St. Louis. Separating them from their families. I couldn't let it happen."

Her eyes flashed, her anger hittin' me like a punch to the gut. This wasn't just a picnic gone south. A gully washer of fear and determination hit me, tumblin' me ever' which way but Sunday. I near to reached out a hand to steady myself.

Stop it! I couldn't handle all these feelin's that were pushin' at me. I wasn't made for it. I was the evil boy in the cellar, the one Ma Josie was rightfully afraid of. The one Boss Rawlins sent to take care of "problems." Where was a soft lady like this schoolteacher then?

"So you were going to hide out here forever?" I thrust a hand toward the dark room. "Real stroke of genius, there, schoolteacher!" I scoffed, tossin' my hat on my blanket.

Her face darkened as her eyes darted away. She bent her head, picked at a thread on her sleeve.

"Well, I didn't have much warning to prepare." she offered, a tad less starchy. She swung her eyes back to me, tears wellin' up, and I rolled my eyes like they was dice on the table. "Well, actually, no warning. We barely made it out before the soldiers brought the wagon."

Well, nothing I can do, I told myself, thinkin' I had my way out. One man can't stand in front of an army.

I heard a mocking laugh in my head. I knew then I wasn't gettin' off that easy. I don't know what I done to earn this pile of horse…

Somethin' nudged my hand. I looked down, expecting Feather. It was the little girl the teacher had been holdin'. I yanked my hand up, out of her reach, my lip curlin' in disgust. Ain't no way I was gonna go round holdin' hands with no snot-nosed brats.

"You stay here, every Joe who rides by is gonna wanna stop in. You're right by the road."

She half-smiled. "I've begun to realize that," her voice wry.

I looked to the oldest boy. Surely an Indian kid would have a better idea of where to hide than this rundown mission.

"Any caves around? Somewhere the Army folks don't know about?"

The pride shone in his eyes at my question, certain of his knowledge. That feelin'd actually come to me, a time or two, when luck had smiled at me. His face sure didn't show it, though. Stony, like many Indian men I'd seen.

"Caves by Horse Tooth Mountain. They difficult to walk. No army man."

I'd run by those mountains a few times. Couldn't remember what they were called on the map, but the boy was right. They looked like back teeth in a horse skull.

"There's water there too?"

"Yes, sir."

I'd just been sir-ed. Liked the respect, I s'pose, but it made me feel old.

And strange inside, all wiggly in my guts.

"Well, then, that's where you need to go. Glad I could help."

"But, but," the school teacher stuttered, moving as if to reach for my arm before she stopped herself. "Couldn't you come with us?"

"Now, look here, lady," I started, when the stark fear in her face swept my breath away. Black, cold, fear. No hope of light. Dadblamit, I was gonna have to learn me some more feelin' words if this kept up. I'd no idea one woman could have this many emotions so close to each other. My head began to pound and I rubbed my hand on my forehead to ease it.

"H-here's y-your revolver back," she held it out to me, and I took it back, shovin' it into its holster at my hip. "You ssent those men off. W-we need ssomeone with survival skills," she rushed on, like she had the trap planned out all along, "Ssomeone who knows how to deal with the more…rough people."

"No way!" I shouted, desperate to fight against her trap. She stiffened and stepped back, the shotgun's barrel raisin' a hair. Good. She was scared. She should be. "I ain't gonna stick around in the mornin'. I got places to go, without no Indian kids."

"I can offer you reward money," she breathed out in a rush. "Keep us safe until my father has a chance to rectify the matter."

Well, hadn't she just hit the nail on the head. She must have seen somethin' in me soften, because she kept at it. "What's your price? A hundred dollars? A thousand?"

I stared at her, mute, while my mind blanked on that number. A thousand dollars? I'd never seen so much money, doubted I'd spent that much in all my days.

I blasted it all five ways to Sunday. Was I ever gonna be back to myself again? What was happenin' to me? Surely, I'd died and this was Hell. That yella-haired lady, that last one. She'd talked about feelin', musta cursed me, 'fore she'd died. Why else was I even listenin' to this crazy schoolteacher? I'd never let feelin's outgun cold, hard logic. I shoved the thoughts down, buried them deep, brought back my fangs.

"Rest up," I growled as I stomped to my corner. "We'll head out at first light."

The sun shone in my soul. That's the only way I could call it. The room lightened up with her relief. I needed to douse this newfound warmth before it got out of hand.

"But I ain't carrying nobody," I added, pulling my hat over my face. "I ain't no nanny."

I lifted my hat a touch to add, "And don't you get no ideas you're the boss of this here trail ride!"

I muttered then, "Dadgum women and children. Just give me somethin' to shoot, 'fore I fly off the handle."

Her disagreeable humph made me feel a mite better.

10

Violence on the Trail

I hadn't ever been one for dreamin', before the grave, or at least rememberin' them when I wake up. But somehow steppin' out of that coffin had brought dreams that taunted me, pulled my insides out. This one felt more like a memory clawin' its way back, a memory I usually shoved way down deep. Don't dwell on the past, that's what I tell myself. No good comes of it.

After Ma Josie kicked me out of the orphanage, I figured I was about nine when they stuck me workin' on the ranch. More like slavery, the way I saw it. No sayin' no for me back then.

Strong for my age, I guess, so they put me cuttin' steers, muckin' stalls, loadin' wagons alongside grown men. But what really shaped me into the man I was today was that Boss Rawlins sent me to "take care" of anyone got in his way. Watched me close during the day, locked me in a room at night like a caged coyote.

Made me strong, I s'pose, all that heavy work, the bloody work. Gave me a mean streak a mile wide. Taught me how to read people, what they chase after. Most folks are like wolves, huntin' the weak ones.

Boss Rawlins, he hated my guts. Kept me around just the same. Made him feel bigger, havin' someone to beat on, to do the work of two of his hired hands. Just an orphan kid, nobody to miss me, right? He shoulda known better. I developed my skills early on, I guess.

I woke up with a start, heart thuddin' like a blacksmith's hammer, to find that boy from the night before starin' down at me. His eyes held a wisdom that sent shivers down my spine. Not many grown men had eyes that haunted like that. He nodded slow, warily, his hand on that smilin' mutt's back.

"Miss Granley is good woman," he said in his broken English. "You hurt her, I kill you."

I understood every word as the warnin' flashed in his eyes.

"Good spirit," he continued, lookin' at the dog.

"What's that supposed to mean?"

He held my gaze, those dark eyes like bottomless pits. "You not alive. Not dead. Stuck in between. Good spirit decides."

I gaped as he turned, walked away quiet-like, and started rollin' up his blankets. I couldn't stop the shiverin' that came on then. Dawn was paintin' the sky a pale pink as I peered out the window.

"Granley," I called, not in the mood for her little-girl name. Didn't budge. "Granley, get those kids movin'."

The boy glanced back, his face unreadable as always, then went to wake the teacher with a hand on her shoulder. She shot up with a gasp. "Oh, it's time already?" She started her rounds, gently coaxin' the kids awake.

One of 'em let out a wail, and that familiar itch started crawlin' under my skin. Never could stand cryin'. It grated on my nerves somethin' fierce, and my nerves was already wrecked, between my dreams and that boy's words. Saddled Hammer quick as I could and waited. Finally, I stomped back in.

"What's takin' so long?" I barked.

She looked up from tuckin' a blanket around a snivelin' kid, her eyes wide with surprise. "We need to use the privy, wash our faces, and eat breakfast, Mr. Colton."

My lip curled in disgust. "Ain't no need for all that fancy washin'. We can eat and relieve ourselves on the road. Let's go!"

"These are not c-cowboys on a cattle drive, sir," she snapped. "They are children."

Her shrill voice set my teeth on edge. "Children or not, they can travel," I growled. The itch was makin' my hands shake. Her blood would probably be bright red, not that dark, sluggish stuff. Seemed to fit her, somehow.

I slammed the door behind me as I stomped outside. What in tarnation was I doin'? I could be long gone, miles away from these grubby little scamps and their naggin' teacher.

But I knew I wouldn't. That thousand dollars had me tied as tight as a calf on brandin' day. I kicked a rock in frustration. Guess it woulda been better just to die that day. Now I was stuck with a pushy dog, a stubborn horse, and a schoolmarm with a dozen kids to keep outta the Army's way. And why not throw a flyin' pig into the barnyard while we're at it?

Granley marched out with the kids in a line, lookin' for all the world like a mama duck with her ducklings. She stopped in front of me, her back straight, jaw clenched tight. Starin' up at me with those syrupy eyes of hers, dared me to somethin'. It hit me like a sucker punch – she expected me to not only let the brats ride my horse, but to pick them up and put them on myself.

Death of somethin', anything, was necessary to make this itch stop gnawin' at me. *Find somethin' quick, or it'll be one of them.*

Took a deep breath, shoved the murderous urge down deep. Didn't like it festerin' there, but it was better than scarin' these kids half to death. They'd get loud and leaky then. Swallowed my pride and reached down, scooping up the first one – a little girl all warm and wiggly. Like holdin' a squirming sack of rotten potatoes.

"Really, Mr. Colton," Granley smirked. "It's not that bad."

The dadgum woman was laughin' at me! I glared up to the sky, hopin' for some divine intervention. The dumb dog just wagged his tail and licked the nearest kid, who giggled in response.

Granley chuckled again. "See? Your dog doesn't mind them."

"Yeah, well, dogs like nasty things," I growled. "Like lickin' their own behinds."

"Oh, Mister Colton!" she chided with a scowl that didn't reach her twinklin' eyes. "Watch your language!"

Picked up the next one, a boy this time. Drool drippin' from his chin like a leaky faucet, straight onto my hand. Took all the patience of a saint not to wipe it off on my pants before hoistin' him onto the horse.

Granley doubled over laughin'. "Oh dear, I'm so sorry!"

"Ain't funny," I grumbled. Made her laugh even harder.

Third one got the same treatment, plopped down behind the others, and I wiped my hands on my dusty trousers for the hundredth time. Took the reins and glared at the kid she'd called Charlie or whatever it was. He just nodded, another kid clinging to his back, and led the way.

Walkin'. Hated walkin'. Boots were made for ridin', not for carryin' a man's weight around on his own two feet. Even worse with kids, always whinin' or needin' somethin'. Seemed like every ten minutes they had to stop for somethin'. Luckily, the teacher kept them in line and I didn't have to deal with 'em much.

My hands itched somethin' fierce, shakin' like leaves in a storm. They craved the feel of the knife in my hand. Guns were for protection, but knives... knives were pure pleasure.

"Need blood, Feather," I muttered under my breath.

The dog's tail thumped against my leg.

"It'll get where I can't stop it," I said, more to myself than him. Tried holdin' off before, goin' long stretches. Knew every kill put a target on my back. I ain't stupid. But then, with each kill, somethin' snapped. Couldn't think straight, just the feel of the blood, warm and slick.

One time I pushed my luck too far, got seen. Maybe that's why the law was after me in the first place. Wondered if my dyin' had thrown them off the scent.

I saw the schoolteacher throw me a worried glance or two. She probl'y could feel the evil comin' off me, the need for death. I kept my eyes off her.

I sighed, forced one foot in front of the other, followin' the kid. What in tarnation was I doin' here? Herdin' these Indian kids, givin' up my horse, walkin' like a sodbuster. Seven kinds of fool, that's what I was.

We came out of the woods, and there they were – two riders in the distance.

"Get close," I hissed. "Let me handle this."

Couldn't tell if they were the same two from the night before. It'd been too dark to see faces well enough then. As they got closer, their intentions became clear as daylight. No good comin' from these two. Wolf scents wolf.

The bloodlust roared loudly, clawin' at my sanity. Fought the urge, pretendin' to be nervous. Didn't get nervous. That was for folks with feelin's, with souls. But it helped draw the prey in closer.

"Well, well, look what we have here," the bigger one drawled, a fat smile plastered on his face. Two of them against one, and a whole mess of kids. "Looks like you got yourself a real interestin' family, ma'am."

Granley snapped her head up, eyes flashin' fire, but she kept her mouth shut, for once. The other one leaned closer, his horse snortin' in annoyance. No good, no good at all. Choices flashed through my mind like a deck of cards bein' dealt, as I came up with a plan.

Glanced at them all, then drew the Colt Frontier and aimed, finger pullin' the trigger, all in one motion smooth as silk. The big one I shot right in the head. Brains splattered outta the back of his head like... well, like brains. Glistened in the mornin' sun like specks of gold.

The other one, closer to the teacher, his horse reared back at the shot, almost throwin' him. I grabbed him by the waist of his trousers before he could react, the world slowing down around me. The familiar weight of the knife in my hand was a comfort, a dark whisper promising release. He looked up at me, fear replacing the earlier arrogance in his eyes.

"D-d-don't," Granley screamed, her voice a ragged thing.

I ignored her. This was mine, this bloodletting I craved. The point of the blade found his throat, a cold kiss before the warmth of the blood erupted. It washed over me, a wave of crimson calm, silencing the gnawing in my gut. His body went limp, the life draining out, pooling around my boots.

The metallic tang of blood filled my nostrils, a sweet, coppery perfume. I breathed it in deeply, like a starving man finding a feast. The world sharpened with clarity as the itch was sated, then I returned, the sound of the children's horrified cries cutting through the silence.

Granley stared at me, her face a mask of terror, tears streaming down her cheeks. The boy, Charlie, watched me with those dark, unreadable eyes, something flickerin' in them... respect? fear?...in their depths.

The teacher rushed to the side of the road and spilled her breakfast between sobs. "You-you k-k-killed them!" Granley finally choked out, tears and horror pourin' off her.

"Yep," I replied, not puttin' the effort of emotion into my voice.

"B-but… they d-didn't threaten us!" she sputtered, her voice rising in pitch.

"Didn't they?" I asked, my hand already reaching for the reins of my horse. This whole charade was wearing thin. I didn't need these people, and the children were a constant reminder of my own younger days.

She didn't respond, just stared at the bodies sprawled in the dust, her shoulders shaking with silent sobs. The children huddled around her, their faces an array of fear, some cryin', but they were quiet, I'd give them that. I shut down the thought of what that could mean. I wanted my money, not any sympathetic thoughts.

"Get their horses and their weapons," I ordered the boy, my voice cold. "We can use them."

He nodded silently, already moving towards the fallen men. Granley remained rooted to the spot, staring at me with a conglomeration of fear and loathing. I sighed, a rough sound escaping my lips.

"Look, lady," I said, my voice weary. "They were trouble. You and those kids are safer without them around."

A hollow lie, even I knew that. They were just two men. Even with evil on their mind, I coulda sent them away. I didn't need them dead, not for any practical reason. It was the itch, the hunger, the ravenous beast that resided within me, demanding its meal.

It was long minutes before Granley pulled herself together, her eyes hardening with a newfound resolve. She walked over to me, her chin held high.

"Aren't you going to give them a proper burial?" she asked, her voice tight.

I scoffed. "What for? They ain't gonna need it."

"It's the decent thing to do," she insisted.

I leaned closer, my voice dropping to a low growl. "Now, what makes you think I give a plugged nickel about decent?"

She flinched but didn't back down. "You're helping us. That's a decent thing to do, isn't it?"

I let out a bark of a laugh. "I want my thousand dollars, that's all. I don't care what happens, long as I get my cash."

She opened her mouth to retort, but I cut her off. "Look, you just gotta understand somethin'. The world ain't black and white, teacher. Sometimes bad folks do good things, and sometimes… sometimes folks who seem decent got a darkness in them you wouldn't believe. Don't you trust nobody in this world, most of all someone like me."

I pulled my hat down low, obscuring my eyes, and turned away, the weight of her stare heavy on my back. The boy finished gathering the spoils, a grim efficiency in his movements, as if this wasn't the first time he'd done this chore. I poured sand on the fire of that thought. Behind me, I heard Granley's skirts rustlin' and turned to find her tryin' to pull one of the men off the road, her stubborn face set and wet with tears.

I sighed and took over the task so we could get movin' again, knowin' she wouldn't back down from this fight. I pulled them to the side and rested their hats over their faces. I wasn't gonna be diggin' no cotton-pickin' graves. The woman musta realized that, 'cuz she just bowed her head over the corpses for a moment before she wiped her face with her sleeve and turned back to me. I shook my head. Fool soft-hearted woman.

We took their horses, heftin' the children up. The kids were silent behind us, their wide eyes reflecting their horror, givin' me an odd sensation inside.

As we rode on, I could almost feel Feather smirking beside me. The urge to shut him up, to silence any amusement, was strong. But I held it back. Because she was right. I was a monster, a wolf in sheep's clothing, leading these innocent souls right into the jaws of danger.

But for now, I was all they had. And what I hardly admitted to myself, what really had me scared, was I wasn't certain I was just in it for the money no more.

11

Horse Tooth Mountains

Silence, blessed silence, stretched for a deceptive eternity. Only the crunch of boots on the dusty earth to break it. Sweat trickled down my temples as the midday sun beat down without mercy. Then, like a crow's raucous caw, the teacher's voice shattered the peace.

"Mr. Colton," she said, her voice clipped but laced with a hint of worry, "The children are getting hungry."

I kept walking, boots crunching on the dusty trail, and squinted up at the merciless sun. It was high noon, maybe a little past.

"Can't they wait? How much farther, boy?" I tossed the question at Charlie, who rode behind me, his face an unreadable mask.

He shrugged, a gesture that spoke volumes despite his limited English. "Maybe four hours. Maybe more. We walk slow."

A long sigh escaped my lips, irritation coilin' tight in me. Glancing back, I met the teacher's gaze. Concern and a ghost of some unnamed emotion, wariness maybe, swam in her brown eyes. It made me itch, a phantom sensation like needing a hot bath to scrub away the stickiness of other people's feelings.

Life had been simpler before this "curse" started twisting me up inside. When had I changed into a man that would put up with this ever needy ragamuffin group? And that teacher! She never let things be, always hoopin' and hollerin' about something until I was fit to be tied. And yet, here I was, walkin' while the grubs rode my horse.

"They can eat while they walk," I grumbled, hoping to avoid the inevitable.

"Mr. Colton, we've been over this."

This time, she didn't just speak; she acted. A hand shot out, grabbing my elbow. My reaction was instinctual, a snarl rippin' from my throat as I spun around, anger flarin' hot and fast like a wildfire. She yelped, eyes wide, instinctively taking a step back. I could practically hear her heart hammering against her ribs.

"And I told you," I snarled, emphasizin' the danger I posed, "I ain't a nice guy. I don't give a…"

The words died before they met the air. Not with all those curious eyes watching. This whole charade – playing protector to a gaggle of scared children and a stubborn teacher – was eating away at me. Between the spooks, my dreams, and this woman stirring feelings I couldn't name, I felt like a cornered beast.

"You gotta understand, I don't feel things, school teacher, not like most people," I forced out, the words tasting bitter on my tongue. "Empty inside, always been. No soul, or something. So, you best be rid of me as soon as you can."

There, I'd said it. It oughtta scare her off, send her running back to whatever fancy life she left behind.

But this woman, Granley, surprised me. She squared her shoulders, chin jutting out like a defiant sparrow facing down a hawk. Sure, fear still flickered in her eyes, but she held her ground.

"And y-yet you are helping us," she said, her voice steady, even if her words hitched some. "What if you have more inside than you think? It's just been buried deep."

I ignored her words, yanking my hat down further, a shield against the world and the unwelcome emotions churning inside.

"Five minutes," I conceded through gritted teeth.

A ghost of a smile played on Granley's lips. Blast it all, I didn't need her gloatin'.

"You best not be lyin' 'bout my reward, neither."

She didn't respond to my dig, just gathered the children around her, her voice soothing as she distributed snacks from a pouch. When she offered some to me, I grunted a refusal.

"I ain't hungry."

"But you haven't eaten since you came in last night," she persisted.

I met her gaze head-on, letting the cold, empty monster lurking beneath the surface come up. A flicker of something crossed her face – pity? Disgust? – before she looked away.

Feather nudged my leg with his snout. I glanced sideways to notice Charlie staring at me. Did he see the same I did? The way the dog seemed… more than just an animal?

"Time's up," I barked, the gruffness back in my voice.

Granley scrambled to her feet, herding the children towards their mounts. She enlisted Charlie's help, pointedly keeping me out of it. I didn't argue. She was getting the message.

Except, when I caught her looking at me, there was something else hidin' in her eyes. Pity, yes, but something else too – a spark of determination, maybe even… hope?

I hated that look. I'd seen it before, the way people looked at me, wanting to "fix" me. I wasn't broken! I was different, made this way for a reason. Not human. They all gave up eventually. Hated that too, especially

Especially coming from this little slip of a girl, barely more than a wisp with her big brown eyes and a habit of biting her pink lip in concentration. Like she could unravel the tangled mess that was me and somehow make everything right.

I clenched my fists, my heart racin', and I wished to push them kids off my horse and beat it outta here. But something held me back. Maybe it was the way her fierce spirit mirrored my own, or maybe it was the flicker of fear in her eyes whenever I got too close to that monstrous edge.

We pressed on, leaving the dusty plains behind and entering the foothills. The path, if you could call it that, became a treacherous mess of loose rocks and thorny shrubs. The children, with their shorter legs, struggled to keep up with the horses. Granley, tried to help them, but her fancy little boots offered little purchase on the uneven ground.

Frustration simmered in me. We were wasting precious daylight, and these constant delays were getting on my nerves. Just as I was about to voice my irritation, Feather froze beside me, a whine sounding as his ears perked. Prickles ran over my skin as I followed his intent gaze, just as I noticed a young girl, no more than six, lose her footing and teeter on the edge of a steep incline.

I was movin' before her high-pitched cry pierced the air. I lunged forward, grabbing the girl by the scruff of her dress just as she tumbled. The fabric ripped in my hand, but I managed with a second grab to haul her back onto solid ground. She clung to me, sobbing hysterically, her small body trembling.

The other children watched, wide-eyed, while Granley rushed over, relief washing over her features.

"Are you alright, Hope? Mr. Colton, thank you!" Her voice trembled with gratitude.

I grunted noncommittally, shoving the girl towards her. The child, still sniffling, buried her face in Granley's dress as the teacher took her. I looked at Feather, cold settlin' into my bones. Feather's whine echoed, the way his body had frozen, pointin' to the ledge. Had he…? I shook my head. Best not entertain those thoughts.

The treacherous terrain continued, demanding constant vigilance. Fallen logs had to be cleared, loose rocks navigated, all while keeping the children safe and the group moving forward. The sun dipped lower in the sky, casting long shadows that stretched like skeletal fingers across the landscape.

"We need to find shelter for the night soon," Granley announced, her voice strained but resolute.

"What you goin' to do, in these caves? Hole up in there, 'til the color of their skin ain't a sin no more?"

She rolled her eyes at me, a flash of amusement momentarily chasing away the worry that kept her face pinched.

Don't guess no one's done that before. Made me feel all weird inside, like there wasn't a monster inside, always ready to come out.

"Hiding in the caves is a temporary solution," she responded. "My father is a Senator. I've written him asking for his help. I sent the telegram off before we left."

Well, that explained all sorts of things. Her pa was in the *government*. Prob'ly rich as all get out, too. 'Course he was, her with her nose in the air offerin' me a thousand dollar reward.

"Why you workin' as a teacher, then, if you're pa's so high 'n' mighty?"

Her gaze was heavy on me, but kept my eyes movin' around the trail, lookin' out for danger.

"I wanted to help children. I love teaching, seeing their eyes light with questions. It makes me feel…a part of something bigger than myself, like I can change the world, one child at a time."

"You're a dadgum fool. World don't change. Best you can do is keep yourself from drownin' along with the other rats."

She was silent for a blessed moment before she said softly. "It's a shame you feel that way, Mr. Colton. I believe the world can change, one person at a time. Even someone like you."

I snorted in disbelief. There was no tamin' somethin' wild, somethin' evil, like myself, no denyin' my itch. She'd get hurt with thoughts like that. I picked up my pace a bit to leave her behind.

12

Interferin' Teacher

We reached the caves as the sun was sittin' low in the sky, casting the valley below us in twilight. The boy and I unsaddled the horses while the younger ones, with practiced ease, gathered firewood. Guess Indians know how to make camp, born to it like they are.

Granley came to me as I got the fire goin', brows drawn together, wringin' her hands. "We're about out of food," she admitted, a touch of desperation lacing her voice. "I only had so much at hand, and no time to get supplies."

I looked at her, guess my jaw dropped a bit 'cause I had to think to close it. "You stole a dozen kids and only had food for a day?"

"Llike I sssaid," she retorted hotly before she visibly forced herself to calm. I was beginnin' to realize she only had trouble with her sounds when she was mad or scared, "I had no time. I didn't hear about their plans to ship them out until I was on my way to the school yesterday morning. I just happened to overhear a conversation with the corporal at the fort."

I raised my eyebrows at her. "What are you tellin' me for?"

"I thought you might be accustomed to living off the land," her eyes lookin' at me, shinin' with misplaced hope. "You could hunt."

I scoffed. "Well, ain't that just fine. Now I'm meant to be feedin' all ya'll."

Granley offered a sly smile, a weapon only a woman could wield. "I rather thought you might enjoy it. Get away from the children for a while. And Chalipun has already set off to find something as well."

Good, I only needed half as much, then. Growling, I bust up on my sore feet, slammed my hat on my head, and stalked off.

With fading light hindering my search, I descended to the creek below the caves. The water ran clear over smooth rocks, revealing the lazy fish darting beneath the surface.

Sharpening a makeshift spear, I waded into the cool water, relishing the relief it offered my throbbing feet. Within minutes, I'd speared four fish.

They offered no comfort for the itch, a fact I'd come to loathe. The creatures bled little, their eyes glassy and lifeless even in death. Disappointment gnawed at me, but the itch was calm enough for now.

Returning to camp, I was met with Granley's warm smile. What did it take to get this woman to back off? I tossed the fish at her feet, a silent command to clean them. My purpose served, I intended to sleep. My plan was to leave before anyone woke. Before that teacher could convince me otherwise. I'd decided that thousand dollars was just a pie in the sky dream. It wasn't worth stickin' around with these kids, and that meddlesome teacher.

Leaning against my saddle, I pulled my hat over my eyes, the chattering of the children a constant murmur. It was strange to hear a white woman speak their language, their voices filled with a strange joy despite their predicament. Maybe people found happiness in unexpected places.

A sour taste filled my mouth, an echo of the guilt I tried to numb with this... existence. Resourcefulness. That's what I called it. A pathetic excuse for the monster I'd become.

"Mr. Colton," Granley's voice broke the silence.

I lifted the brim of my hat a fraction, enough to see her holding out a large, charred prickly pear paw, piled with cooked fish, her eyes glintin' with challenge.

"No," I mumbled, pulling the hat back down.

A rustle beside me alerted me to her presence. She sat close, the nearness sending a jolt through me. Was she eating? The thought of a full stomach was tempting, yet the memory of past hunger pangs was a deterrent. These days, finding food wasn't usually an issue.

"Thank you for your help," she said softly. "I should've expressed my gratitude sooner."

Gratitude. A foreign concept, one I couldn't readily access. The polite response was unfamiliar territory. Instead, a strange pressure built within me.

"Welcome," I blurted out, the word catching.

Silence stretched between us. She didn't retreat, her presence both comforting and unsettling. Maybe she was finished eating.

"Mr. Colton," she began, her voice firm, "we need your protection. Chalipun is just a boy, and we have nowhere else to turn."

I scoffed. "I ain't no hero, lady. You're better off without me."

"But you're all we have," she insisted.

"I'm telling you," I growled, rising to tower over her, "you don't want me around."

Her lips thinned, eyes widened as she drew back from me, but her voice held steady. "I understand your concerns, but…"

I cut her off, my face inches from hers, hoping to intimidate. "I'm leaving in the morning. That's final."

Anger lit her face, but she held her tongue, for a moment, anyway.

"When you say that we are better off without you," she began cautiously, "What do you mean?"

Frustration bubbled up in me like a pot o' beans boilin' over. This woman was like a pesky mosquito, buzzin' around a scab a fella can't stop scratchin'. "You can't fix me," I growled, my voice rougher than a badger's hide. "Just let me be.

She cocked her head, studyin' me like a hawk after a field mouse. "Maybe not," she finally said, her voice steady as a preacher's amen. "But God might have other plans."

I let out a snort, a harsh sound like a coyote coughin' up a hairball. "Honey, God's about as real as a jackalope in these parts. You best hightail it outta here and get some shut-eye. Hope you and them kids live to see the light of day come mornin'. 'Cause with me around, that ain't no sure thing."

Her jaw clenched tighter than a snare trap, but her eyes held me like a rattler fixin' to strike. "Y-you're ssscared," she said, her voice low but clear like a church bell. "That's why you're actin' all mean like a cornered varmint."

Them words hit me like a mule kick to the gut. Scared? Me? I scoffed. This little schoolmarm, all fancy talk and foolish faith, didn't know beans about bein' scared. Fear was a luxury I couldn't afford, not with the darkness roamin' around inside me like a hungry wolf.

"You ain't got a lick o' sense about what you're spoutin'," I spat, anger boilin' up like a geyser to cover the raw spot her words left.

"Mmmaybe not," she said, her voice gainin' some spunk like a filly learnin' to buck. "B-but I know this much, Mr. Colton: There's good in everyone, even those lost in the shadows. Sometimes, all it takes is a gentle nudge in the right direction."

Her words hung in the air, a challenge wrapped in a kindness that left me feelin' like I swallowed a tumbleweed. I looked away, the firelight dancin' on the cave walls like crazy spirits. What did she know about the darkness clawin' at me, the hunger that gnawed at my soul like a starved coyote?

Why did she keep pushing? Didn't she understand the danger she put herself and those children in? Or could be...could be a part of me craved that normalcy, the warmth of human connection.

"You can take that sentiment and shove it," I pushed back, her gasp feedin' the fire inside. "I'm not lost, and I'm definitely not scared. Yer just a fool woman, tryin' to feel safer by keepin' the wolf on a leash."

I felt her glare even though I refused to look at her. After long moments, she moved off, and at last I could breath again.

Silence settled back down, thick as molasses, broken only by the fire cracklin' and a cricket chirpin' its lonely song. The fire's warmth seeped into my bones, a comfort against the icy grip of the itch that thrummed beneath the surface.

My eyelids got heavier, my breathin' evened out. As I drifted off, a strange image flickered in my mind: a hand reachin' out, not in fear, but in understandin'. The teacher's hand. I shoved the image away, cravin' the familiar darkness like an old blanket.

But for the first time in longer than a snake sheds its skin, a seed of doubt had been planted. Could there be somethin' more? Somethin' beyond the darkness that choked the life outta me? Sleep, uneasy as a spooked horse, finally took me, leavin' the question hangin' heavy in the night air like a gunsmoke haze.

81

13

"You shot me!"

"The fact of the matter is I'm glad you stayed," the schoolteacher replied to my stompin' around the cave, "but it was your choice, so you can stop growlin' like a bear with a toothache about it."

Frustrated, like a steer caught between a lasso and a branding iron. Cur dog on one side, this woman on the other, both with my end in sight. "I might've stayed," I growled, shoving my boot on so hard the whole thing near about flew off my foot, "but that doesn't mean I gotta be happy about it!"

"Oh? Then spill it, Mr. Growly-bear. What changed your mind?"

Growly-Bear? She made me sound like a child's toy. I opened my mouth, ready to retort, then glanced at Feather who thwacked his tail excitedly. My retort died in my throat. Granley arched an eyebrow, then a triumphant grin split her face.

I gritted my teeth so hard I thought they might crumble. Shoving my hat down further, I stormed out of the cave entrance.

"Where you headed?" she called after me.

"Those young'uns need dinner, don't they?" I hollered back without turning.

Hunting for food wasn't exactly my forte. People? Now that was a skill I had honed to a fine point, useless as it seemed right now. But my hunger had always been a darker thing than most experienced.

That woman had me cornered, and she knew it. Nagging at me like a pesky fly. All I wanted was some space, a way to keep her at arm's length.

She's different, I admitted grudgingly, even if the thought itself made my blood boil. Why she didn't have the sense to be scared of me no more, I didn't know, but her trust ate at me like carbolic acid on a wound.

Reaching the mountain peak wasn't much of a climb, but it offered a clear view of the flatlands below. I scanned the horizon, getting my bearings. The fort sat westward, maybe a day's ride, less if you pushed your horse.

It gave me some pause, something to chew on. Less chance of the army stumbling upon us out here, further off the beaten path.

Leaving the mission had been the smart move. Off the main roads, harder to find, less likely to attract weary travelers. The only worry now was that it also made a perfect hideout for someone looking to lie low. I'd seen the darkened spot of an old campfire before we laid our own. Might not be the only ones using this area, but hopefully, we'd be alone as long as we needed it.

Deciding it was best to scout the perimeter, I walked with a cautious eye, ears pricked for any sound. My boots crunched in the sand and I pulled my collar high, tryin' to keep the flies off me. Birds sang as the breeze gusted through the canyon, bringin' the scent of dust and early wildflowers. Circling the camp a few times, I found nothing out of the ordinary.

Satisfied, I headed back down to the creek, enjoyin' the cold water on my overused feet. I speared us another mess of fish, replaced my boots, and made my way back to the cave.

Suddenly, something slammed into my shoulder, like a mule kick, followed by the crack of a gunshot. Staggerin' back, I dove for cover, scrambling to figure out where the shot came from.

My arm, throbbing like a hornet's nest, still worked. No broken bones, at least. I crawled back towards the cave, blood blooming bright red as it trickled down my wrist and hand.

"Mr. C-c-colton!" Granley shrieked, dropping a rifle. A rifle! This woman just shot me! The realization dawned on her at the same time, her hand flying to her mouth, tears welling in her eyes. She rushed to my side as I reached my feet.

"Y-you're b-bleeding!" the words stuck on her tongue in her panic. "I'm ssso sorry, I didn't know it was you!"

Frantic, she started tugging at the shirt covering my shoulder, the one now sporting a bullet hole.

I shoved her back. "You shot me!"

She moved around me, comin' back and yanking at the fabric on my back. "It didn't go all the way through."

My jaw clenched. "Obviously."

"We need to get the bullet out," she declared, barking orders like a sergeant. "Chalipun, get a knife hot over the fire! Disinfect it!" My shirt came loose, and I instinctively pushed it back down.

"Leave me alone!"

She stood in front of me, her voice firm despite my growing dizziness. "Listen here, Eli Colton. That bullet needs to come out, and fast. My mother was a war nurse, and she taught me a thing or two about tending to wounds. So get that shirt off!"

She pushed me onto a log and ripped open my shirt again. A gasp escaped her lips when she saw…everything. Hell's bells.

I knew a dozen questions would come flooding now. I swore under my breath. The scars itched sometimes, but otherwise, they didn't bother me much, not as much as that itch inside. Only ached and pulled a bit when I stretched certain ways.

Boss Rawlins back then, he loved pain. He'd tie me down and go to work on my back, carving me up like a Thanksgiving turkey. Those few years, I got real acquainted with the feel of his knife. Until one day I was finally big enough to pay him back in kind.

Granley barked orders like a seasoned general, the kids jumping to obey like trained soldiers. The woman had only packed a day's food, but somehow an entire infirmary fit inside her bag. You just couldn't figure women.

And those kids. I had a bad feelin' 'bout them…I'd rarely known little ones to be so quiet. So watchful. And it called up a part of me I fought to stomp down, the part that remembered those fearful moments of expectin' the worst.

I gave in to her demand, knowin' she was right about the bullet. Not wantin' a broken tooth, I took my knife out of its leather scabbard and put the leather between my teeth.

"This might sting a little," she warned, her voice trembling slightly.

I huffed a chuckle unwillingly. She looked pale, even the knife seemed to wobble in her hand. Fear, like she'd admitted. This woman didn't want to hurt me. Reaching out, I took her wrist with my good hand. Looked into her worried eyes.

I took the leather outta my teeth. "I don't feel pain," I lied, the words tasting like ashes in my mouth, not sure if I was protectin' her or me. "Just like I don't got no soul."

A shaky breath escaped her lips, as I put the leather back into place, then nodded at her. Steely resolve settled in her gaze and her lips firmed as she focused on my shoulder. The searing pain from the knife eclipsed the throbbing gunshot wound. I grit my teeth hard enough I was sure I was gonna bite through that scabbard, my muscles locked up tight.

It felt like she was digging for gold, forever, but eventually she pried the bullet out, holding it up triumphantly like a trophy. Bright, bloody red stained her fingers. I swallowed hard, a dryness constricting my throat, as the itch raised its ugly head, the thirst for blood as real as any physical thirst.

Her hands worked quickly, stitching the wound shut.

"You lied, Mr. Colton. That had to hurt you just as much as any other man."

"And you shot before you knew who you were shooting at!" I retorted, my voice weak but defiant.

She finished bandaging my shoulder. "You need to rest. Don't want to reopen the wound. You lost a lot of blood."

"Been through worse."

Her lips pressed into a thin line. Her eyes flickered towards my torso, the part hidden by the shirt. I knew she was wonderin' about my scars, just as I knew I wasn't gonna tell her a thing.

"I know," she said softly, "and I know you won't listen anyway. Doesn't mean I won't speak my mind."

Burning pain lanced through my shoulder, but I gritted my teeth and pulled a new shirt out of my pack. Maybe I could patch the other one, after I washed the blood out. I looked at it, stuck my finger through the hole. It wasn't too bad. Once I deposited the kids in their orphanage, I could find someone about my size, follow him home, how I'd always done.

"Might as well save your breath," I grumbled.

"That wouldn't be right. If I see something that needs fixing, I have to speak up. Always."

Of course she would believe that.

One of the younger children, a girl named Goyan, approached me, her big brown eyes filled with concern.

"All better?" she asked shyly.

Before I could answer, Granley spoke quickly. "Yes, Goyan, he's all better now."

Goyan didn't seem convinced. "Kisses!" she declared, launching herself forward and planting a gooey kiss on my cheek.

My first instinct was to shove her away, but a flicker in Granley's eyes stopped me. Instead, I gently scooped Goyan under her arms and placed her back on her feet. I wiped the damp spot on my face with my sleeve.

"Yes, Goyan," Granley said, a hint of amusement in her voice, "kisses make everything better."

Goyan giggled and nestled in beside me. Granley packed up her makeshift medical station, a wry smile playing on her lips.

"Looks like you made yourself a friend, whether you like it or not, Mr. Colton."

Hell's bells indeed. I let out a groan, more of annoyance than pain. Maybe this little detour wouldn't be so bad after all. But the thought of being stuck with a nagging school teacher and a band of kids... well, that was a whole other story.

14

"A chill where she'd been."

Friend, my foot. That kid stuck to me like mud on a hog. Every time I set her aside, she came right back, gigglin' like it was some game. Chalipun and I took turns makin' circuits around the camp, after makin' sure that woman wasn't gonna shoot either of us while we was at it. I'd done decided we had to keep watch, in case someone come upon us.

He was practically a man, even if he had some growin' to do, and I figured he'd be some help. I think he caught everything with those watchful eyes of his. Prob'ly more than I wanted him to.

He came back from his circuit with a couple rabbits, so we had dinner. Well. They had dinner, the memory of rabbit cooked over a campfire a cruel taunt on my muted senses.

Being halfway between alive and dead meant existing in a colorless world, devoid of taste or joy, a hollow shell where a life used to be. Why did I still breathe? Why bleed?

"Chalipun, I'll take first watch," I told him as he ate. "You can take the other."

He nodded, those dark eyes flashin'.

"I can take a watch," the school teacher piped in, like a jaybird that can't resist a juicy worm.

"Chalipun and I got this." I didn't look at her.

"There's no reason I can't take a turn and let both of you get more rest."

87

"You're a woman," I growled, placin' my hand heavily on her shoulder to encourage her to sit back down.

Granley's jaw clenched and nostrils flared as she shook me off hotly. Good.

"A w-woman who managed to shoot you!" she pointed out, her voice laced with defiance.

"A woman who shot her only protection!" I shot back. Knowin' arguing with the stubborn female wouldn't get me nowhere, I pulled on the mask of charm, the one I used when it suited me. It helped things along, sometimes.

"We wouldn't be restin', worryin' 'bout you."

She scoffed. "No reason to worry about me. It's not like I'm going to war!"

"Don't have to have no reason. Ain't I right, Chalipun?"

The boy's eyes held mine steadily. There was somethin' in them, somethin' I couldn't put my finger on.

"Miss Granley sleep. Men watch."

I nodded my thanks to the boy. She looked back and forth between us, her lips pressed into a thin line.

"You know you can't make me sleep. Why not let me help?"

"If you get yourself hurt, who's gonna take care of all these kids? You think about that? I don't know nothin' 'bout kids, and you gonna leave 'em all to the poor boy?"

I could tell that argument loosened her seat on that high horse she was on.

"I'm hardly going to be injured keeping watch," Granley countered, her voice wavering slightly.

"Now you don't know that," I replied, havin' to curb my chuckle.

She looked up at me, a knowin' look creepin' in her face.

"You sound an awful lot like you care, Mr. Colton. A soulless man like you claim to be would act in his own best interests, regardless of the well-being of others."

It took a moment to change horses, from my charmin' mask to myself, the darkness bubblin' up.

"And what makes you think I'm not?"

I could practically see the bees buzzin' in her head. She gave me a little half-smile, like she'd done figured me out.

"Touche," she said softly.

I didn't know that word, but I understood what she meant. I'd won this round, but I wasn't sure how high the stakes were. She took a breath.

"Very well, then, I shall leave the watch to you men. I will do as you suggest, and get some sleep."

The school teacher got the children ready for bed, had them say their prayers. If that wasn't the strangest thing, seein' all them Indian kids kneelin' over their blankets and prayin' to a white man's God.

"Do you pray, Mr. Colton?" she asked, all prim and proper, suggestin' every decent man does.

"Only when someone bigger than me made me," I shot back.

"Hmmm," that no-good sound. "Then I will pray for you."

"Don't bother yourself."

"It's no bother," she countered, her voice gentle, "Speaking to my Father about you."

She was a peculiar lady, for sure, and somehow, she didn't seem two-sided like most them God-fearin' folks were.

She lay down with the little ones, thought she'd gone to sleep with them. But it wasn't long before she got up, straightened her skirts, and came to sit with me, makin' me tense up like a bronc 'bout to buck. I said nothin', ignored her, hoped she'd leave me be. She was quiet for a fair piece, but then she spoke.

"You were a boy when it happened?" she whispered.

Her words were a punch to the gut, takin' my breath away in shock. I clenched my teeth against the nausea that rose up. I never was much of a talker, but I ain't never told no one 'bout growin' up. Wasn't 'bout to start now, not to her. She already knew too much.

"You know what, yer a fool woman," I spat, hopin' she'd go back to her own business. "You're pokin' around where you don't got no right to be. Shut up and leave me be."

That only bought me a minute of peace, but truth be it didn't help me none, 'cuz the memories come floodin' into my kerfuddled mind in spite of my words. I began to shake, like I'd caught a chill, clenchin' my fists.

A tense silence followed, but then the woman opened her mouth again. "I-I've seen scars like that before," Granley shared, her voice thoughtful. "A boy came in with them a few years ago. His father had a…p-predilection…I guess you'd call it. Liked to see him hurt. He…Once he talked about it, he sseemed to feel better. Like removing a splinter, the wound was still there but allowed to heal."

I squeezed my eyes shut, hatin' the moan risin' from my throat, wantin' to shove her away. I ground the heels of my hands into my eyes, sendin' sparks through my head, tryin' to curtail the images that flashed in my head.

Ma Josie screamin', spittle flyin' as she walloped me long after I'd curled on to the ground, then dragged me into the pit of the cellar. Cryin' for hours, beggin' to be let out, for a drink of water, anything to show some humanity. Knowin' somehow, I deserved the beatings, the isolation.

Boss Rawlins' eyes glintin', as sharp as his knife, as he pushed me down, that crooked board in the wall all I could focus on through the pain. The wrongness of it all, the justice in what I'd brought back on him in the end. The feel of my blood, his blood, all warm and thick mingled together in my mind

My teeth cracked. I made an effort to loosen my jaw. I wasn't gonna talk to her, no way, no how. What in tarnation did she think to get done? She was diggin' same as she'd done for that blasted bullet, but this pain was worse, much worse.

"You sure are some sorry, no-good teacher," I accused, hatin' her in this moment as my stomach twisted itself inside out. "Traipsin' all over with them kids, an' you didn't have no plan, not even any food. Takin' on a stranger like me, you don't what I done. Puttin' them in mortal danger."

She gasped, and I knew I'd hit the mark, her body stiffenin' next to mine. Spurred on by my success, I kept goin'. "It's like you don't care about these young 'uns at all. They'd been better off shipped to the orphanage."

She took a deep breath, smoothed out her skirts with a tremblin' hand. When she turned back to me, I knew I hadn't stopped her probin'. Why'd she have to be such a dadgum stubborn do-gooder?

"You know, I've seen a lot of pain and misery, Eli, working with these children. I know what happens in this ugly world. I'm gonna tell you the same thing you told me…I can't help if I don't know what happened."

I felt a knot stoppin' up my throat. Tried to swallow it, but it wouldn't go down. I curled in on myself, like I'd protect my gut in a losin' fight, turned away from her.

"You can't help me none, Granley," I forced the words past the swelling. "No one can."

My words hung heavy in the air, and I cursed my flappin' trap. "You don't know that," she countered, her presence a pressure on a blister about to pop.

I looked at her then, sittin' beside me. Her face was open, earnest, clear that she thought if I told her my secrets, everythin' would be comin' up roses.

When the words came, they fell out of my mouth like a dog's sick, and there was no callin' them back, no stoppin' them.

"Me tellin' you that my own mother tied me to a tree and left me when I was just a li'l kid, that's gonna help? Or that the headmistress of the orphanage thought I was evil, locked me in the cellar?" Shards of glass were rippin' me up on the inside.

"And sure, she sold me to Boss Rawlins when I was all of nine, so I could work twice as much as any of his hired hands? Send me to kill off his enemies, and I came to like it, crave that power? He liked his boys young, and bloody? You gonna help me with any of that, teacher?"

And dang it all if that pretty little woman sat calmly through the flood, eyes waterin'. She reached out with a feather-light touch, testin', landin' on my arm.

"I'm so sorry, Eli, that you had no one to show love to you."

The back of my eyes began an unfamiliar prickle, my nose tinglin', a memory from the distant past. Tarnation. I huffed a breath, trying to keep it reined in, angry, embarrassed. Blast! Thunderation! Blue blazes, no! I turned away as one escaped, the shock of that one only causin' more to rise. I hadn't cried since I was prob'ly six. What was she doin' to me? I was unmanned.

Granley leaned over, put her arm around me, her head on my shoulder, and held me while I cried. And I let her, let her closer than I'd had anyone since I could remember. When I'd stopped, she touched me lightly on the head, like a priest blessin' a baby, and walked back to lay with the little ones again.

There was a chill where she'd been.

My eyes followed her, as she settled down, unsure whether I felt shame or…hope? I'd not known that feelin' - did other people experience it like this? When her eyes flicked to mine, she smiled, a soft thing. I nodded, stomach twistin' in an entirely different way, wonderin' what she thought of me.

Remindin' myself to keep my eyes facin' outward, to keep from fire blindness, I shifted back to the mouth of the cave. My eyes were achin' and swollen, the shadows outside fuzzy, and I kept rubbin' them until my eyelids burned.

I was relieved when I woke Chalipun up halfway through the night to take his turn. The boy was bright eyed and ready to go right away. I knew those eyes of his missed nothin'. He'd heard everythin', and I couldn't quite meet his eyes.

"Miss Granley sleep?" he asked.

"Yeah," I said roughly. "Once she stopped tryin' to get me to talk."

A hint of a smile glinted in his face. "She strong woman. But talk much."

Yep, that boy'd do all right.

I settled myself down, thinkin' to just rest my eyes, but I slipped off to sleep easier than a baby on a bottle.

15

Goyan

I woke up with a weight pinnin' my arm. Panicked awareness slammed into me like the hammer on a chambered bullet. I turned my head and found a mat of dark brown hair. Confused, I sat up, stunned to see the little girl who'd been wrapped around me. Then I noticed the chill of a wet spot on my shirt.

That Goyan had made water all over me! My shirt, my blanket, her dress, all soaked through.

"Aw, by Harry, no!" I roared, the sound echoin' through the stillness of the mornin', settin' her beside me.

Granley bolted upright, eyes sleepy but voice firm and prim. "Mr. Colton, watch your language! Whatever is the matter?"

"That girl pi…tinkled all over me!" I stammered, fumbling to unbutton my shirt, trying to keep the wet patch away from my side, ignoring the throbbing pain in my shoulder. My ears burned hot as memories of last night flickered through my mind, and I kept my eyes well away from Granley's.

Granley peeked down at Goyan, who somehow remained blissfully asleep. "Oh!" she gasped, then a smile tugged at the corners of her lips. "Oh, dear!" she choked out, a giggle escaping before she could contain it.

"It ain't funny!" I growled, pluckin' at my urine soaked shirt to try to keep it away from my skin as I removed it, my nose wrinklin' at the pungent smell.

"No, no it's not," she agreed, laughin' anyhow. I glared at her.

Grinnin', she stumbled to her feet, brought me her blanket. Did she seem more comfortable around me now? I watched her, warily.

"Here," she said, holding the blanket up for me. I took it as I tossed my shirt close to the fire to dry. Tarnation, I hadn't even washed the blood out of my other one yet. The only two shirts I had.

Granley stooped to pick up the girl. "Oh, Goyan," she whispered. "You poor thing."

Right, she was the poor thing. I was the unsuspectin' lunkhead that got caught in the flood.

The girl opened her eyes sleepily. "Uhoh," she mumbled, a frown creasing her tiny forehead. "Wet."

"Yes, darling. Let's get you out of that wet dress, shall we?"

Granley expertly unbuttoned the girl's dress and slipped it off, revealing a nauseating sight. Small, discolored, rough circles marred her back, each about the size of the end of a cigar. The school teacher's mouth tightened into a thin line before she met my gaze.

"You weren't the first child to be mistreated, Mr. Colton, and I'm afraid she won't be the last."

Suddenly, the air crackled with tension. "Mister!" Goyan shrieked, makin' me wince, holding her arms out to me.

Granley snorted, a sound oddly reminiscent of a horse, and grabbed another blanket, wrapping the shivering child in its warmth.

"Mister!" Goyan repeated, her voice gaining volume.

"You'd best hold her, Mr. Colton," Granley said, a hint of amusement dancing in her eyes, "unless you enjoy the sound of a screaming child."

She watched with an air of quiet satisfaction as I gingerly bent down to pick up the little one. Goyan snuggled against me, her tiny arms wrapping around my neck, planting another sloppy kiss on my cheek. I tried to rub it off with my shoulder, hissin' when it pulled at my wound. Tiny hands patted my cheeks, offerin' comfort.

A fierce surge of protectiveness welled up within me, an unfamiliar sensation that sent a shiver down my spine.

Stop it, I mentally growled, pushing the unwanted emotions away. Ever since wakin' in that grave, I'd been feelin' things best left alone, and I was pretty sure it had somethin' to do with that dog.

"She won't pi- relieve herself on me again, will she?" I mumbled, more to myself than to Granley.

Granley snorted again, a sharp sound that cut through the tense silence.

"She can control herself," she explained. "She just has accidents at night sometimes. All this upheaval has probably upset her little system."

A sudden realization struck me. "She's not old enough to be in school, is she?"

"She's only four," Granley said, her voice soft. "So no, not quite old enough in most circumstances. But I run an orphanage and school together, you see."

She spread my shirt and Goyan's dress by the fire, draping them carefully over a fallen log.

Curiosity battled with a deep-seated fear of bein' weakened by emotions. I wanted to know more about Goyan, about Granley, yet a part of me recoiled from the vulnerability such knowledge might bring.

"Who?" I finally managed to ask, the word rasping, like a blade on a sharpenin' stone.

Granley stopped tending to the clothes, her gaze meeting mine directly. It was a look that dared me, challenged me. That woman had me on edge, a tightly wound spring ready to snap.

"Starting to catch feelings, are we, Mr. Colton?" she teased, a glint in her eyes.

"No," I denied reflexively. But even as the word left my lips, a primal need to protect Goyan, to keep her safe, bloomed in my chest. It was a feeling so foreign, so unexpected, so dadgum strong, that it scared me.

Her fingers brushed against the stubble on my face, sending a jolt through me. By Harry! Those weren't the teacher's feelings stirring within me. They were…Mine.

The realization slammed into me like a runaway wagon. Shame burned hot in my gut. What was I doing letting myself feel this way? Getting attached was a luxury I couldn't afford. It never ended well.

"She was adopted as an infant by a family," Granley said quietly, her voice thick with emotion. "Her mother had died from smallpox. But it turns out, her adopted parents tired of her. Unwanted again, they dropped her back at the orphanage."

Tears welled up in her eyes, glistening like dewdrops on a spiderweb in the morning light. "I had to care for her wounds, Mr. Colton, knowing that I was partly responsible for them. I was the one who had placed her with that family. In my naivete, I thought it was a happily ever after story waiting to happen."

A story I'd craved for myself, back in those foggy memories of the orphanage, before the darkness took hold. A family. Someone to love me.

The image flickered to life in my mind: a dark, dank cellar, the echo of my own screams bouncing off the cold, stone walls. Back then, I'd still had the capacity to feel, before the relentless cruelty had beaten the emotions out of me. I shoved the memory away, a bitter taste rising in my throat.

Those days were long gone. I was far stronger now, encased in an armor forged from years of hardship.

Granley was watching me, her gaze filled with an unsettling empathy. "It brings things back, doesn't it?" she asked softly.

The little girl, oblivious to the emotional turmoil brewing around her, grabbed my face with her chubby hands, squeezing my cheeks together. I was drowning, flailing for air but finding none.

"Some," I admitted, my voice a hoarse croak, hatin' my honesty.

She waited, expectant, for me to elaborate. But the well of words had run dry. I couldn't share that suffocating darkness with her, not yet.

"I need some air," I muttered, pushing myself to my feet.

Goyan's lower lip trembled, and she let out a whimper that pricked at my newly developed conscience. Ignoring the pang of guilt, I strode out of the cave, the girl's wail echoing behind me.

The crisp morning air tickled my skin, a balm to my roiling emotions. I needed space, time to think. Climbing the rocky path that led up the mountainside, I pushed myself further and further until the trees thinned and a panoramic vista unfolded before me.

Feather materialized at my side, his brown eyes filled with concern. "Don't even start," I growled heatedly.

He whined softly and nudged my hand with his head. All I wanted was silence, a break from the gully washer of emotions.

But silence wouldn't come. My mind was a chaotic storm, churning with fragmented memories and unwanted feelings. The image of the headmistress, Ma Josie, materialized, her face twisted in a hateful sneer. She'd worn her hair pulled back tight, her face perpetually flushed.

When she yelled, spittle would spray from her lips, and she wielded her cane like a weapon. Boys were the targets of her cruelty, and sometimes, after a session in the cellar…

"Leave me alone!" I roared, the sound echoing through the stillness of the mountaintop.

Memories flickered: a fleeting moment of kindness, a single hard candy offered as a reward, the ever-present uncertainty of whether today would bring Ma Josie as an angel or a devil or some confusin' mixture of both.

I knew then, with a chilling certainty, that I wouldn't leave, no matter the reward. Not until they were safe. They may not have been mine to protect, but something primal, something I couldn't explain, compelled me to stay.

Nobody protected me, a cynical voice taunted within. But a stronger voice answered that I could be the one to keep them safe from the evil that had plagued me.

Feather yipped and darted off, chasing after a butterfly or some other fleeting distraction.

I had to go back. There was no choice.

Steeling myself, I began the descent, each step a descent into the unknown. I built my walls back up, brick by stubborn brick. I couldn't let them down. Never again.

Reaching the base of the mountain, I rejoined the group. Granley looked up, hope lightin' her eyes. I didn't know why she was so determined to breach my defenses, but one thing was certain – she'd have better luck tamin' a rattler. My walls were stronger than her.

16

"Let's Dance."

My gaze swept over the children, a stoic mask in place as I grit my teeth against the throb in my shoulder. Taking my post near the cave entrance, I scanned the woods, full of mesquite grown tall this close to water. The sun reflected off the sandstone of the mountain face, bakin' me in its relentless fury.

A jolt of icy fear hit me when Feather growled, low and threatening. My gut clenched, a sickening premonition of what was to come. Moments later, I heard the ring of a hoof on a rock from outside the cave, the unmistakable metallic jingle of a bridle. We were no longer alone. I shushed the kids as my heart began a rapid thud. I looked back into the cave.

They were just kids, huddled together like frightened chicks. Goyan, with her infectious laugh and gap-toothed grin, now clutched at Granley, her eyes so wide I could see the whites around them. I couldn't let them get hurt. Over my dead body.

I hadn't felt the itch this strong in days. It washed over me, almost like dark armor, gatherin' for the fight. The primal urge for violence, for blood. It was a familiar demon, one I'd carried for a long time. But seeing those scared faces, so innocent, so defenseless…somethin' else, somethin' strange, stirred in me. A twisted sense of duty, a need to protect what couldn't protect itself.

"You and the kids hide in the back," I rasped, my voice tight with urgency. "We got company, and I don't think they're here for a picnic."

98

Her face was drained of blood, her eyes widening in terror. "W-what? H-h-how d-do you know?" Her voice trembled.

Run! That's what every instinct screamed at me. But the thought of those kids filled me with a fierce protectiveness that stampeded right over the self-preservation screamin' in my head.

"I know. Get them kids outta here!"

"Mr. Colton," she started, but I didn't have time for her questions.

Fear lent my grip a vice-like quality as I grabbed her wrist, forcing her to meet my gaze. "Now, Miss Granley!"

She shook off my hand, her eyes wide with some blend of fear and defiance. But she did what I said, herding the children towards the back of the cave, their small figures disappearing around a bend in the rock face.

Chalipun materialized beside me, a rifle held steady in his hands. I was younger than him, when I made my first kill. Somehow, I knew he'd faced such violence before. He'd do.

"Don't shoot 'till you can see them plain," I told him. "Keep as much of yourself hidden as you can. I'm gonna slip around, catch 'em from behind."

He nodded, a slight incline of his head, still no expression on his face, eyes clear and aware. Yep, like I said, he'd do.

I pulled my Winchester out of my things, stickin' a handful of bullets in my pocket, and and crept to the side of the cave, seeking them through the thorny brush. They were ridin' single file, ten of them. Fifteen bullets in the rifle, six bullets in the revolver, I thought. I couldn't afford to miss, doubted I'd have time to reload. They came in, easy, relaxed, like they'd been here before. I thought back to that black spot in the cave, the sign of past campfire.

They didn't know we were here. They walked their horses, slouchin' in the saddle, one of them havin' a smoke as he rode.

Like a pack of wolves comin' home to the den, they snaked through the rocks and trees, silent and deadly and confident. My heart hammered a frantic rhythm against my ribs, a drumbeat urging me on. I was close enough to see their faces, one with a crooked nose and narrow eyes, another with a broad forehead and cruelly twisted lip.

I recognized both from the wanted posters I'd shared space with in that dusty jail cell, their crimes a violent list to match my own. Like knowin' like, wolf scentin' wolf, I knew they had to die. Wasn't nothin' else gonna keep that teacher and those kids safe.

With a silent prayer, I stalked closer, my heart calmin' with the familiarity of the hunt. The calm that hit right before the storm thundered through. Mebbe this wasn't my fight, not to start. But luck had a twisted sense of humor, puttin' that teacher, those kids in my path. I couldn't leave them to these men. I knew what dark things they brought.

Let's dance.

I yanked the last one out of the saddle as he rode past, a fat man perched on his horse like a sack of potatoes. I took him out of the fight with a single, well-placed blow to the head with the butt of my pistol, not wastin' a bullet. One down. The satisfaction was small and fleeting, just an echo. Without wasting a moment, I melted into the shadows, the trees offering scant protection.

It wasn't long before their shouts erupted, a cacophony of surprise and anger. They'd realized their friend was missing. Now they'd be cautious, every rustle of leaves setting them on edge. Nine left to deal with, twenty-one bullets ready.

I lined up the sights on my Winchester, took a shot at the nearest one from behind a tree, the acrid odor of gunpowder sharp and acrid, sharpenin' my senses. I hadn't had time to practice with the thing, and my shot went wide, just wingin' one of 'em.

It was enough to send the lot of them swingin' around to look for me. I ducked back down, crawled 20 paces away as they shot up the bushes around where I'd been I felt that shoulder wound open back up, the wet stickin' my shirt to my skin.

Come on, you chewed up scalawag. Hold it together a bit longer, I told myself as I lined up the rifle again. I shot one in the back before I hightailed it to another location, tryin' to keep them guessing.

Thought I'd gotten away free 'till I looked down, the dark patch on my trousers, crusted with sand. Didn't feel it yet, but it looked like it'd just grazed me.

I should cut my losses and beat it. Didn't make sense for me to stick around. Wasn't none of my trouble. Memories flooded me, meltin' with the here and now. That dank cell, the yella-haired lady, blood of so many. I wasn't a good man. Men like me didn't stick around for trouble not their own.

The outlaws were almost to the cave - I'd run outta time. Goyan's face came unbidden to my mind. All the others, too. Granley. They didn't deserve what skunks like these men would do.

I grit my teeth together, knowin' I was gonna do somethin' stupid for those kids and that dadblamed woman. Pretty sure I'd regret it. Then again, mebbe not. I'd prob'ly be dead instead.

I stood up where I was, between the trunks of two trees, Colt Frontier in one hand, Winchester in the other, ready to meet my Maker, if it came to it. I'd already died once. Should be layin' in a grave now. Heart beat steady, ready. Nineteen bullets left. Eight targets between Granley and safety.

"Lookin' for me, fellas?" I hollered, standin' sideways, mostly behind a tree trunk, a smallish target, I hoped.

They turned their horses like one of them fancy cavalry drills, all eight at once. Their guns all aimed at me. I smiled, knowin' Death was in my eyes, weapons at the ready in my hands.

"You shoot me, I'll get at least two of you before I go down. That's 2 outta 8. Any of you willin' to risk those odds?"

The indecision flickered in all the eyes but one. Most men, they don't want things bad enough to risk life or death odds like that. Land sakes, they prob'ly wouldn't risk poker odds like that. But, when the dander's up, one'll do somethin' stupid.

And there's always one.

That one narrowed his eyes as he sighted me, his revolver raising like it was moving on it's own accord like a snake in the grass, and I knew then it was all goin' to turn to a bag of nails. Bally rotten luck.

Time moved like molasses in winter. I shot that one square in the chest, he crumpled and fell as his horse sidestepped. Eighteen bullets, seven men. But his buddies had been drawn into the fight. My next bullet took another one of 'em in the shoulder, but he still raised his gun. Seventeen bullets, until I shot again, knocked him outta the saddle. Fifteen bullets, six men.

I was walkin' toward them. Musta looked like a haunt from the cemetery, I suppose, marchin' toward them without regard for their bullets. The bullets tugged at me, one in my arm, another my thigh. It'd hurt a heap later. If I was still above snakes.

I took my sight, and one fell to the side, his hip quickly turnin' dark, but he hadn't tapped out, dadgumit, so I shot again. Thirteen bullets, five men. I saw another fall from the side of my eyes. Chalipun musta used the rifle. Good kid. Four men left. Somethin' punched my midsection. That one was gonna be a bad one, I thought in the back of my head, but didn't dwell on it, the thought passin' by like water in a creek. I was only thinkin' of keepin' those men from hurtin' those kids, my mind only in one direction. Protect at all cost.

I shot at another, my hand trembled and I barely clipped my target. Took me several shots to down him. The smell of blood and gunsmoke was gettin' strong. Dang my melt, I was gettin' weak, musta lost a lot of blood. I was having a hard time walkin', even staying upright. I needed to end this quick, or I was going to be deader than a can of corned beef and not able to help nobody.

I heard screams comin' from the cave. The kids. Another bandit fell, clutching his side. I turned toward the cave. Had to protect those kids. My shot went wild, hit a horse. He reared, dumpin' his rider. How many men was that? How many bullets? I'd lost count, somewhere in all that. I stumbled toward the fallen rider, movin' slow, like wadin' through hip deep water.

Granley had a pistol in her hand, fired it past me. I turned back around, aimed, and found I was out of bullets. I pulled my knife, started forward as another rider fell. I grabbed the reins of the nearest rider, slit the horse's throat, fell atop the rider as the horse went down. Stabbed him in the neck good as he shot me in the chest.

I fell back, knowin' I was dead. Somehow, I got back to my feet, stumblin', blinkin' away the darkness to look around me, ready to take on the next one. They were all down. It took a moment for that to settle in. They were all down. I'd done it. I'd kept them safe.

I heard my breathin' slow, my blood thickened in my veins. One beat, two. Gunsmoke burned my nostrils.

I turned back, looked into the cave. I saw the younger ones, still huddled in the back. Chalipun stood slack at his spot, lookin' into the cave, dark eyes glistenin'.

Granley was on her knees, crying. And a small body in her arms, still. Too still. I stubbornly shuffled to her, before my legs gave out.

"Goyan."

Her body was limp, lifeless. Something broke in my chest, then, tore me inside out. I'd failed. I looked around me again. No, not failed. Just hadn't won. No fairy tale endings. They were all unhurt, except that poor, small girl. The teacher looked at me, tears fallin' freely.

"She went to get you. I didn't see her until she fell."

"My fault," I tried to say as my body began to grow cold, and I listed to the side.

"Oh, Eli, no!" she gasped, as her eyes searched me, her voice full of sadness and regret.

I know what I looked like. I had probl'y half a dozen holes in me, or more, some of 'em were real bad. I couldn't feel them no more. I wasn't gonna make it. But that was okay. She would. The kids would.

"'S okay." My voice sounded funny in my head, like it was comin' from inside a barrel. "Take care of 'em."

I laughed, a strange sound. What was that feelin', made me feel warm and soft inside? Like a flower pushin' out of a crack in the road, unexpected and bright. Was that really how it felt? Carin' for someone?

I think I died then. Last thing I knew of was Granley's voice in my head. Dander-headed woman. What would she remember of me?

17

Awake

A white-hot fire ragin' through my insides was the next thing I knew. Darkness surrounded me, punctuated by blindin' flashes of light like a storm brewin'. Whispers, like the rasping of demons, filled my ears, their meanin lost in the haze of agony.

Sometimes, I thought I heard Granley's voice as the devil himself taunted me. "Eli," I heard her call.

I wrapped myself in the solace that she and the kids were still alive. I'd forgo the pearly gates for them, accept the pain rackin' my soul.

Light exploded in my head, blurry figures dark against the light.

"Eli!" Granley's voice came to me, nearby, a beacon in the storm of pain. "I'm here, Eli."

I turned toward her voice. My eyes blinked, my vision cleared. She was there beside me, chestnut hair mussed, eyes shadowed. I tried to speak, to assure her I was alright, but my throat felt like I'd swallowed sand. Panic clawed at me. Was this it? Was this the price I'd paid for my actions? To drag this woman to Hades with me?

"Eli," her voice, a lifeline thrown to a drowning man, cut through the fog. "You're alright. You're safe."

I reached out a shaky hand, the movement a symphony of pain. "Don't be here," I rasped, the words scraping raw against my throat. "Shouldn't be here with me."

"This isn't…well, this isn't where you belong," she agreed, a faint smile playing on her lips. Relief washed over me, a bittersweet tide. I wasn't dead. Not yet. Black took over again.

"Eli, be still, you'll hurt yourself further," she demanded in that school teacher voice.

I didn't know I'd been movin'. I opened my heavy lids, focused my eyes. She was leanin' over me, her forehead puckered. Her eyes were blacked, like she hadn't been sleepin'.

"Goyan," I managed to crack out. My throat burned like I'd swallowed fire.

She smiled. Didn't make sense to my thick brain. She shouldn't be smilin'. Goyan had died.

"G-goyan just b-bumped her head. She's already back to her old self."

I closed my eyes. There was a rock in my throat I kept tryin' to swallow, but it wouldn't budge.

"Hhhere," Granley said, "Drink some water."

She had a glass, poured a bit on my lips.

"You've been at death's door three days. The doctor said it's a miracle you pulled through."

The glass shook, spilling on my face.

"Oh, Eli! I thought y-y-you had d-died!" She held a tremblin' hand to her mouth as her face crumpled.

Danged if the woman wasn't cryin'. Made me hurt inside all funny, for her to cry.

"Shhh," I told her. "'M not dead." Tarnation, it took all my strength just to talk.

"Y-you were b-bleeding all over and I d-didn't know what to do so we finally got you on a sled and w-we had to bring you all the way back and y-you were just laying there bleeding the whole way and you stopped breathing halfway back and when Dd-doc saw you he looked like you were already d-dead and he almost didn't even try to treat you and I had to scream at him to get him to do anything and then the c-colonel came and I was so afraid!"

The woman was shakin' and cryin' and looked for all the world like she needed a stiff drink.

"Colonel?" I croaked. Where'd the cavalry come from? Had they been trackin' me?

She blinked at me, wiped the tears from her eyes, straightened herself up. "Well, yes, the cavalry had been following the band of criminals. The Miller gang, they called them. They'd robbed a stage three days ago, killed everyone on it." She paused, smilin' at me. "You're a hero, Eli."

I laughed at that lie, a ragged sound that scraped my throat, disturbin' my wounds and turnin' into a groan. "Not me."

"I'm afraid so. You took out the entire gang. All but two will recover enough to go to prison. You rescued me and a dozen orphans."

I mulled that over in my head. The door opened. A tall man, that age where he had the wiles but hadn't lost the strength of youth, clean-shaven, with deep eyes that bored into me, entered. He was wearin' a shiny tin star. I knew my time was up. I was gonna pay for my deeds now, back to that fate I'd somehow slipped loose of.

"Good morning, Sheriff. He's awake and speaking."

The sheriff nodded at her, "Ma'am. Thank you for sendin' for me."

"Of course."

He stood, lookin' awkwardly at her, twistin' his hat in his hands.

"If you don't mind, ma'am, there's some things the boy and I need to discuss in private."

I knew what was comin'. I'd have to be brought to justice, same as those I'd fought off. There were a lot of crimes I had to answer for. Never mind I'd already been hung for them, I'd somehow escaped the death sentence.

She looked from the sheriff, then to me, and back again, tryin' to figure out what was goin' on. Her face set stubbornly.

"Go on, Granley," I croaked. "It'll be fine."

She looked me over, her lips pressed into a thin line as she turned to the sheriff.

"Just for a moment, Sheriff. He's not out of the woods yet."

"Yes, ma'am."

She nodded, turned and walked out the door. He looked at me for a long moment, his gaze like a physical weight, pressin' down on me, findin' my tender spots. I was a bug under a magnifying glass under his eyes, every secret laid bare.

"I'm Sheriff Alvarez, Mr. Colton. You're the hero of the hour," he said, leanin' over me. "There's reward money waitin' for you, for takin' care of that gang. What's more, the Senator'll likely have somethin' for you, you savin' his daughter and all."

He watched me closely, like he was waitin' for me to make a wrong move. He'd probably seen my posters before. He was just bidin' his time, gettin' me well, 'fore I was hauled back to jail. I understood.

"Give it to the orphanage," I said. "I won't be needin' it." Figured I'd most likely end up behind bars again leastways, if not hung again.

He nodded thoughtfully, pursin' his lips as he looked out the window, 'fore his gray eyes turned back to me.

"You bear a strikin' resemblance to one of my posters. Name 'Will Carter' ring a bell?"

I looked him in the eye, waitin' for him to say it, to take me back where I belonged. I'd go. Do it all again. Dyin' twice does somethin' to a man's mind. "It does."

He looked right back, his eyes diggin' into mine. I wondered what he was findin' there, why he was hesitatin'. This sheriff, his eyes were old, calculating. He saw right through me.

"Trouble is, I sent a telegraph inquiry 'bout this 'Will Carter', The record says that man was hung an' planted."

He was givin' me a way out. I didn't understand why, but I was glad for it. I wasn't near as ready to push up daisies as I'd been not so long ago. Somethin' unfamiliar, bright, began to grow in my chest. Was it…hope?

"He was."

"Hmmm. Got any guesses 'bout that?"

I looked him in the eye. I knew what he wanted - reassurance that I was safe to be out in the world. Could I give it? What if the itch came back? Would I be able to control myself?

"That man's dead. He won't trouble no one no more."

I meant it when I said it. Hoped the itch was gone for good.

Sheriff's eyes crinkled, just a tiny bit. As much of a smile as that man was likely to give, I reckoned.

"Good to know. Stick around for a while, son. Patch yourself up. You'll be a new man before long."

Did he just wink at me? I stared at him, wonderin' at that wink and his last words.

He opened the door to step out. "Ma'am," he nodded.

Granley rushed back in, her eyes worried as she checked all over to make sure things were put right, relief relaxin' her face to find me all in one piece. That woman worried more than anyone I'd ever seen. She gave me another drink of water.

"You should rest, now. You can't overdo things."

My eyes were already closin' of their own accord.

And maybe I dreamed again, because I thought I felt an ember in my gut, burnin' hotter than any wound. Could I outrun the darkness, become a new man? The thought flickered before her cool touch on my brow chased it away with a whispered "Thank God."

18

"Hades-made tin pot."

Next time I woke, Granley bustled in, a steaming cup in hand. "Good morning, sleepyhead. Doc says your stomach's up for some broth. Here you go."

The woman was as relentless as the wind. You could pitch yourself against it, but it was so much easier to just go along.

She helped me sit, handed me a cup of warm, steamin' broth, the scent rich and mouth-waterin'. She sat in the chair beside the bed, watching patiently as I drank.

"Sheriff Alvarez mentioned you donated the reward money to the orphanage," she said softly, "That was very kind of you, Eli.."

Heat crept up my cheeks, as I kept my eyes on the mug in my hands. "It was nothin'."

"You earned that money. You should have kept it. I also owe you the money I promised you."

"Those kids need it more than me."

She pursed her lips, clearly torn. "Daddy got me named as the headmistress. The orphanage is permanent now, not under the army's purview. He cut a deal with the commander to leave my children alone."

"Good."

She worried her lip with her teeth. Somethin' was makin' the woman batty. She eyed me, a question in her eyes.

Granley hesitated, then blurted, "Actually, Eli, I could use some help around the orphanage. Would you be interested?"

I scoffed, unsure I'd heard right. "I don't know nothin' 'bout caretakin' of no orphanage."

"Well, you see," she countered, her voice firm and a tint of pink on her cheeks, "I suspect you have more experience with orphanages than I do. I think you would be a great asset. Try it - at least until you heal fully."

I couldn't meet her eyes. "I'm not exactly the best man to be around kids, Gra...Miss Granley."

"Ffor crying out loud, it's E-e-emma," she exclaimed. "After all we've been through, surely we can dispense with formalities. And I think you are exactly what is needed, Eli. After everything you did..." She cut off, her eyes growing shiny. She looked away, biting her lip.

I stared at her, workin' through the thoughts in my head. Sure, I wanted to stay more than anythin'. She was a right pretty girl, and I'd gotten fond of those kids, as odd as that was. But...

"I ain't a decent man," I confessed, my voice rough with somethin' akin to shame. "Time was, there were posters out for me. Some may still be hangin'."

She wasn't gonna be put off so easily. Her brown eyes held mine, as stubborn as that hammerhead horse of mine.

"I've seen all manner of men, Eli," she muled up. "You strike me as decent enough, considering all you did for us. Give it a month, see how it works out. It'll take you that long to heal anyway."

She sure was a hard-hittin' woman. Gotta respect that. And truth was, I didn't want to leave town. Mebbe it was being all shot up, but I felt different. Like mebbe I could be...somethin' more. Somethin' human.

"You talk to Sheriff Alvarez," I sighed, givin' in, too tired to fight. "Have him talk to your pa 'bout it. They think I'm good for it, I'll do it."

The triumph in her eyes told me I'd as much as stepped in her trap. Thing was, I couldn't find it in me to care. Then I realized I drank the broth, enjoyed it even. Were my tastebuds alive again?

She looked at me curiously. "What is it?"

I grinned up at her. "That's the best d...uh...broth I've ever had."

She glowed at me. That's the only way I can describe it, like a sunbeam. "Thank you, Eli. I'll bring you more in a little bit. Let's see how you handle this, hmm? Brady, I mean Doc, said only broth for a few days. He wanted to make sure everything was patched up in your intestines."

There was a tap at the door before it swung open, and a young man with dark hair, spectacles, and a long mustache stepped in. His eyes went to Granley, checkin' on her before he turned to me.

His smile was friendly, open. Trusting. It was like I could almost feel that dark part of me, the part I'd hoped was gone, perkin' its ears. I shoved it down, stomped on it for good measure.

"Good to see you awake, Mr. Colton," his voice was firm and clipped like an Northerner. "We like our heroes alive here in Spring Ridge."

Caught off guard by his openness, I froze, unsure. The sheriff at least had met me with some distrust. That, I understood, I knew. I fell back on my usual mask, the one I'd used to finangle my way in tough situations before.

I gave my best winnin' smile. "Well, this hero appreciates bein' alive, Mr…"

"Brady Finnagan, most just call me Doc," he grinned as he moved beside me and set his black bag down. I wondered if they sold those in special doc stores or somethin'. He rummaged inside, pullin' out various contraptions that glinted in the sunlight before he looked up at Granley.

"I'll need his shirt off, Emma," his voice softened as he spoke to her.

She reached for my buttons 'fore she caught herself and both she and the Doc stared at her hands as her face reddened, the tension thick. Doc coughed, lookin' away.

"I-I'll j-just take this back to the kitchen," she chirped, over-bright, as she spun and dashed out the door.

Doc's eyes followed her as she left, then turned back to me. He measured me, curiosity in his eyes. "She did very well tending your wounds until I was able to take over."

"Thought I was a goner, for sure," I mumbled, avoiding his gaze. This whole situation felt…strange. Here I was, injured and vulnerable, surrounded by the kind of people I would have targeted, back before… I didn't quite know what to do, never had no one worried about me, checkin' on me.

He reached out for my shirt, like Granley had done. Instinctively, I flinched away, a jolt of pain lightin' up my body from the movement. My face heated and my ears prickled. What was happenin' to me? And I was stuck here, in this bed…and I needed to relieve myself. Could I walk? Could I even stand?

"Pardon me," he murmured, lettin' his hands fall to his side. "Of course, if you would remove your shirt for me. I can assist, if you just ask."

Flyin' teakettles, it hurt to breathe, to hold that cup of broth to my mouth. Could I really get my shirt off on my own? It was doubtful. But I didn't want it off, no how.

I pulled a grin again. "You know, I'm feelin' right as rain, Doc. I'm a tough ol' coyote. Give me a couple days rest, I'll get outta yer hair."

Doc's smile faded. "Look, Mr. Colton, I treat plenty of tough guys who hate being fussed over. But trust me, you're in no shape to be a hero right now. You've lost a lot of blood, and need continued treatment to ensure your wounds do not get infected and that I've tied everything together as it needs to go."

I clenched my fists as I considered, finally givin' a quick nod and allowin' him to undress me like a child. My face flamed at my helplessness.

After he had me bare before him, he began to inspect each wound, unbandaging and cleanin' and rebandaging. He went on to describe the stitched furrow in my thigh, the wince escaping my lips a testament to the lingering pain. Doc's touch was firm but gentle as he prodded the wound, sending a fresh jolt through me.

"Bullet grazed clean through the muscle," he muttered, his brow furrowed in concentration as I grit my teeth to the pain. Next, he moved to my hip, his fingers brushing against the bandage there, lightin' it on fire.

"Nasty one here too. Took a while to dig that lead out." With each description, a wave of nausea knocked me back. The weakness I'd been fighting all day slammed into me, a physical manifestation of my fear.

A strangled gasp escaped my lips as I struggled to breath, my heart hammerin' like a runaway freight train. Black began to tunnel my vision. Where was my knife? My eyes darted frantically around the room, landing on the empty nightstand. "Tarnation!" a sob broke through, completin' my shame.

I needed somethin' to protect myself, I thought as my ears began to whine. I'd never been so soft-bellied in my life, weak as a drowned kitten, like a turtle trapped on its back. "Where's my knife?" I rasped, lookin' to the small table hopin' to find it. All there was was that glass of water.

I clumsily reached for it, anythin' to protect myself from his threat as I lay helpless. I flung it at him, shoutin' as half a dozen hot pokers stabbed through me with the movement. I heard the glass shatter against the wall as darkness raced in from the edges of my sight, blindin' me, and I struggled to push it back.

"Get out!" I snarled, afraid of the weakness in my voice, the black fog cloudin' my head. Too close to that helpless boy I'd been.

I had to get out! I struggled to throw back the covers, groanin' at the effort.

"Relax, Mr. Colton. There's no need for weapons here. Besides, if you think you can get to the door without passing out from the pain, be my guest. But you'll most likely reopen those wounds I just patched up."

I'd not made him the slightest bit nervous. None of these people were afraid of me. I'd lost myself, the man I'd fought to become, one who wouldn't be crossed. A worm I was, once again, just as I'd been as a child, soft. Exposed.

Silence hung heavy in the air. Shame washed over me as I realized how out of control I was. I'd once thought I was calculatin', above emotions, and here I was lettin' them rule me. I gritted my teeth and nodded, a grudging acceptance of my current state. I was a shiverin' mess, a trapped animal.

To his credit, he was quick about it, didn't say nothin' else. He changed out the dressin's, poked and prodded without any sympathy to my pain, stuck some tubes in his ears connected to a shot glass shaped thing on my chest and stomach.

"Everything seems to be as it should be." He helped me put my shirt back on then turned his attention to restorin' things to his bag. "You are not to leave this bed today, do you understand, Mr. Colton?"

"I need to relieve myself," I mumbled into my lap, my face burnin' fierce.

A shallow metal pan thumped between my legs. "I can assist, if necessary." This time he allowed his mouth to quirk up.

I grabbed the pan and debated throwin' at him, but the need to make water was fierce. "No," I fumed. "You can leave now."

Doc chuckled softly as he shut the door, leaving me alone with my thoughts and that Hades-made tin pot.

19

Leavin'

I was awake, watching the trees blowin' through the window, feelin' a ghost of the wind play with my hair, when there was a scratchin' at the door.

"Feather?" I called hopefully, cursin' as my movement pulled at my wounds. I'da never thought I'da wanted to see the dimwit dog like I did now, trapped in this bed.

The door opened with a blur of brown fur as Feather bounded in, jumpin' on the foot o' the bed and crawlin' to me. "Where ya been?"

"He's been pawing at the kitchen door for the past three hours," Granley huffed. "You've got another visitor."

My eyes popped up to the door. She'd dressed finer than I'd seen her afore, her mahogany hair done fancy swept up on her head. She had Goyan on her hip. L'il thing was suckin' on her first two fingers, as she rested her head on Granley's shoulder. "Hurt?" she asked, like she'd done in the cave.

"Just a smidge, tumbleweed," my voice not my own, so soft and gentle.

She leaned toward me, reachin', her hands openin' and closin'. "Kisses," she demanded.

Granley carefully placed Goyan beside me. Instantly tiny arms wrapped around my neck, her wet face pressed against my cheek, soft and warm. I shoulda hated it, but fer some reason it made me warm inside. That thought made a knot begin to tighten my gut.

My heart began to stampede. Feather wiggled closer, his tail thumpin', like he knew.

"Better?" Granley's hand did a poor job hidin' her smile. I squinted at her as the girl patted my other cheek.

"You shouldn't enjoy this so much," I tried to growl, but I couldn't put the threat in my words no more.

She laughed at me full on then. "You don't know what to do with us, Eli. It'll be all right. You'll figure out we aren't a threat and you don't have to snarl at us like a bear in a trap."

She might as well sucker punched me in the gut. I can't do this, I thought. Gotta get outta here, afore I get them hurt. Feather snuffed at my leg.

"Owie!" Goyan had found the bandage on my shoulder and leaned down to kiss it, losin' her balance.

I jerked to catch her, piercin' pain shootin' through me. I sucked in a breath and held it.

Granley started to pull her away. "Don't, she's fine," I stopped her, "Ain't ya, tumbleweed." Don't know why I started callin' her that, nor why I kept her there. I'd never been one to cotton to little ones, not even when I was one myself.

Granley hovered like one o' them jeweled hummin' birds. Couldn't tell if she was worried more 'bout me or the kid.

"She's small for her age, you understand, and should be speaking better. She barely talks at all." Granley chewed her lip. "And she's terrified of men."

I read the trail she was layin' and the itch ruffled its feathers again, wantin' to take care of those who'd hurt the girl. Waste of good air, they were. Soon as I could get outta this bed and hold my irons steady, I'd…

Feather nosed me again while Goyan played with my hair. His tail thumped against my leg.

"Eli?"

"Huh?" There was a furrow 'tween her eyes as she studied me.

"Is this too much? I can take her and bring you some broth, and let you rest."

Goyan bent down and crawled to Feather, began to mess with the dog's ears. Feather licked her cheek, made her giggle. He wiggled beside me, soakin' up her attention, thumped his tail some more. Like a reg'lar dog. But I didn't think he was. He was somethin' more.

I looked out the window, watched a big dust devil travel down the street, feelin' its twin in my gut. I clenched my fists, my teeth grindin' together. How was I gonna keep my dark down? It was risin' up, like I'd heard them oil wells spurtin' from deep under the ground, blottin' out, chokin' me with it's foulness.

I needed out, needed to keep the dark away from Granley, from the kids. I hadn't done what I did just to have my itch jeopardize their safety. My heart pumped fit to explode.

All a sudden, was like a coal train'd been set on my chest, my lungs squeezed. "Granley!" I gasped, clutchin' for her arm like a drownin' man, my vision sparkin' on the edges.

"Eli!" She shook my hand off, pluckin' the kid off the bed and then her face was so close to mine I could feel the heat of her, see the bits of color in her eyes. "B-breathe!"

I was dyin', the world blackin' out, the dark takin' over, a roarin' in my ears. A rattler's bite struck my cheekbone as vaguely registered that she'd slapped me. I coughed, then rolled to my side, heavin' like a horse been run to the ground. Granley's hushed voice reached my ears, but I couldn't pay her much mind as my insides tried to come out onto the floor. From the pains that lit up I wasn't sure I hadn't been set a'fore a firin' squad.

"Y-you hhhear me, Eli?" I caught a glimpse of her eyes, so close to mine, her frantic voice difficult to hear over the poundin' of my heart. "P-p-push that air out!" I gasped as my lungs found space for air. "Again," she demanded. "Out! In!" My eyes stung.

Granley's cool hands swept my hair back as I wiped my drool with the back of my hand, shaky as a newborn colt. There was a furrow between her brows as she plucked at the sheets around me. I felt a burn run through me, my cheeks lightin' up, an' I couldn't meet her eyes. Half a man, I was, but full of evil.

"Get out," grit out, like one o' them old men sittin' on a porch.

She pretended she didn't hear me, tryin' to put me to rights, but I had to have her out. She couldn't be here with me. I couldn't even look at her. Her presence was like salt rubbed into a wound. "Get out, Granley. Right now. I-I don' wanna see you."

"Eli-" Her eyes went wide as I glanced at her, her face pale.

"Don't you hear me? Go away!" The words hurt me like a bullet, but they needed to be said. She couldn't be here, I had to make her safe. My very bones were filled with the dark. I could hurt her, and the thought of that tore me apart.

Her eyes narrowed and the mule in her rose up. "Nnno." she countered. The air in the room chilled as she glared at me.

"Granley," I grit out, "You don't leave you're gonna see my lily-white behind, 'cuz I'm gettin' out of this bed.

She flushed, holdin' my eyes stubbornly before she turned, that largish nose of hers held up high, and walked through the door, slammin' it behind her. I looked out the window, saw the dust risin' in the clouds, my heart just as dirty. I knew what had to be done.

Doc came in not long after that, as I was swingin' my legs off t' the side, breathin' through the fire burnin' in half a dozen places.

Gone was the friendly Doc. This was a severe physician who'd take no guff from his patient. He come in with no preamble, fell to feelin' me up. I allowed it, with some grumblin', 'cuz I didn't have the air to fight him.

"Miss Granley reported you experienced a breathing attack earlier?" his voice even as he moved his listenin' contraption around my chest.

"It weren't nothin'." I wasn't gonna give him no reason to hold me here. Not with the dark swirlin' through me. I'd done been through wounds such as this afore, don't know what kept me here 'till now.

"Hmph. Get back in bed. You shouldn't be walking as of yet," he said dismissively as he replaced his instrument. "It's not even been a week. You'll tear things open."

"Look, I'll lay out my all cards plain to see. I'm leavin' today. I figger you can help me, or I'll just get by as best I can."

"You're lucky to be alive as it is, you stubborn fool," he snapped as he glared at me, arms crossed. He wasn't a small man, and I was weakened. He could keep me here, if he wanted. "You try to leave today, you'll be lying on the road bleeding out before the sun sets."

I let the Death rise up in me when I looked in his eyes then. The itch was there, diff'rent somehow, but undeniable, just the same. The air between us crackled with unspoken danger. His jaw clenched as he narrowed his eyes, widenin' his legs a might, like he was bracin' himself for a fight.

"I cain't stay, Doc. I gotta go. Don't you get it? I'll bring somethin' bad to bear."

He studied me for a while, his blue eyes piercin' into me, like I was a trail didn't make sense. Somehow, he wasn't afraid, and it wasn't 'cus he was blind to the darkness I'd showed him, nor because he was a fool.

The man simply knew what was inside me and accepted it, like he was familiar with the dark. Maybe I wasn't the first he'd seen, I didn't take the time to wonder on it just then.

"You aren't gonna make anyone happy if you do this," he finally stated.

I just glared at my hands fisted in my lap, shame and anger burnin' my ears.

He sighed, resigned. "Very well. If I can't convince you to stay, let me wrap things up as best as I can before you go. Then you must take it easy on yourself, no heavy lifting, no sudden movements, do you understand, Mr. Colton? You start bleeding again, you might not make it."

He began to wrap ever'thin' over again, tight to make me grunt an' groan. If I wasn't mistaken, he took pleasure in it too, judgin' from the small upturn of his mouth and the spark in his eyes. Then I got clothes on me, borrowed, since I s'pose mine weren't fit for rags after it all. I sat on the bed after that, shakin' and sweatin', knowin' he wanted to tell me "tol' you so."

But in due time, I got myself to the stable an' dragged the saddle onto Hammer, who didn't 'preciate that I had to mount from the wrong side to accommodate my wounds. Sweatin' like a pig on Sunday, I rode outta town, my teeth breakin' with the pain each step of the horse brought.

20

Alone on the Road

The air hung heavy and thick with an impendin' storm, suffocatin' me as much as my turmoiled thoughts. I lay forward, resting my arms on the saddle horn, my eyes closin', dozin' in the saddle. Sweat plastered my shirt to my back, and a metallic tang filled my mouth. Regret weighed heavy on me, haunted by the shocked look on Granley's face as I turned on her, like a rabid dog.

A glance at my leg revealed the stain of an opened wound, a reminder of my foolishness. Looked like it'd stopped, though it would prob'ly open up again when I moved. I cursed as I looked 'round the empty trail, knowin' I needed shelter.

As if it had been called forth by my need, my eyes lit upon a half-fell down shack a bit off the road. I pushed Hammer to it, takin' him 'round back, so he wouldn't be seen from the road, 'fore I slowly slid off, my bum leg givin' out.

I clung to the stirrup, pantin' as I waited for my legs to work again. Hammer was gonna have to spend the night in his saddle, no way I'd manage heftin' it again. I grunted as I loosened the cinch. I could give him that, at least.

After a breather, I righted myself, grabbed the blanket and bandages Doc had made me take, and made my way into the place, scuffin' up dust with each step. Smellin' of varmints and sun-rotted wood, the wanin' daylight shone dimly through cracks in the walls, lit on the thick cobwebs lacin' throughout.

Glancin' around, I made sure the one-room shack was empty, findin' a spot in the corner where the floorboards looked whole. I used my boot to scrape it clean, best as I could without angerin' my wounds.

With a grimace I laid the blanket down, easin' myself to the floor as well as I could. I sat for long moments, pantin', as I waited for the pain to subside. I looked my wounds over, rebound them best I could. I weren't no Doc, but it wasn't half bad, I didn't suppose. If it mattered.

It wasn't cold, despite the storm. I shouldn't need a fire, but my bones wanted one nonetheless. I didn't have the wood, didn't care to gather it. Someone had already scavenged the furniture, not that I had the strength in me to break it down. No fire tonight.

The wind began to pick up, howlin' at the windows, the bushes outside scratchin' on the walls like somethin' from the world below. The cobwebs became specters from the other side, to condemn and curse, or to plead and beckon, I wasn't sure. I shivered, unsure if I had a chill or if it was the creepin' dread coilin' around my heart.

The thunderstorm hit hard as night darkened the sky, lightning interrupting the black and leaving ghosts in my eyes. A sudden weighty thud of a large creature moving into the house had me grabbing my gun and shouting "Hold it right there!" My heart hammered an erratic rhythm, fear at bein' weak when I needed to protect myself.

Wet fur pressed against me, a cold nose pushed into my neck.

"Feather? Where ya been?"

A tail thump echoed hollow on the floorboards. I lay back down, just realizin' how much I'd hurt jumpin' like that, fool dog. Lay there a spell, listenin' to the thunder rumble like a herd of spooked cattle and the wind howlin' like a coyote lost in the night. Them scratchin' sounds at the walls turned from varmints to somethin' worse, somethin' clawin' its way outta hell itself.

Seemed the very darkness I'd took pride in had turned into the very thing I hated. How had I been any different from Ma Josie, Boss Rawlins, preyin' on the weak? Guilt burned through me, hot and heavy. I'd hurt so many, their fearful, pleadin' faces flittin' like phantoms in the moonlight, just because I could, because that blasted itch drove me. Then that yella-haired woman, the one that'd cursed me.

"Haunted by the ghosts of your deeds," I murmured, my mouth dry. Was she the reason I climbed out of that grave? How else could I explain what had happened to me? Had the sheriff's wife believed right? Were spirits hauntin' me, even now? I'd never believed in them things, but now…

I'd been layin' in that coffin for no less than three days, maybe more. How else could I account for it? And Granley had said I stopped breathin' - had I died again? As much as I wanted to dismiss the superstitions, "smoke and mirrors," like I'd told the sheriff's wife, I couldn't explain what had happened to me.

Cold sweat slicked my skin, despite the warmth of the night. What if dyin' wasn't the end? Maybe I had more trail than I'd thought. The only comfort was the steady drone of Feather's snores beside me, that strange, altogether eerily knowin' dog. Finally, I drifted off myself, takin' refuge in a sleep that was more like a hold-your-breath kinda waitin' game.

Granley and Goyan are walkin' beside me in the meadow, the soft sun shinin' gently in Granley's brown hair, turnin' it a rich honey color. Goyan is talkin' a storm, reaching for the wildflowers, spinnin' in circles, her voice bright and sweet. Granley's laughin', her eyes shinin' with joy, the tiny wrinkles I'd not even known I'd noticed scrunchin' together as her cheeks bunch in a smile.

Then I notice her brilliant red necklace, around her fragile neck, scarlet jewels that begin drippin', spreadin' slowly down her lily white blouse, like the yella haired lady who cursed me. Her eyes widen in horror and time slows as she grabs for her throat, the red tricklin' through her fingers, my heart freezin' in disbelief.

I look for Goyan, only to see her crumpled on the ground, her pretty dress only a canvas painted with red, a terrible revulsion creeps over me as I find the source of the blood - my very hands, still holdin' that cursed knife, slick with their life blood, and a awful sound rips from my throat, like that of a broken creature.

I turn back to Granley. She looks at me, her eyes pleadin' with me to save her as she falls toward me, reachin' for me. I rush to her, catch her small tremblin' form in my arms, hold her as her eyes flicker from life to the emptiness of Death.

Then again, she's beside me, in that beautiful meadow, smilin' at me. And it plays out again. And yet again. I'm powerless to change it, to alter the course of events. Then there was buzzards, peckin' at my decaying body, relentless. I wave at them, try to get them to fly off, but they're persistent.

Then a warm wetness on my face. I opened my eyes to Feather lickin' my face like I'd smeared it with jelly.

I felt chilled to the bone and sore down to my soul. I gritted my teeth as I forced my achin' body up, my knife a heavy weight on my thigh. Shakin' and weak, I untie it in its scabbard, use it to hack out a shallow hole behind the shack, each hard-won groove in the hard earth a relief to my soul.

I bury it there, like a funeral for my itch, spittin' on the dirt when I'm done. Granley's pale and lifeless face flashes before me, like a lightnin' strike in my soul.

"No more," I vowed, to myself and whoever else cared to listen, my voice so hoarse it was nearly unrecognizable to my ears. "Never again," I try to convince myself.

Then somehow I dragged my broken body back onto Hammer, heading once more away from the innocents. They were alive for now. It was clear to me, the more distance between me and them, the better.

But ol' Hammerhead, he took the bit in his teeth again. Mebbe he was mad 'bout spendin' the night in the storm. Dunno, but he turned me back the way we'd come, no matter how I sawed at the reins.

And Feather-Brain, I knew he was laughin' at me. He weren't no friend of mine. He'd come, when I was restin' peacefully in that coffin, havin' gotten my just desserts, and torn my life asunder. I was alone, just as I'd always been.

Since the dadgum horse wouldn't turn, I tried to get out of the saddle, fallin' right onto my rump in the middle of the road. I lay a moment, catching my breath, as Hammer stopped, looked 'round at me like I was some kinda fool. He wasn't wrong.

I managed to get to my feet, head swimmin' dangerously, picked up my hat, started limpin' a crooked line the other way. Feather grabbed hold o' my pant leg, pulled at it. I kicked at him, hissed at the pain from my foolishness as I nearly tipped over.

"I ain't goin' back there!" I shouted at him. "It's the only way to protect them! I don't want to hurt them!" I kicked at him again. "Leave me be!"

The dog nudged me toward the horse, insistent, his tail waggin'. I shooed him off, standin' there, my mind spinnin' as I tried to think past the poundin' in my head. Another tug on my pant leg nearly sent me back into the dirt. He wasn't givin' up, wasn't gonna let me run away, save them innocents from myself.

I limped back to the horse, my body feelin' weak, battered. I leaned in defeat against his big form. His solid body was a fleetin' comfort. I knew I'd just end up back there, if I didn't do somethin' to keep myself away, because the biggest part of me thirsted for another taste of what I'd had there. Hurt, alone, I wanted nothin' else but to see Granley's face.

"I won't be able to stay away," I sobbed into his black neck, and he just stood there, my only comfort. They would die, my darkness would get them sooner or later.

The knowledge settled, heavy and bitter. There was only one way to break this pull they had over me. I did the only thing I could think of that could save Granley and the children, the thing that should've happened after my hangin'. I should be dead in that coffin, not walkin' free to kill.

A lone tear escaped, mournin' what couldn't be, as I stuck that Colt Frontier between my teeth, the metal of the barrel hard and cold. I cocked it and squeezed the trigger. I fell like a child's doll.

21

Alive or not-quite dead?

I woke again to Feather lickin' my face again, like wakin' from a dream, fuzzy and unsure. I looked around, found myself in the corner of the shack, sunlight filterin' through the cracks like spring's first shoots. I scrubbed my eyes to clear them, my arms shaky and heavy.

Then I noticed somethin' in my mouth, hard and greasy and metallic. I turned to my side and coughed up a twisted lead slug, the size you'd get from a .44 Colt. It thudded heavily on the dirty plank floor, a message from beyond that my attempt at endin' things was rejected. Bile replaced the tang of the slug as I realized there was nothin' more I could do.

Anger filled me, hatred for whatever force insisted on keepin' me to this plane, to harm innocents, prey on them like a rabid wolf. A raw scream ripped from my throat, wordless and brutal, my hands pullin' at my hair in fury and despair.

As I breathed, saw-bladed knives twisted in my side and shoulder wounds. I just laid there and considered what might be real and what might be dream. I wondered if I was alive even now, or just not quite dead. Sure hurt like I'm alive, I thought as I groaned and rolled over to my back, contemplatin' my next steps.

What did it all mean? What purpose did it serve? Why was I still walkin' the earth, when so many others were not?

Feather pushed his body beside mine, tail floppin' and stirrin' the dust in the streams of sunlight. He nudged my knife, still in its scabbard, toward me, almost like he was reassurin' me I could control it. I picked it up, brushed the dirt off, noticed the teeth marks from Granley's surgery.

Her smile flickered before my eyes, gentle and trustin', the way I'd felt after I'd…Sure, I was shamed, but I'd also felt that prickle of hope. What if…what if talkin' to her could do somethin' for my itch?

"You dug it up, huh?" He snuffled into my arm, tail waggin' faster. I thought back to the cave, wondered what Granley thought of my leavin'. Wondered why I cared. I'd died to protect her and those kids. Maybe…I hesitated to even put a thought to it…maybe I wouldn't hurt them.

The crimson necklace around Granley's throat burst into my head. Feather nudged me, and then I recalled the determination I'd had to protect them at the cave. I'd done somethin' beyond myself, got these unfamiliar emotions that somehow felt…good. If I could do that for them…surely I'd be able to keep myself from hurtin' them.

I decided then, I'd go back, leastways 'til I'd healed. Or until the itch became too much to bear. I'd leave before it got too strong, but the pull back to that sleepy town, to that kind woman, was unrelenting. Granley was prob'ly fit to be tied, with me leavin' the way I did.

Sure enough, wasn't long 'fore Chalipun scuffed at the doorway. I pulled myself to a stand, leanin' against the wall so's I didn't sway, feelin' woozy as a drunk on New Year's, puttin' my hands on my hips to hide their tremblin'. His eyes flickered over me, but his face didn't change. A man in a kid's body.

"Granley send you?" I croaked, strangely light-hearted at the notion. I bent to grab the blanket, sendin' the slug spinnin'. I snatched it right quick and stuck it in my pocket, ears burnin' at what I'd done, or tried to do.

It didn't miss Chalipun's quick eyes, but he didn't mention it. He'd prob'ly felt shame at some point too.

"She mad?" I asked, half hopin' she was. It would mean she cared, like maybe I meant somethin' to her.

He grinned, steppin' forward to hand me a note. "You have luck she no come."

I scoffed at the note, ears pricklin' as my face heated yet again. "Just like a schoolteacher," I complained. "You read it. I cain't read worth a plugged nickel." Went to put my things back into the saddle bags, ignorin' the note.

His smile fell, his hand droppin' before it raised again. "You try?"

I shot a look at him. "Why, cain't you read, neither?

He was scowlin', embarrassed like I'd been, but refused to lower his eyes from mine. Tarnation, that boy was somethin'. "I sit with Goyan, help her."

I rolled my eyes, finally gettin' my footing with him, as I threw the saddle bags onto Hammer, tightened the cinch back up. I'd have to make sure he got a good groomin' and oats, to make up for spendin' the night in the saddle. "Well, don't we make a team o' two legged jacks. Fine, give it here."

I unfolded it and squinted at the writin'. I'd not learned much more than block letterin', so it was like readin' track after a rain, but 'ventually, I got the gist. Silly woman was threatenin' to send the army after me iffen I didn't get my sorry hide back to town so's I could heal up and help out at the orphanage.

High-handed, interferin' woman. I clenched the note in my fist, glared up at the kid. He grinned back at me, prob'ly guessin' what was in the note.

"Land sakes," I mused at her shenanigans, off kilter for a moment at her bravado, then turned back to Hammer. I grit my teeth as I pulled up into my saddle.

"You got a horse?"

He nodded and run off.

We wandered into town at a snail's pace, my wounds unable to take more jostlin'. I rolled my shoulders, hissin' at the pain, tryin' to relieve the feel of the eyes watchin' us come in.

Chalipun led me to a big house I guessed was the foundlin' home, blue paint just beginnin' to curl from the sun. It was set back from the main street with a sprawlin' yard, large cottonwoods spreadin' dappled shade with their spring buds, and a small stable hidden behind.

That batty lady musta been watchin' out the window 'cuz she met us at the stable, her face dark and thunderous, and began talkin' a mile a minute.

"D-don't you ever do that to mme again, d-do you hear mme, Eli C-colton?" She fought to get the words out, her mouth as uncooperative as a wild bronc.

Her fists clenched, and she was blinkin' fiercely as tears pooled in her honey eyes. "G-going off on your own without t-telling anyone, and you wounded close to death!" Her arms flung up before she crossed them in front.

"What was I to think?" she added, voice waverin' as her shoulders came down, the wind out of her sails for a moment.

I took a breath to answer, but she started up again, bound and determined to have her say even if her words wouldn't come easy.

"Y-you are going to mmarch in there right now and lay down and rest," her finger made no mistake about where I was to go. "I made a room all up for you. Y-you are going to get healed up and then I have a whole list of things I need done, but y-you are going to start on the small things.

"I don't need y-you straining and reinjuring yourself any more than you already have. Ch-chalipun will bring Doc by to check y-your wounds again to ensure you haven't done yourself a grave disservice."

She finally took a breath so's I could get a word in edgewise. "I done come back, Granley," I spoke gently, like you would to growlin' dog. "Reckon I'll try it out. Got spooked is all."

Then to top it all off, the waterworks come to her honeyed eyes, her voice hitchin'. "I-I was afraid y-you'd end up d-dead on the road, and I'd never know what happened to you." She put her hand to her mouth and turned away slightly.

And what was I to do with that? Her tears burned into my heart. "Nah, ol' skunk like me's harder t'kill than all that," I offered gruffly, my tongue thick.

She patted my good arm, her touch feather light and warm, as she wiped her eyes, my body stiffenin' like some wooden cigar statue at her touch. "You aren't invincible, Eli. I'm glad you're back."

"Yes'm," I grunted, my throat constrictin'. I turned to escape this scene, my eyes prickin' dangerously, but Chalipun had already taken care of Hammer.

"Come with me, I'll show you your room." Her scent wafted to me as she drifted past, somethin' soft and sweet that somehow brought peace to my soul. I followed, one leg after the other as I trudged after her.

"Yes'm." To tell the truth, I could do with a lay down, feelin' a bit wobbly kneed. Feather followed like a shadow.

"I put you in a downstairs room, so you wouldn't have to attempt the stairs," she said as she opened a door.

That room was better'n most anythin' I'd ever had, clean, with a bed and a chest of drawers, a flowery wash basin on top. A thick braided rug covered a large part of the wooden floor beside the bed. I dropped onto the pink coverlet, hatin' I prob'ly got dust all over it but unable to stay on my feet.

"'Preciate it, Granley," I muttered as my eyes closed.

It took her a moment to ken my meanin', but at last she shut the door. I sighed, my muscles little by little lettin' go. I didn't bother with my boots, doubted I had the strength to pull 'em off. I fell back on the covers and was sawin' logs 'fore two shakes of a hound's tail.

I woke to Doc openin' the door. Clutchin' my side, I rolled to sittin'.

"No offense meant, Eli, but I'd kindly ask to put an end to our visits. Your excursion likely has not done you a bit of good."

"Don't give me no guff, Doc. Granley already done shook her fist at me."

He snorted as he made quick work of his inspection, the sharp whiff of whatever stingin' medicine he used to douse my wounds burnin' my nose. "I imagine. I never thanked you for what you did for her and the children. It's no secret to those around here, Miss Granley holds a special place in my heart."

His words hit me like a freight train, 'cuz I hadn't even realized what I'd started thinkin' 'bout Granley. Of course she should have a man like Doc, honest and well-thought of, not some mangy varmint ridin' a bad wind like I was.

"Don't mention it, Doc," I muttered as I stared at the callouses on my hand, tracing the scars on my knuckles. I shouldn'ta come back. It'd been a long while since I'd had to keep my mask on for so long, hidin' the dark from folks. Even now it tried to claw its way out, itchin' deep inside.

Feather nosed open the door and jumped into my lap. Scents of cookin' filtered through the open door, salted pork, I guessed. I briefly wondered if I'd be able to taste the food. I heard the kids laughin', a new sound that made me feel curiously happy. They hadn't laughed durin' our journey, watchful and quiet like some of the kids I knew at the orphanage, kids that had seen too much.

My attention drifted back to Doc as he huffed at the dog, then addressed me, wrappin' his profession around him like a cloak. "Well, you've held up fairly well. Take it easy for another week or so and you should be right as rain."

"Ain't my first rodeo." I pulled my shirt back on as Granley appeared in the doorway.

"Dinner's at the table." Her eyes flicked to Doc Flannagan, her cheeks pinked, before they landed on me. "Will you join us, both of you? We haven't had a chance to speak, Eli, but your position includes room and board."

"I am grateful for the invitation, Miss Granley. I'd be pleased to dine with you and the children." Doc took his bag, dismissin' me, and moved through the door.

Granley…Miss Granley fidgeted for a moment, her eyes skitterin' across me, color high. I thought she might say somethin' but she just pressed her lips together before she turned to follow him.

I wondered at that as I finished buttonin' my shirt, briefly considerin' ignorin' the summons. She deserved a man like Doc, not a sidewinder like me. Best thing I could do for her was keep my distance, make sure he had an openin' to slide in.

But the smell of that salted pork made my mouth water, and I had to admit to myself that I yearned to be included in the hearty laughter that drifted in, somethin' I'd never really been a party to. I firmed up my chin and limped in the direction of the kids' voices.

22

The Cellar

I had me a whole list of things to be done. Kept myself busy with the small things while I healed up. Quiet I was, keepin' that dark in, afraid it would spew forth. I stayed in my room, if I wasn't workin', fearin' to go to town, certain I'd be lookin' for the weak among the flock.

The kids'd come by, interested in somethin' or other I was doin', and I'd grump at them, thinkin' I'd make 'em run off. They had no more sense than a rooster crowin' at midnight. Weren't nothin' like I remembered livin' in the orphanage. The kids here had food for their bellies a'plenty, schoolin', and Miss Granley instead of Ma Josie, who was more likely to hand out a hug than a beltin'.

But day was I made it to the item on my list I'd been puttin' off. "Build shelves for canned goods in the cellar." I'da ignored it another week or two, 'cept she'd asked me when I'd get to it, gave me some story about how she'd put things on the ground but was afeared they'd rust down there. I could do a lot of things, but I couldn't stand to disappoint that woman.

I'd never considered myself a cowardly man. I stood at the top of those dark steps, narrow an' rough, the chill, moldy air waftin' up toward me. The scent was too familiar, set my heart to flutterin' like a spooked bird. I was just waitin' for her hard push to send me sprawlin' down those stairs, like it'd happened so many times before, and I near turned tail.

I took my time, there at the top, tremblin' like a leaf in a tornado, the dark chasm open before me. But I had my boards in one hand, the lantern in the other, an' I pushed one boot in front o'the other, seein' ghosts of my past in the darkness.

My breath huffed like a horse just run a race, an' I began to hear that awful woman's voice with each squeak of the steps, each whoosh of my beatin' heart. She had a way o' talkin', all smooshed together, like she'd just drunk a fistful o' raw liquor.

'Course, she was meaner than a sidewinder whose tail'd been trampled most days, but liquor made her worse'n the devil himself. Each step brought her voice closer, 'till I could nearly feel her hot breath on me, the reek of her rotten teeth.

Evil boys don't sleep in beds. Step. You're a nasty one, Will Carter. Step. I'll give you a cookie if you're good. She would taunt us, her voice sickly sweet, like gangrene. It was her game, the promise of a reward, the inevitable disappointment, then the brutal punishment - step.

The remainder of the steps stretched on, yawnin' before me like a dragon's open mouth, the lantern castin' demon's shadows in the depths. The musty scent of damp earth reminded me of wakin' in that grave. The boards shifted, nearly slippin' out of my slick hands.

Gonna beat that sin outta you. I flinched as I felt that stick of hers on my back as she walloped me - step. Come here an' give Ma Josie a kiss. I shuddered with the memory of being pulled close to the witch - step.

Back down into yer hole, you little snake! She screamed at me, her voice richocetin' in my ears.

When her phantom hands grabbed me, sharp and cold, I threw the boards to the bottom, the crack of their impact on the hard dirt like a gunshot. Blinded by my terror, I pounded up the stairs, trippin' and scuffin' my palms on the rough stairs. I finished the climb on my hands and feet, leavin' the lantern burnin' on one of the steps.

Got myself out the door, chest burnin' for the fresh air. I needed the light to remind me Ma Josie wasn't here, I wasn't in her cellar. The ever present odor of horse manure, the sound of the leaves in the breeze, brought me back to the here and now. I headed straightaway to the saloon, desperate for somethin' to push those memories back down. Liquor's sweet numbin' drew me in like a mirage's lie of water.

Place was empty, 'ceptin' for one old timer who sat nursin' a glass like he had naught to do. I had myself a couple, catched my breath, let my heart slow down, the shakes settle. But I still felt her hands on me, makin' my skin crawl.

She'd want us to hug her and kiss her like she was our real mama, then would beat the livin' daylights out of us at her whim. Never knew which one we'd get, from day to day, from hour to hour, even minute to minute, angel or devil. I'd spent my first couple years chasin' after her love, 'fore I began to hate her.

I drank the last one slow. I watched the bartender as he tidied up, wipin' the infernal dust off glasses, the old man in the corner as he fiddled with somethin' in his pocket. They both glanced at me every so often, wary but not alarmed. I rubbed my fingers over the notches in the wood. Anythin' to take my mind off that woman.

Feelin' a mite calmer, I stepped out of the saloon, pausin' a moment in the shade, allowin' my eyes time to adjust. He was right there, the perfect prey. Alone, unaware. I kept track of him from the corner of my eye for a bit, the dark risin', fillin' me with the need to shun my helpless past, show my claws.

I had the plan, it would be so simple, to follow him, pull him between the buildings, do my thing. Sate that itch. No one the wiser. It wouldn't take long, five minutes if I got him good. You slice through the lower part of the throat, they can't even scream. My hands twitched as I readied myself.

I heard a dog bark, sharp and loud. It stopped me cold, pushed the darkness back like a thief caught by light. I didn't move toward him, and he moved off, the chance lost. I sucked in air like I'd been drownin' and just come up for air, and the dark left me. For the first time, I didn't feel the need to see his eyes turn into Death.

That was good, right? Why'd I feel so out of sorts?

I shoved open the orphanage door, my head spinning. Somehow, I'd made it back without a thought. Before I could stumble towards my room, a tall man, almost my size, blocked the way. He wore a fine suit, a stark contrast to my dusty clothes. His smile, warm and familiar like Emma's, crinkled the corners of his eyes framed by a hoary beard and mustache.

"You must be Eli Colton," his voice boomed. "Jeremiah Granley. I owe you a debt of gratitude, son. A mighty big one."

Dumbfounded, I stared at him. His expression turned concerned.

"You look like you've seen a ghost, son. Here, sit down." He ushered me towards the settee, his big hand surprisingly gentle on my arm.

"Probably not the best lookin' ghost you ever saw," I mumbled, collapsing onto the soft cushions.

He chuckled, a touch strained. "Perhaps not. Water? Something stronger?"

I met his gaze, searching for a reason for his gratitude, for the way his eyes seemed to hold a hidden story. He waited for me patiently, like he had all the time in the world, just lettin' me get my words out

I licked my lips, my knee dancin' a jig, tryin' to keep it all in, but it slid out anyway. "I didn't kill him," I finally blurted, appalled that I was spillin' my secrets. "Could've, but something stopped me. The darkness… it didn't win."

His smile faltered. He didn't pull away, though, something I hadn't expected. He pursed his lips a moment, eyes shadowed as he looked to the glass in his hand, swirled it, before he looked back to me.

"That sounds like a victory, Eli," he said carefully, pulling a chair closer, its legs screechin' on the wood floor.

A shiver wracked me. Ma Josie's words echoed in my mind: "Evil boy," "snake," "sinner." My ears rang with her words, and I covered them with my hands, squeezin' my eyes shut. I was breakin' apart inside, all those awful things in my heart come slidin' out, like vipers out of a den.

"I am evil," I rasped, and like they'd done with Emma in the cave, the words wouldn't stop. They just kept pourin' outta me. "Killed them all, didn't care a blasted bit. Wanted more. They hanged me for it. I died. They buried me. But… I wasn't dead. And the dog, he helped at first, like a second chance.

"But this time… this time it was me. An' I… I—" Tears pricked at my eyes, my voice choked with fear. "What if Ma Josie's right? What if I am evil? What if I can't hold on? I gotta protect Granley, the kids, but I'm always pulled back…"

Before I could crumble completely, the man surprised me again. He wrapped his arms around me. My skin crawled at the contact, the usual urge to fight, to flee, warring inside me. But… something held me there. A sense of… safety? A warmth that slowly untwisted the lasso that was cinchin' my insides. He waited until I relaxed before he let me go, sittin' back and clearin' his throat.

"Let me tell you a story, Eli," he said, his voice gruff but calm, eyes droopin' slightly with regret. "A story of my own. Years ago, during the war… I was a young hot-head. I led a charge, a reckless one fueled by rage, my own darkness. Men died, Eli, good men. Like you, I should have died there.

"And on that battlefield, staring death in the face, I found myself in a place of utter darkness. A voice offered me a choice… a second chance, but with a burden. The stain on my soul is still present, Eli, but…I think I've succeeded at keeping it at bay, all these years.

"So you see, my boy, I do not doubt your story, nor that if you are offered a second chance, you are worthy and capable of it."

It was then I heard Miss Granley's footsteps on the hollow boards approaching. I hurriedly rose and faced the window, trying to erase all evidence of my tears.

"D-daddy, you're here!" I heard their embrace behind me. "Oh, Eli, I didn't see you there. So you've met Daddy!"

"Yes'm" I said, keepin' my face averted, hopin' she didn't see the tear streaks that were surely there. "I gotta go…do somethin'." I rushed outta that room like a coyote with his tail lit on fire.

23

The Apaches & the Cavalry

I made it to the cellar the next day, sweatin' like a pig and knees knockin'. But I repeated Senator Granley's words each time that Ma Josie's voice broke into my head, quieten' her words. Each hammer blow put a coffin nail in those memories.

But the next day was Sunday. And as I'd healed, I was no longer excused from the town's salvation meetin'. Granley'd washed and starched my shirt, and I'd buttoned it high. It recalled the feel of the noose to me, had me sweatin' through my shirt in no time. We walked up to the whitewashed buildin', them Indian kids following behind Granley like ducks in a row. Once again the darkness rose to its feet, sniffin' out the prey that gathered there. I locked my muscles tight, kept my eyes on the preacher's feet.

What's worse, every li'l biddy wanted to cluck over me, and I could feel my false front wearin' thin. The itch was risin', like a spirit from the grave. The spring in me got wound tight, sat tight through the singin' and the prayin' and the preachin', just waitin' for me to let loose my hold for a moment and let it shoot free. I don't rightly recall a word he said, not that I gave much weight to them preacher folks, my experience being worse than good.

When it was all over, I skedaddled outta there afore half of 'em had rose up from the pews, hopin' nobody'd follow me. Wasn't sure how I'd handle the suffocatin' attention if someone did. My feet hit the earth outside that buildin' like my boots was on fire, swashin' through the grass as I beat it outta town.

I'd found a hollow, not too far off, where a creek run through, leastaways during the spring, and I beat it there, unbuttoning my shirt and rollin' the sleeves up, tryin' to get my air.

I sat myself on a rock beside the water, put my head in my hands. I was as tuckered as if I'd been on a hard day's ride, tuckered as all get out, like a bronc fightin' the saddle.

Feather come boundin' up a moment later, tail waggin' and brown eyes soft, knowin'.

"I could feel it, wellin' up inside. It wanted them all, easy pickin's."

He pushed his big shaggy head against my leg, like he was reassurin' me I could weather the storm. I ruffled his floppy ears, acceptin' the comfort he was givin'.

"I'm worn out, Feather," I sighed, keepin' my eyes on the the cottonwoods and mesquite across the way.

He laid down, his heavy head on my foot, with a grunt. I sat an' just listened to the birds sing, until my insides weren't knotted no more.

The followin' weeks, however, brought me a sliver of relief, I felt less saddle sore, the itch inside mellowin' to just a faint tightness in my soul. I sat at the table for Granley's dinners, with all them kids, Goyan in my lap more often 'n not, and Senator Granley. Sometimes Doc Flannagan too. Granley, she flitted about like a happy lark as we passed the dishes and helped the kids. And I couldn't help it, my eyes followed her like flowers to the sun.

And mebbe I was different now. Most days, Granley'd come find me whilst I was doin' my chores, bring me sugared vinegar or some such, talk for a bit, leanin' close enough I could smell her flowery perfume. I never talked much back, not knowin' what to say, but it didn't seem to stop her.

She was the happiest person I'd ever known, somethin' that usually called the dark up in me, but I…I basked in her sunshine like a lizard on a rock. It both confused and soothed me, left me all a'kilter with its newness. I kept everythin' she said locked up in my mind, to pull out in my quiet moments and examine, to bring a bit of her with me where ever I went.

"Don't you ever wonder what their lives would have been like," she asked me one day, "if they'd stayed with their tribe?"

I wasn't a complete dolt, and kept my thoughts to myself. She wouldn't want to hear that they'd prob'ly become murderers and thieves. Not Granley. She hardly ever seemed to need my replies anyhow.

"I don't speak their language well," she admitted after a moment's silence. "I don't know any of their stories, their traditions."

I guess I didn't see why that mattered, but I wasn't an educated man. Guess I didn't know too many of white man's traditions either, which is why I always felt out of sorts around Granley.

"Do you know they are forcing them to act like white men?" she asked.

"Yes, ma'am," I answered, wonderin' where she was goin' with this. Seemed to me it'd be better for them if they could pass as white. This world wasn't too kind to anyone who was different, somethin' I'd learned from harsh experience.

"I want to give them a chance to choose. I want them to know their heritage, but be educated enough to move in our world. If the government had their way, everyone would be the same. Can you imagine a world like that, Eli?"

I felt ignorant. I hadn't imagined it, nor could I see a problem with it. Things were what they were. Best a man could do was ride whatever horse he was given.

"If everyone is the same, then there's nothing to discover about the world. It would be like eating steak and potatoes every day."

I didn't see nothin' wrong with steak and potatoes every day. I liked steak and potatoes.

"I know you like steak and potatoes, but what if there was nothing else to eat? No fried chicken, no stew, no pie? Just steak and potatoes, day in, day out."

She turned to me, her eyes big and earnest. "I'm afraid one day we'll wake up and the world is only steak and potatoes, and no one will know how to make anything else."

Something twisted in my head, and I could see what she was gettin' at. Them kids needed to learn about their kin, or it would be lost forever. One generation was all it would take to snuff out their way of life. And I knew the white man's world wasn't any vision of perfection.

I ain't never learnt much about Indians, but I figgered I could do sommat about that. Knowin' each tribe had their own language and to-dos, I talked with Chalipun, found out the kids most all come from the Mescalero Apache tribe. Then I took up the Senator, feelin' all twitchy and my palms slick.

"I figger mebbe we need some more help around here," I ventured, one night as we sat on the porch, smokin' and lookin' up at the stars, like was our habit after dinner. Feather snored beside me. "A housekeeper, maybe another handyman."

He humphed, a surprised puff of smoke escapin' his nostrils. "Do we now?"

I nodded to myself. "You know, Gr...Miss Granley, she's awful busy, runnin' 'round all the day long, tryin' to get everythin' done."

"That so?"

I cleared my throat, leaned forward to rest my elbows on my knees. "I been thinkin'," I tried to sound like it'd just occurred to me, "Mebbe I'd head over to the reservation, find someone who can talk to the kids. Speak their language, tell their stories."

There was a pause. Two puffs on his pipe before he responded, tone doubtful. "I see."

We sat in silence for a few minutes, almost like he wasn't gonna answer. My leg began to do a jig. It was a stupid idea. Why would anyone want more Injuns around? There were wild parties still attackin' folks. Everyone knew someone who'd been struck dead. The stories ran rampant across the plains.

"You know that never occurred to me," he spurted in disbelief, his hand hittin' the arm of the chair, makin' me jump. "That's a splendid idea! There's no need to ride all that way. I'll send a letter."

I guess I was surprised when they come up on a wagon. These weren't no rampagin' savages. Dressed in hand me down clothes, they looked...like their souls was paper thin. And that Senator had done brought in more than a housekeeper an' handyman.

A small army of those Indian folk arrived, 'long with a mob of kids. Granley, she lit up like a bonfire on Mayday when she realized what was happenin'.

"Eli C-colton, you are behind this," she whispered as she rose up on her toes to kiss my cheek, her hand grabbin' my arm. "You wonderful man!'

"Your Daddy did it, not me," I growled and took myself off some distance. I ain't forgot that Doc had his dibs, and they'd make a right pretty family. But that kiss meant somethin' to me, the first I could remember that wasn't tainted with hate. I felt it carve itself into my memory, warmin' me up inside like a fire'd been kindled in my soul. I knew then I'd do just about anythin' for that woman, no matter if she was another man's girl or not.

There was a whole lotta hoopla as Granley fussed to make them all a space, glancin' at me every li'l bit with a sparkle in her eye. She set to orderin' storage rooms cleared, beddin' aired out, like a General overseein' the army, but through it all that mouth of hers never stopped smilin'.

A young Apache woman, whose name I'd been told was Washtay, sat beside Goyan, speaking softly in their native tongue. I can't even say in words the look on that child's face before she giggled and lit up, talkin' more than she'd done in a week. An' maybe the dust got in my eyes an' I had to turn to clear it out.

As everyone bustled about, settlin' them Apaches in, a plume of dust rose in the distance, a company of riders approaching at a fast clip. The cloud billowed closer, revealing a company of weary Black soldiers at the forefront, hooves poundin' the ground and tack janglin'. An officer, his pale face flushed cardinal red, rode amongst them. They must have come from the Fort nearby. I could guess the reason, easy 'nough.

Granley, spotting the riders, marched towards them, a determined glint in her eyes, like a fightin' cock. Fool woman was gonna get herself locked up, if not shot! I pondered what to do for a beat, then followed discreetly, keeping to the side of the buildings. I wasn't gonna let her face these soldiers alone.

I quickly took stock, began makin' my plan. Judgin from the looks his men cast his way, the officer didn't inspire no fond feelin's in his soldiers. I wondered if mebbe all I'd have to do was get rid of him. I hated to do that, 'cause then I'd have to run, but I'd do it for Granley. No way was I gonna let her come to harm.

As Granley reached the soldiers, the officer dismounted with a huff. "Miss

Granley," he barked, his voice tight. "Seems my orders to leave these 'savages' to stay here have been…misinterpreted."

Granley met his gaze unflinchingly, determination set by the lift in her chin, the set of her shoulders. She was magnificent, like them rich people's horses, full of blood. "C-colonel Rrandolph, sso nice to meet you again," she gritted, her lips tremblin' with effort. "T-to what do I owe the pleasure?"

The officer's scowl deepened, his flush darkenin'. "You know why I'm here, Miss Granley! I've come to return these 'savages' to the reservation."

He stepped forward aggressively, and I darted to Granley's side, widenin' my stance. The soldiers behind him stiffened, their horses snortin' anxiously, bits clinkin'. Their eyes seemed to hold indecision. Was that sympathy I saw in their eyes? How far would they follow commands? I tensed, readyin' for a fight.

Townspeople had begun to gather around us, like wolves scentin' blood, a low murmur buildin'. Both anger and sympathy warred in their faces. Tension was racketin' up, like the pressure before a storm. My hands fisted, while I worked to keep my body loose.

"They h-have every right to be here," she returned, hands on her hips. "We requested them, as teachers for the children."

The Colonel's face became apoplectic. "They threaten everyone here! Didn't you hear about the settlement by Limpia Creek? Twenty-three dead, by these Indians!"

"Nnot 'these' Indians!" Granley retorted hotly, takin' a step forward, fists clenched. That dadgum woman was gonna break the camel's back. I readied for my move, watchin' that Colonel's every move for the slightest sign of aggression.

I'd get him first, then the one with the insignia on his shoulder, looked like the next in command. I wished for my rifle, even a second revolver, to give me more rounds to get off. Maybe that'd give them pause, give Granley enough time to get away.

Just then, Senator Granley emerged from behind the wagons, a wide smile plastered on his face. "Colonel Randolph!" he boomed. "What a surprise! I see you've brought our…" he trailed off, gesturing to the Apache newcomers with a twinkle in his eye, "…additional guests."

The Colonel's jaw clenched. "Guests? Senator Granley, these are—"

Senator Granley held up a hand, silencing him. "Ah, but Colonel," he said, his voice smooth as butter, as good as any of those fancy lawyers at my trial, "perhaps you haven't seen this." He reached into his coat pocket and retrieved a worn document, handing it to the Colonel.

"This," he explained, "is an official document granting these Apache families and elders permission to leave the reservation and seek a new life here."

The Colonel scanned the document, his face a mask of disbelief. I watched as Granley's shoulders came down, her anger replaced by a satisfied smirk. The soldiers, too, relaxed slightly in relief, their postures less rigid.

Finally, the Colonel lowered the document, his gaze flickering between Senator Granley and the Apache families. "This… this changes things," he muttered, regretful.

"I should say it does," Granley piped back.

The officer glared at her, jaw tight, clearly torn between continuin' the argument and foldin' his hand. He musta decided more dignity came from retreat.

With a curt nod to the Senator, the Colonel wheeled around and barked orders to his men. They remounted, the dust rising once more as they turned to leave. The crowd gathered in the street, always eager for blood, began to go on their way.

As the last soldier vanished over the horizon, and Granley turned back to orderin' them Apache folk around, Senator Granley let out a triumphant laugh.

"Times are changin'," he commented. "The line of civilization no longer needs to be held with an iron fist. Wouldn't be surprised if that Fort is decommissioned in the next few years."

24

Granley

I spent a lot of time thinkin' in those days. I guess things was goin' all right then, an' I had lots of time while followin' the to-dos on Granley's list, callin' on Chalipun to help with trackin' some o' them high-falutin' words she used for normal things.

The three Indian men, two of them elders with faces like dry-rotted leather, followed my lead an' helped mightily. Chalipun would join us when the schoolin' was over. Between all of 'em, we understood each other well enough to rub along easy. Not that I talked much, 'cept when I had to.

One of the older men was Nantan, whose quick eyes missed nothin', not a flap of a bird nor a stir of the wind. He was wary at first, for some reason relaxin' once he realized Feather came with me. He tracked what I did with the mangy mutt, like he knew the dog was somethin' out of the ordinary. Feather liked him too, an' always greeted him for a ear rub when we come out.

Joseph, a tall man for an Indian, laughed easily, his wrinkles set in a smile. He always smelled of chicory, which he'd chew as we worked. At first, I'd flinched at the sound of laughter, expecting some kind of jest at my expense. But Joseph's laughter caught on like fire to tinder, and soon I was grinning despite myself.

The oldest was Bodaway, stiff with age, but the others clearly respected him, stopped what they was doin' and listened when he talked. He was somethin' of a wise man, I guessed, 'cuz the women would come and ask him 'bout things too. And I'd catch his eyes sometimes, and I could almost see my past in them. Didn't know what to make of that, as spooky as it was, 'cuz he didn't treat me no different.

It didn't seem possible I'd been hung dead, nor that the dog was somethin' special. Shootin' myself seemed a far-off nightmare. My injuries had healed right quick, leavin' only shiny pink scars to remind me of the shootout at the cave. It was easy enough to toss it off like it hadn't happened, to only think about the here and now.

Mebbe I was I loony, and none of it had happened. But every time my thoughts started to go down that trail, the feel of the noose slippin' tight 'round my neck pulled them right back on track, shook loose those doubts. Bodaway would give me a look, his eyes glintin', holdin' a knowing. And maybe I'd imagined it, but a couple o'times he'd rub his neck as he looked at me, and the air would crackle around me.

There was somethin' other about these men, somethin' beyond my reckonin', like all the other strange events that'd happened. It all started with that yella haired woman, Feather and the rock. I didn't know what to make of it all, so I just kept on, workin' on Granley's list, as the mysteries swirled in my mind like dust devils.

***

The mornin' sun slanted through the high, dust-filmed windows of the small chapel. The overheated smell of so many bodies was accented by the sharp perfume that tickled my nose as I shifted on the hard wooden pew, grippin' my hat on my thigh. Why'd services have to be so blasted long, I wondered, not for the first time. Granley sat beside me, smilin' as she joined in the unfamiliar hymn, her father a deep baritone on the other side.

Religion'd always seemed like a coat people would put on, ready to come off at the "Amen" at the end. Ain't never met folks who were truly kind like the Senator and his daughter. Even the preacher, with his fire-lit shock of hair, had greeted me with a genuine smile every Sunday. It was a might disconcertin', I reckon, but it kept me from protestin' when Granley seemed to expect me to attend.

I twisted my head a might, catchin' a glimpse of the Apache kids sittin' on the back pews. The older ones took care of the younger ones, keepin' them quiet. I'da thought there'd be more of a to-do about them, but Granley seemed to have worn down any protests before I'd come onto the scene. Sure as anythin', her next weeks would be full of pushin' for the adults to be allowed in. The woman was a force of her own, a little tornado in gingham.

I realized my knee'd begun to jitter with sittin' still, and settled it with effort. The preacher came to the front, red hair wavin' in the slight breeze, a slight man with a boomin' voice. Good. Just the sermon, a hymn, then I could skeddaddle, if the previous pattern held.

"Brothers and Sisters!" he thundered, arms stretchin' out to take us all in. "We are all unworthy of heaven's bountiful blessing. Not a one of us belong at the Lord's feet! None here are saints, no, not one of us! We have all strayed far from the path, succumbed to sin's dark temptation!"

I tensed, the words chillin' me to the bone, as if he spoke directly to me. Were his eyes lingerin' on me, more so than the rest of the pew-sitters? Was it possible he somehow knew of my dark past, the itch that still burned inside?

His voice softened as he continued, a smile lightin' his face. "But we shall not despair! Even the most wretched sinner can find redemption! 'My grace is sufficient for you,' Apostle Paul spoke to the Corinthians."

My head snapped up, attention focused on that preacher. My heart began a rapid drumbeat, a strange emotion beginnin' to flutter inside.

"The blood of our Lord Jesus Christ, shed on the cross, washes clean our transgressions, no matter how deep the stain."

A full on shiver ran through my body, knockin' my hat to the floor. I bent to get it, my mind whirlin' like the wheels of a runaway stage. I'd never heard this talk of forgiveness, of cleansing. Hellfire and brimstone, damnation, eternal punishment…those were messages I'd been accustomed to. Could it be, could I be…clean of the blood that flooded my past?

I shook my head, barely containin' a laugh of disbelief. Nothin', nobody, could be as stained as my tattered soul. I tightened my grip on my hat, wantin' to escape but knowin' it would disappoint Granley. And that was one thing I'd bite off my tongue before I'd willingly do.

So I sat through the remainder of the sermon, dredgin' up the evil deeds that I'd done, wonderin' when my reckonin' would come. Because blood had to be paid with blood, and I'd took more than my fair share.

***

Granley come out with her pitcher of sugared watermelon vinegar as I was workin' on the new dormitory. After passin' out the glasses, chattin' for a moment with the other men, she smiled, eyes sparklin' as she looked up at me through her lashes. "Eli, could you come help me?"

"Yes'm," I mumbled, heart beginnin' to dance erratically at her attention. I followed her to the side of the house, wonderin' what on earth she needed there.

Once we was in the shade of a small redbud, she looked 'round, like a kid who'd stole from the candy jar. I realized then we were hidden from the men, hidden from the street. That wasn't good, not for her.

I started to step away, but she grabbed up my my roughened hand in her soft, delicate ones, holdin' me in place as sure as a rein-tied horse. She grinned up at me, eyes glintin' with a warmth that made my insides clench. I stiffened, willin' myself to not reach for her, not hold her against me like I wanted.

"I really d-did want to thank you," her eyes held mine, steady. "I know D-daddy sent the letter, but you listened to me and started it in motion."

I scuffed my feet, slidin' my eyes away from hers.

"It weren't nothin'" I rubbed the back of my neck to get the burnin' to cool, shiftin' feet, torn between pullin' my hand away from hers or keepin' it there.

"It meant a great deal to me, and I wanted you to know it." She hadn't let loose my hand yet, and I found my eyes drawn to her lips, a strong urge to kiss her come over me. The light, flowery scent of her teased me, lit me up in ways that were new and strange.

"Miss Granley-" The words flew from my mind like a bird outta the brush, struck dumb. A choked, nervous giggle escaped my lips. Thunderation, I was actin' a right fool. I needed to get out of there, away from her.

She leaned toward me, her lips pushin' forward a tiny bit, soft, pretty, a little bit of shine to them. Struck me then, no matter what Doc wanted, she wasn't interested in him. It was me she'd hung her bonnet for.

The realization had me frozen, like a frog in lanternlight. Scared and amazed all at once. "Eli?" She blinked up at me, those honeyed eyes soft and gentle.

The nightmare from the shack slammed back into my mind, the image of Granley with that gruesome crimson necklace, my cruel gift to her. I snatched my tremblin' hand from hers like it was burnin', took a step back, shaken. I panted like I'd been runnin', horror rattlin' through me. I knew the truth - I was still a danger to her. I glanced to the side, lookin' for an opening to bolt.

"I've killed men…women," burst from my mouth, and I steeled myself to the terror and disgust I knew I'd find in her eyes. Sure, she was sympathetic to the pitiful boy, but she'd surely disdain a murderer. "In cold blood." I stuck my hand out, keepin' her at a distance. "Stay away from me, Granley."

A furrow formed between her brows as she drew back from me, like I'd known she would. Like I needed her to. A woman like her would never choose a man like me, should never be with a man like me.

"W-w-what?" The confusion, the flash of fear, tore me inside, pullin' my guts out through my throat. I needed her afraid of me, while at the same time, I desperately wanted what she offered.

"I'm a murderer." I forced myself to be blunt, to keep my voice cold, not wantin' her sunshine to try to fight my darkness. She had to stay away. It was the only way I knew to keep her safe. If I had to scare her to get it done, I would. "They done tried an' hung me for it."

Her eyes searched mine, wide, hurt, questionin'. "W-what are you ssaying, Eli?"

"I gotta get back," I growled through the tightness in my throat. "Don't wanna no one to say I'm shirkin.'"

I stumbled away from her, ignorin' her call to me. But when I looked at them Indians workin' with me, saw Joseph, his arm slung around Chalipun as he showed him the way he'd fit a corner together, I saw the dark welling of blood on their throats too. And I wanted it, wanted the thick, sticky, copper of it, to chase life into Death. I thirsted for it, that itch risin' like a mountain lion from its perch. Bodaway turned to look at me, and I saw the knowledge of what I'd done, what I could still do, in his eyes.

I turned, hid behind a bush next to the shed, and upchucked until my stomach was peelin' from my backbone. Darkness swirled my insides, crushin' me in its grip. Then, like I was again that small boy in the orphanage, I curled in on myself as tears fell like raindrops, my fist in my mouth to quiet the sound. I mourned, alone, like always.

25

First Kiss

"Eli?" I woke to Granley's soft voice as she rubbed my shoulder. "Are y-you all right? You didn't come in for supper."

Her catchin' me out here, the concern in her voice, cinched the knot in my gut. Tense, I rolled myself 'till I was sittin', my back to the shed wall.

"You should stay away from me Granley. I'm no good." Burnin' with shame, I rubbed a hand down my face, hopin' to hide my swollen eyes, hopin' the tears wouldn't come back. Not in front of her.

"Nnonsense!" she insisted, but her voice was tremblin' like a lamb's first cry.

I grabbed her arm, my grip tighter than I'd intended. She gasped, and I loosed my fingers a touch, sorry I'd hurt her. I sat, waitin' for her to look me in the eyes. "Granley, I've killed so many..."

"I know y-you sssaid, b-but they were outlaws..."

"No! You don't get it, darlin'," the endearment slipped out, nearly unnoticed as I pled for her to understand. "I was the outlaw!" I all but shouted at her. "I told ya, they tried an' hung me. For some reason, I crawled back outta that grave. But I see..."

A chicken bone lodged itself in my throat as I worked to speak, bile risin'. Her face was pale. I took my hand away from her arm, and she fell back onto her rump.

"I see what I could do to ya, to everyone here." My voice cracked, the next words forced and raw. "An' it…it breaks me, Granley."

I waited for her to escape, to curse me, to give me the boot. But she sat there, drew her knees up to her chin, and studied me. Didn't inch away, didn't lift her lip in disgust. The silence stretched between us, so thin it could snap, an eternity.

Finally, she took a deep breath, whispered, "Well."

I could almost hear the gears in her mind turnin', but I didn't dare to look into her eyes now. I needed her to hate me, but I didn't want to see it. I was breakin' apart inside while I waited for her to curse me.

"That's rather a lot to take in," she admitted.

She was too kind, too good, to curse me. I had to make my point, and right quick before I gave in to her light.

"You don't want me. I shouldn't even be here with ya. You go take that Doc Flanagan fella," I urged her, voice thick. "He'd treat you right, give you a good life. Just not me…not me."

My breath came freer than it ever had, a weight I'd not even noticed lifted. She was silent another moment, as we sat, and I began to make plans to ride out.

"That's why Sheriff Alvarez wanted so urgently to speak with you, when you woke." Her voice had gained some strength as she puzzled it all out. "He recognized you."

"Yes'm." It was dark enough I couldn't read her face well. I gave her time to think, it was best I could do for her, 'sides push her away from the snake in her life.

I looked up at the stars, wishin' up to whoever was up there things were different, that I could allow her next to me.

"Did you tell Daddy?" she asked all of a sudden.

"I did," I mumbled, avoiding her gaze.

"So both Daddy and the Sheriff know you were…"

"I was hung, sweetheart. Guilty, and hung until I was dead. I don't know why I'm back, why I crawled outta that grave, but I ain't gonna pull you down with me."

She squeezed my arm gently. "We are friends, aren't we, Eli?"

"I s'pose, but-"

"Well, then you can tell me these things too," she declared, her eyes shinin' with trust.

"Granley, I-"

She put her hand on my arm again, stopping me. "Sso both Sheriff Alvarez and Daddy thought I was safe around you. I happen to agree," her voice brooked no argument. The woman had missed her calling. She should have been a general. "You have given me absolutely no reason to think that man that was hung and buried was the same man as the one I see in front of me now. I think you are outnumbered, Eli Colton."

I opened my mouth again to argue.

And the woman leaned forward and kissed me when I had nowhere to run. All I could think then was about her soft lips on mine, a hint of vinegar sour and fruit sending tingles down to my toes, and how perfect she felt against me. My cold heart warmed, like feet before the fire.

Both her hands had ended up on my shoulders as she looked up at me, and the moonlight caught her eyes as she smiled. I was kerfunkled, kerbobbled and plain flummoxed.

Hope raised my spirits, fragile like butterfly wings. It could be possible, that I could redeem myself, could tamp down that itch that still called to me.

"Come get your dinner. I kept it warm for you." She stood, reached her hand out as I stood too, and led me back to the house, my steps wooden.

The Senator watched me come in with her, glanced to our hands. I stiffened, only for him wink at me as he turned to head up the stairs, as if givin' us his blessin'. I was again dumbstruck by this family, the way they saw through me but trusted me just the same.

I ate what she put in front of me, listening to her chatter about the kids, and the Apaches come in. And for once, I thought we could be together in the future, doin' the same thing, 'cept with our kids up the stairs. And it didn't freeze me cold, or send me runnin'. The opposite, I felt like warmth had touched my soul for the first time.

She put her hand on my shoulder, touchin' me again, an' it was almost like she spread angel dust on my soul. The cutest dip appeared between her eyebrows.

"Are y-you certain you are well, Eli? I didn't…What I did-"

I couldn't stop the grin as I remembered her lips on mine, the hint of a tingle returnin' at just the memory. "You done just fine, Granley. I should thank you, I guess."

She laughed. "Are you ever going to call me E-e-emma?"

I gaped for a moment. "Uh…mebbe."

She kissed my forehead as I was sittin' there, then moved away. "Goodnight, Eli," she called as she left the room.

"G'night, Gr…uh, Emma." Her laughter tinkled from the stairs, light and warm.

I sat and pondered if mebbe she was right, and "Bloody Bill" Carter really was dead and done. I prayed it was so, because I couldn't leave her now. I couldn't make my legs walk away, not like I'd done before. My heart was hers, for whatever purpose it served.

Next day, her smile as she brought out water was like a desert flower bloomin' after a rain. And it didn't pass by unnoticed. Them Apache men began hootin' and elbowing each other, pattin' me on the back with congratulations. Gr–Emma laughed at their antics as she left, winkin' at me, burnin' my cheeks hotter than the sun on Sunday. Nantan grinned approvingly, declarin', "Strong woman bring young warriors!"

My face burned hotly as I ducked my head. S'pose men and women are about the same everywhere, always dancin' 'round one another, pulled together by some unseen force. And those that've done that dance, they like seein' it in others. Maybe it brought memories of this rush of feelin' that overcome my numb heart.

I threw myself into my work, harder than usual, thinkin' maybe I was buildin' something that would be standin' when I was long gone. And it felt…well, I don't hardly have words for it. It was new and strange to me, these thoughts of a future.

That night, though, Doc Flannagan came for dinner. And he noticed right off that Gr-Emma sat next to me instead of her Daddy when we all sat at the table. His color was high, and I was tensing for a confrontation, knowing what he'd told me about his intentions toward her.

He was, as I'd said, a good man. He waited until we was almost done with the dinner before he asked, "Have there been some new developments I don't know about?" with a big smile that didn't quite reach his eyes.

Emma jerked beside me, but the Senator laughed. "You have a quick eye, Doc. My Emma's lassoed herself a suitor."

I could feel the heat comin' off Emma's cheeks. Mine were a bit warm too.

Doc Flannagan barked a laugh, and thought it was a might forced, it was also pleasure that Emma had what she wanted. Knowin' he didn't hold a grudge had my muscles meltin' like wax of a candle. I knew I wouldn't have been able to do the same, in his shoes. "Yes, that sounds just about right."

A gasp of outrage from beside me had the Doc turning to her. "You know he's right, dear. You were never one to wait around."

"Well, seeing as how I've got two apple pies in the kitchen, you might have wished you had held your tongue!"

She flounced thataway and brought back the desserts, some of the kids helpin' with dishes, and a big bowl of clotted cream. He got his pie anyway, then bid an early farewell, and I wondered how I woulda done in his place. I would have been hard pressed to walk away with kind words, instead of misery.

"Don't worry too much," the Senator advised quietly, when Emma and the kids'd gone. "He knew it was a long shot, the way she never looked twice at him."

I couldn't help but feel outta place, like a mockin' bird in another's nest. "You sure you want—-"

"Never a doubt, son."

26

Shoppin'

I s'pose I didn't know the first thing about courtin' a fine woman. I was starstruck, for sure. But that woman, once she got the bit in her teeth, she plowed on how she wanted. Her and Hammer would've made a fine pair, 'cept she was a sight finer lookin'.

"You will be taking me to the church social Saturday," she told me one mornin', light and breezy as a lark.

I'd a spoon of oats headin' up, and I set it down, rattling it against the china. It took me a moment to recover from her straight shootin'.

"Yes'm," I replied, my voice a tad gruffer than I'd intended.

"I was thinking," she kept on, a divot appearin' between her eyes as she glanced away from the stove to me, "Maybe you would like to get some new clothes for it." Her tone was soft with her suggestion, but she held my eyes.

"Naw, I ain't never had no use for fancy git-up," I answered, the words tumbin' out like chickens out of the coop. I was suddenly nervous somethin' was goin' on in her head I wasn't privy to.

The loss of her smile, the slump in her shoulders, nigh broke me in half.

"Eli Colton, you better be taking this courtship seriously," the steel come out in her voice, coverin' over her hurt.

I felt a pang of guilt wash over me as I realized I'd let her down somehow. Emma deserved better than a no-account outlaw like me, someone who still fought that itch, wrestled mightily with the darkness inside. I didn't know the first thing about how to act in polite company.

"Of course I am, Emma," I muttered, unable to meet her eyes.

I heard her sigh before she touched my shoulder, her scent reachin' my nose. "Eli, I meant that I *want* you to go get new clothes. You've been wearing the same two pair of worn trousers every since I've known you. And those shirts were hand me downs to begin with. Get something nice for the social."

"Oh," I responded like a dolt. "But you said…"

She laughed gently. "I know, I was trying not to be so bossy. I didn't realize you'd be so literal."

Well, how'm I supposed to know? I grumbled to myself, feelin' like a newborn colt, long legs and awkwardness. The feelin' was entirely too commonplace around this woman.

"I'll do it first thing," I reassured her, forcing a smile. I couldn't shake the feeling of unease that gnawed my insides. This was just the beginnin', and I was plum ignorant about women like her. If I didn't keep on my toes, I stood to lose her to someone like Doc.

Watchin' her work, the weight of her expectations pressing down on me like a heavy saddle, causin' a shadow of the itch to rise up. I pushed it back down, locked it in a box. Would I ever be strong enough?

So, I ventured into the dry goods store, lookin' for ready-made. The dust motes danced like tiny spirits in the streaks of sunlight that filtered through the big shop window. Inside was hot as Hades, smellin' of coffee, tobacco, and the ever-present dust.

I found the clothin' in the back. I got my hands on a pair of gray cotton trousers, shook 'em out to put it up to my hips, checkin' on the fit. A'sudden, the shopkeeper, a plump, older woman in a blue dress come bustling by, causin' me to jump. Her eyes lit on me like a chicken findin' a juicy worm as I fisted that pair of trousers tight.

"Eli Colton!" she crowed as her heels tapped on the scuffed floorboards, comin' at me like a charge of the cavalry. "I've seen you in church, with the Senator and his daughter."

"Yes'm," I replied cautiously, wishin' I had space to fall back, to scurry away. Attention had rarely been a good thing, in my experience.

"Welcome to town. Mrs. Clara Sinclair," she beamed, extending her hand like a man waitin' for a howdy'do shake.

I kept the shake brief, palm sweatin' against her fragile, cool hand. "Good to meet you, ma'am." I tried to turn away, but she was like a too friendly cat, windin' around my feet, trippin' me as I tried to walk.

"And that twinkle in young Emma's eyes whenever you're around…" she began, her voice trailing off meaningfully. My grip tightened on the trousers, crumpling them like newspaper goin' into the fire.

A choked laugh escaped me. Could she see through my carefully constructed mask? "Can't say, ma'am," I mumbled, shifting under her scrutiny, sweat pricklin' my skin. I hadn't thought I'd have to discuss ever'thing between me and Emma when I'd stepped inside for clothes.

She leaned forward, like she was gonna whisper a secret, her gray eyes wide. "And those Indians!" she confided in a hushed voice. "Some folks are worried she's bit off more than she can chew." Her eyes darted around the shop like she was afeared they were sneakin' in from the shadows.

I don't know that I was surprised by her comment. I knew well enough there was a lot of fear of Indians. I pondered my response for a moment, angry for Emma's sake.

"They ain't done nothin' to worry about," I responded stiffly, still clutchin' the trousers with a fist, a poor shield against this dragon of a woman.

"Well, yes," she waved her hand like wavin' away a fly, dismissin' the subject. "I suppose between you and the Senator, there won't be any problem."

Her gaze landed on my hands, and she smiled again. "Well, let's see how those fit," she declared, taking charge.

Speechless and face burnin', I obeyed, holding the trousers against my hips.

"A tad short, but it'll do in a pinch. Going to the social with Emma, are we?" she asked knowingly.

Dumbfounded, I could only manage a "Yes'm," feelin' like a calf roped and branded before it could react. What business was it of hers?

She chuckled warmly. "You remind me of my late husband, when he was young. So handsome but a tad tongue tied with the ladies," she sighed wistfully, before she shook her head at herself.

"This will do for now," she tutted, "but you should go to Lila Prewitt for somethin' that fits proper. Maybe a nice coat and vest too. You want Emma to be proud to have you on her arm, wouldn't you?"

"Yes'm," I mumbled, overwhelmed by her forceful personality. The heat of the shop seemed to intensify, and the fear of losing Emma tightened its grip.

"You'll need a shirt and collar, a nice tie too." She moved with practiced ease, pulling items from shelves. "We'll have you lookin' like a proper gentleman in no time."

Putting on a false front was nothing new, but this was different. These people weren't out to get something from me, and I wasn't lookin' to cull the herd. It was hard to understand why this kind woman was fussing over me.

She held a blue shirt against me, a stark contrast to my usual brown work shirts. "Brings out the green in your eyes," she declared, a surprising observation. "And a burgundy tie for a pop of color," she added, draping it around the shirt.

"I ain't never worn one of them fancy ties," I blurted out, heat rising in my cheeks. Ties were more suited for rich folks, not a drifter like me.

Mrs. Sinclair chuckled, the sound warm and reassuring. "Nonsense! It's not fancy, it's put-together. Here, let me show you." She gestured for me to stand still and with practiced ease, demonstrated how to tie the ribbon.

The movements were surprisingly similar to how I secured my saddlebags. Self-consciousness sparked within me – maybe there wasn't such a vast gulf between this new world and my old one after all.

"There you go," she said, stepping back to admire her handiwork. "Looks mighty spiff on you, Eli Colton."

"Thank you, ma'am," I mumbled, feeling a unfamiliar warmth spread through my chest. It might be possible for me to navigate this social scene after all, with a little help from kind strangers and a determined woman by my side.

Mrs. Sinclair brought my things to the counter as a Black cavalryman strode in, pullin' his hat off as he paused just inside the door. Her smile flickered as she noted him, her movements falterin' for a moment. "I'll be right with you," she asserted.

"Yes, ma'am," he replied, his voice deep and smooth and timid. He stood calmly, a tall, silent sentinel while she rang me up, her smile once again as wide as the summer sky. "Tell Emma hello, dear," she said, handing me a neatly wrapped package.

"Yes'm," I muttered, suddenly aware that she'd treated me as an upstandin' citizen, when I was anything but. I skedaddled out of there like a cat with its tail on fire, my mind a'tumblin'.

27

The Church Social

The sun hung low in the sky, the shadows casting skeletal fingers across the dusty streets. I stood in front of the mirror in my room, a stranger with my trimmed beard and pomade in my hair makin' it a couple shades darker than the usual hay color. My fingers fumbled with the unfamiliar buttons of my fancy blue shirt, the double breasted kind, the new fabric stiff against my skin.

Already feelin' the fine shirt stickin to my sweaty back, my stomach churned like whitewater in a river - a nervous knot that wouldn't loosen. I wasn't entirely certain what I'd be comin' across at a church social. I'd never attended a social event beyond a poker game at a saloon. The thought of letting Emma down felt worse than facing that blasted noose.

Feather sat at my feet, his tail thumping against the floorboards, his understanding gaze calming me. I'd never stepped out with a woman before. I'd never even taken one them saloon girls upstairs. Any need I'd felt was drowned out by the need to hide in the shadows, keep my guard up. Puttin' myself out there, showin' my belly, had me tremblin'.

Before the gallows, I'd never thought I'd be takin' a good woman to a church social, wouldn't have even wanted it, but now there was a lightness in my being that surprised me. Had I ever felt joy, in that first life? For the life of me, I could only remember achin' with pain and emptiness. An emptiness I'd tried to fill with the blood of others. I resolved anew to follow the straight and narrow from here on out.

With a final tug, I managed to fasten the last button of my shirt and straightened my collar, the crispness pokin' into my throat, remindin' me of the formality of the occasion. My hands trembled slightly, and I fisted them, tryin' to get them to steady. It took me four tries, but I got the tie knotted. It was a might crooked, but I wasn't about to untie it to try again. It would just have to do as it was.

As I stepped out of my room, my breath was cut short by the sight of Emma standing at the top of the staircase, her eyes bright and her cheeks pinked with excitement, the very picture of beauty. She wore a fancy purple dress I hadn't seen before, the shimmerin' fabric swishing softly as she descended the stairs.

"H-hello, Eli," she greeted me with a warm smile, her voice soft and musical. "You look very nice."

"You're beautiful," I blurted, words tumblin' like a cowboy off a bronc, overwhelmed with disbelief that I could belong here, with her. Heat crept up my neck, reachin' my ears, but I wouldn't take it back. It was the honest truth. "More beautiful than any girl I ever laid eyes on."

She giggled, cheeks pinkin' and eyes dancin'. "Thank you, Eli," she cooed. "You look pretty handsome tonight too." Her approval warmed my heart straight through. She smelled like flowers after a spring rain, everythin' about her good and fine. Again I was awed that she'd made up her mind to latch on to me.

The Senator's house echoed, strangely quiet tonight, the usual bustle and laughter replaced by a heavy silence that seemed to hang in the air like a shroud. Portraits of her dignified ancestors glared sternly at us, remindin' me I was just a man tryin' to bury his past. I straightened my shoulders, determined to be worthy of this woman.

Together, we made our way towards the field beside the church, the sound of our footsteps echoing in the empty hallway. Outside, the night air was cool and crisp, a contrast to the heat still comin' off the baked dirt, the stars twinkling overhead like distant angels in the darkness.

As we walked together towards the church grounds, a sense of unease prickled at the back of my neck. It was as if I could feel a shadow lurkin' just beneath the surface of the outwardly peaceful town, a secret waiting to burst forth. I stuffed it down, determined to make this a pleasant night for Emma.

At the church, the Senator greeted us with a warm smile and a proud glint in his eyes. "There you two are. Emma, my dear, you are a vision! And Eli, you've cleaned up real nice, my boy."

Doc stood nearby, his usual cheerful demeanor muted tonight. His dark eyes held a flicker of something unreadable as nodded at Emma on my arm.

"Miss Granley," he stated formally, his lips twistin' in a mimicry of a smile, "lovely as always."

Pleasure shone out of her eyes, "Thank you."

"Good to see you, Eli," he rasped, shaking my hand, not quite meetin' my eyes. "Enjoy the social."

I nodded, my throat tight with unspoken words, as he turned away quickly to speak to another group. A pang of unexpected sympathy stabbed at me – the knowledge that the woman he desired hung on my arm. Once again, the thought rose that she'd be better off with him, but I stomped on it like a scorpion in the corner.

The night was clear, the field filled with a bonfire and trestles of food, chicken and pies and spring vegetables. The sound of laughter and conversation filled the night air, but I couldn't shake the feeling of foreboding that hung over us like a dark cloud. Was I just imagining the whispers of the townsfolk, the wary glances exchanged between neighbors, or was it real? It all added to my unease.

As Emma and I mingled with the townsfolk, I felt increasingly out of place. The men in their starched shirts and polished boots, the women in their finery and lace – they all seemed to belong here, while I was an imposter in my newly bought clothes and dusty hat. Odd, as Will Carter hadn't had much trouble minglin' with other folks. Or, I suddenly thought, maybe he had and hadn't been aware enough, or carin' enough, to notice.

Emma's hand slipped into mine, a warm anchor in this sea of unfamiliar faces. "You're doing just fine, Eli," she whispered, her voice a soothing balm to my anxiety.

I followed her around as she flitted, like a beautiful bird, from group to group. I was a silent shadow to her cheerful chatter. I tried to subtly wipe my palms on my new trousers. The violin and banjo I supposed would be enjoyable to most, but it blasted my ears like a donkey's bray, the high notes makin' me wince.

"Eli, w-would you mind fetching us some punch?" Emma smiled at me with a touch on my arm, turning away from a group of ladies she'd been chatting with. Grateful for a distraction, I scanned the crowd, my gaze landing on a group of men gathered around a crystal punch bowl.

Taking a fortifying breath, I plastered a smile on my face, hopin' it wouldn't crack under scrutiny, and approached the group.

"Evenin', gentlemen," I greeted with a nod, my voice a touch too high.

The men turned to face me, their expressions ranging from curiosity to mild suspicion as they took in my presence. One of them, a burly fellow with a bushy mustache and a weather-beaten hat pulled low over his brow, stepped forward to address me, his meaty paw thrust in my path.

"Well, well, if it ain't Eli Colton," he rumbled with a note of disdain. "Jeb Boone. My wife's been all a twitter about you and Senator Granley's daughter." His eyes flicked to Emma, his mouth tightening. "How's her Injun school goin'?" he asked, a slight sneer twistin' his mouth. The other men puffed up beside him, like cocks readyin' for a fight.

His gaze lingered on me a beat too long. My smile faltered for a moment, but I quickly recovered, forcing a chuckle to give me time to think of a reply. His words hung in the air, an almost palpable threat.

"Can't blame a man when he finds a fine woman like her," I confirmed, trying to keep my tone light and friendly, unfamiliar to my ears. "She's a force of change," I added, noticin' the men relaxin' slightly. "And the Apaches have been a great help."

We stood in awkward silence for a moment as I wondered if I'd misstepped. "This sure is a great get-together," I mentioned, forcin' a smile, hopin' for the tension to blow over.

The men exchanged glances, their eyes flickering with a mixture of disquiet and amusement. Another man cleared his throat before pipin' up, "Ain't that the truth. We don't got a lot of entertainment 'round these parts, but we sure do know how to throw a good ol' church social."

I chuckled nervously, my gaze shifting between the men as I struggled to find common ground. "Well, can't argue with that," I replied with a weak smile. "I reckon a little socializin' never hurt nobody."

The men nodded in agreement, their expressions softening slightly as they relaxed in my presence. I pointed to the punch bowl. "I've been sent on an errand. Best get back."

They chuckled, makin' light-hearted comments about bossy women, as I turned away from the group. I tried to settle myself as I filled a couple of tiny cups with the bright punch, the hornets in my guts slowly settlin' to a dull buzz. For the first time that night, I thought maybe I could belong in a place like this, full of kind folks.

When I got back to Emma, she smiled at me as she took one of the thimblefuls of punch, and my shoulders relaxed a hair. "You did well with them," she murmured. I smiled back at her, but I wasn't so certain.

She turned fully to me. "I mean it, Eli. It'll get easier." I nodded at her, grinnin' to relieve her worry, half believing her despite my doubts. I hoped she never heard the doubts the people of the town had voiced about her school, and the children in it.

28

Lost Girl

I didn't realize how quickly things could change. Emma had said her goodbyes and taken my arm to walk home. The festive mood evaporated like a drop of water on a hot pan as a hush spread over the crowd.

"Sarah!" a woman's voice cried frantically. She rushed to Jeb Boone, nearly pawin' at him in panic. "Sarah's disappeared!" she clung to him as she began to sob.

Parents began to gather their children to them, to ensure their safety, before the men broke apart, determination in their faces, a turn about from their earlier joviality. A low mutter snaked through the crowd, laced with suspicion, and I caught a snatch of it - "Dirty Injuns..."

My gut clenched with dread, both for the safety of the missing girl and the feeling that the crowd was a pile of tinder, just waitin' for a spark to ignite into a wildfire. If it went up in flames, Emma could be hurt in the crossfire. While I cared about the Indians I was fast befriending, it was Emma I could not bear losing. I instantly regretted leaving my firearms at home.

Emma come over then, her forehead puckered, eyes filled with tears that had not yet spilled.

"Eli, do you think you could help?" she asked, a tremor in her voice as her hand trembled on my arm.

Torn between helping find the girl and protectin' the most important person in my life, I still nodded, unable to refuse her. I didn't see how I'd be much help, since I wasn't much of a tracker, but the desperation in Emma's eyes spurred me on as I chased after the others. Lanterns were brought out, their light spreading around the field like stars.

As we joined the search party, a surprisingly strong pang of fear gripped me for the missin' girl. It was a feeling I wouldn't have recognized before the morning at the cemetery. Before, I wouldn't have cared if a kid went missin'. Now, fear for the girl, Sarah, clawed at me, as I imagined Goyan in her place, alone and afraid.

Half an hour later, we'd circled the field like a flock of noisy vultures, callin' for her, the smoke of the dyin' bonfire seemin' to dampen our calls. We'd not found hide nor hair of Sarah with the night shrouding the field. Like her ma had said, she'd disappeared without a sign.

The tension was tighter than a lasso on maverick, the men millin' around, goin' over things a second time. Discouragement hung heavy in the air as the men regrouped, makin' plans to spread out from the field and search the wilderness around the town. Just then, Chalipun come runnin', a tall figure trailin' behind. Nantan. The men beside me stiffened, their faces hardenin' with suspicion and hostility.

I grit my teeth, muscles coilin' to throw myself into the ruckus to protect the Emma and the boy. Nantan could surely take care of himself, but if either one of them got hurt, I'd never live with myself.

"He listen to the earth ," Chalipun explained, voice urgent. "He find girl."

Nantan stood silent, dark eyes measurin' the men around him. He was not blind to the aggression in the air. Boone puffed up, takin' a step forward, but I laid my hand on his shoulder, grippin' tight.

"Give him a chance. You want her found, don't ya? You got a better idea?"

Boone glared at me, then at Nantan, his jaw clenched like a vice, eyes narrowed. The fear for Sarah in his eyes wrestled with his distrust. He fisted his hands but gave a reluctant nod, not quite lookin' at the Apache man, who watched with dark, steady eyes.

Nantan returned the nod gravely, then turned and began castin' for sign. Nearly an hour crawled by before Nantan gave a sharp cry, breaking the oppressive silence. We all rushed toward him, earlier animosity forgotten in the face of a glimmer of hope.

"She go this way," he explained, pointing to a soft imprint of a child-size boot heel.

Chalipun watched carefully, as if he were tryin' to absorb Nantan's knowledge. Hesitation flickered across the faces of the crowd, but the desperation to find Sarah outweighed their prejudice.

I paused for a moment as they began to move, the entire crown followin' behind the Apache man. The urge to help was unfamiliar but strong, pullin' me along with the crowd despite my apprehension. I'd never been called to help so much as I'd been the last few weeks. Never cared enough, been eager to prey on the weak instead. Somethin' was surely different inside me.

Swallowin' my confusion down, I crouched beside Nantan and Chalipun, eager to learn as he pointed silently to the evidence of her passage, hidden in the dark. Nantan's sharp eyes caught things I never would have noticed on my own, bent grass, a twig with a fresh break, a scuff on a rock, soft imprints of portions of a child's boot in the sand.

Nearly the whole town followed like wraiths, eerily silent, as he cast for signs like a hawk searchin' for prey. He frequently dipped gracefully to the ground to show us the signs he found, nearly invisible to my eyes. His dark eyes studied the earth intensely, slowly bringing us closer to the girl.

The men behind us watched but didn't interfere, as if they were afraid to break the spell. I could hear the river ahead of us when we stopped and he spun around, scanning the area.

"Child!" he called, and a whimper responded. My chest eased as the men of the town surged forward, relief and urgency etched on their faces. They found Sarah in the water, clinging desperately to a tree that had fallen into the river.

"Daddy!" she cried as Boone waded into the river and lifted her out of the water. "I slipped," her small voice wet with tears.

Boone cradled her in his arms as he stepped past us, walkin' quickly back toward town. He paused a moment and took a step back, his eyes flickerin' between me and Nantan.

"Thank you both," he muttered, with a curt tip of his head, before he continued back to town.

We all followed his progress, Nantan beside me. The mother sobbed in relief as soon as we appeared. A collective sigh of relief seemed to ripple through the crowd, and I was pleased to note some eyes regarding Nantan with more curiosity and kindness than hostility.

Emma glided to me with a teary smile, the Senator followin'. Nantan remained at my side, straight and silent. Mrs. Sinclair approached, her eyes red-rimmed but full of relief. She twisted her hands as she faced Nantan. "Thank you," she said, her voice thick with emotion. "I think we would have lost my granddaughter if we'd not had your eyes to help us. We all owe you a debt of gratitude."

Nantan gravely dipped his head as he acknowledged her thanks. "Children are precious," he rumbled simply.

Those words settled heavily on me. It was a stark reminder of the fragile innocence of childhood, a concept that had felt distant from my own life for so long. Yet, here I was, standing beside a man who, despite the prejudice he faced, had readily offered his skills to save a child.

A newfound determination filled me. If the town could accept Nantan and the others, maybe I didn't have to fear my mask slippin so much. The hope that bloomed within me was fragile, but with each passing moment, it felt a little stronger. Maybe this town could accept me even if I showed my true self, the man behind the false veneer I'd kept on for so long. That man was changin', like corroded silver under the polishin' cloth, shinin' where so long he'd been black and ugly.

29

Ride with Emma

The mornin' sun already beat down on the dusty streets of our little frontier town, causin' waves to rise up from the dusty street. I leaned against the weathered wood of the stables in the shade of a nearby tree as I waited for Emma, holdin' the reins to Hammer and her mare Bella. I'd put the strange lookin' ladies' saddle on her mare, wonderin' how on earth woman stayed on a horse with the confoundin' thing.

Butterflies danced a jig in my stomach, eagerness warrin' with apprehension. I looked forward to time with Emma, but I was still afraid she'd see somethin' dark in me that would send her runnin'. I didn't think I'd survive somethin' like that.

Folks milled around as I separated the weak like a wolf among the lambs, as a matter of habit. A woman walkin' alone between two shops, a man with a distracted air passin' by. I shook my head, tryin' to clear the darkness from my thoughts to somethin' more pleasant, more worthy of this fine woman. But I didn't feel the itch, like I usually did, instead feelin' almost like…like I was lookin' out for these people.

Emma emerged from her father's weather-beaten house, a vision in her riding attire, her amber locks glinting in the harsh sunlight like strands of pure gold. My heart skipped a beat at the sight of her. I was like a colt just born, all legs and awkwardness. I noticed with a shock her skirt hem was raised on the left, so that I could nearly see the top of her tall boots.

"Mornin', Emma," I greeted her with a tip of my hat, my voice ragged.

"Mmorning, Eli," she replied with a smile that could melt a man's heart, her voice as sweet as molasses.

"You ready for our ride?" I asked, trying to hide the nervous flutter in my chest.

"Absolutely," she said, her eyes twinkling with excitement. "I've been lookin' forward to it all week."

I turned to her mare, realizin' that the stirrup was set high behind the horse's shoulder, so that it looked near impossible for her to mount on her own.

"How?" I turned to her with confusion.

"There's a mounting block," she pointed to the stable door, where a wooden stair led to nowhere. "Or you can just give me a boost up," she added, with a smile. My heart began to thrum.

She came up to me, and laid her hand on my arm, her riding crop attached to her wrist bumpin' against my hip. "Just put your hands together," she instructed with a calm I didn't share. "When I step on them, lift me up." Then she laughed, "not too hard or you'll send me over the other side."

With a silent prayer to the heavens for strength, I offered Emma my linked fingers, her weight slight as I gently, fearfully, lifted her up. My face heated as I tried to figure out how she fit on the strange protrusions of the saddle.

She maneuvered on top of the saddle, arrangin' her strange skirt that seemed to be cutaway on the backside. Once she seemed settled, I mounted Hammer and we set off down the dusty trail that wound its way through the rugged countryside, the rhythmic beat of our horses' hooves echoing in the stillness of the morning.

As we rode, Emma regaled me with tales of her adventures at the schoolhouse, her laughter a melody like the call of a black-throated sparrow in the desert. I listened intently, hangin' on her every word, grateful for the distraction from my own troubled thoughts.

But despite Emma's best efforts to keep the conversation light and cheerful, I couldn't shake the feeling of unease that gnawed at me like a hungry coyote. The weight of my past sins hung heavy on my conscience, a constant reminder of the darkness that lurked within me. The blood on my soul would stain it forever, holdin' me apart from the peaceful folk of the town.

The sad truth struck me…I didn't even remember the faces of all of my victims. They'd blurred together, I realized with shame, too many to keep the details separate. How could I ever hope to be worthy of someone as pure and good as Emma?

Lost in my own thoughts, I nearly missed Emma's question.

"…and what about you, Eli? Tell me something I don't know yet about you."

I hesitated, unsure what to say, unable to think beyond my shameful past. She knew of it now, and it didn't bear repeatin'. What else was there to me? I was rocky ground, nothin' for seeds of good to root into among the stones of my sins, choices I couldn't take back.

"Well, I ain't nothin' special," I finally replied, my voice gruff with emotion. "Just a man tryin' to make his way in this world."

She grinned. "Go on, you can tell me something."

My mind stuttered, graspin' for anythin'. "I had a dog once, a black and white mutt I'd found. Sam. He was pretty smart, I taught him to do tricks. He'd shake your hand, just like a person. I had to hide him from Ma Josie, though. He'd tuck into my blanket, down by my feet, at night. I…"

I stopped, realizing where it was going. I'd killed that dog. Slit his throat even while I cried. But then a new memory surged forward. Ma Josie had…she'd shot my dog.

Emma studied me with those perceptive blue eyes of hers, pullin' out my secrets. "We all have our ghosts, Eli," she said softly. "But you don't have to tell me if you're not ready. Just know that whatever burdens you carry, you don't have to carry them alone."

Her words struck a chord deep within me, stirring emotions I had long tried to bury. Ma Josie had shot Sam. I'd only killed him 'cause he was hurtin', dyin'. How had I forgotten that detail? All these years, I'd carried that weight, that knowledge that I was evil for killin' that dog, thought that was my first step into the darkness. My skin prickled with the memory.

For the first time in a long while, I felt a glimmer of hope, a spark of light amidst the dark pull that threatened to consume me.

"Thank you, Emma," I roughed out. "I appreciate that more than you know."

I huffed a breath, my chest tight, not quite able to speak. We rode on some more in silence, the dust risin' behind us like a brown cloud. I couldn't shake the feelin' of somethin' watchin' us, a prickle at the back of my neck. Off in the distance, I thought a glint of somethin' catch the sun.

My heart fluttered for a moment. Pullin' up short, I scanned the horizon, squintin' through the glare. Whatever it was, it wasn't movin' now. Figurin' it was just a trick of the light, I nudged Hammer back onto the trail. But I still had that feelin' nigglin' in the back of my head.

As we wound around mesquite and prickly pear, the words worked their way out. "I…I hadn't remembered all of it, not till just now." I couldn't keep the hate out of my voice when I spoke the next words. "I had to put him down. Ma Josie shot him."

"Oh, Eli!" Her response was instantaneous, her eyes were wide and filled with empathy. "I'm so sorry."

Emma's gentle understanding warmed me like the first light of dawn after a long, cold night. Her willingness to accept me, flaws and all, was a beacon of hope in the darkness that clouded my soul.

A roadrunner ran across the trail before us, its loud repeating cackle causin' Bella to take a sidestep and Hammer's ears to flick. He snorted, tossin' his head a moment to let me know his displeasure. I waited for them to settle down for a few paces before I spoke again, truths that I had to let out.

"I ain't never met nobody like you, Emma," I admitted, my voice barely more than a whisper. "Someone who sees the good in me, even when I can't see it myself."

She frowned, that pucker in her forehead appearin'. "I'm not perfect, Eli," she chided.

She was silent a moment, before she went on. "I've been told I'm horribly stubborn and too independent for my own good."

I grinned at her, knowin' exactly why she would have heard that. But somehow, those things that'd annoyed me so much at first had become…

exactly what I liked about her. "No, you're perfect, darlin'," the words flowin' out like I was again that honey tongued devil, 'cept now I meant them.

She was blushin', a pretty pink dusting those cheeks, coverin' over the freckles. I wanted to press my fingers there, check if the skin felt hot. She stirred up somethin' in me, somethin' fierce and strong. She bravely went on.

"I'm not," she insisted, a playful pout not quite hidin' the hurt in her eyes "My nose is too big and my mouth is too narrow."

Somebody had told her that, hurt her precious heart. I couldn't let that stand. I stopped Hammer beside her mare and reached toward her.

"I like your nose," I murmured, tappin' her nose, "it suits your determination." I then gently traced her mouth, "And especially your mouth. I've never known anythin' as soft and good." Her lips were soft, like a down feather, and darkened with my attention. Her lips parted in a small gasp. I sucked my own lips in, bitin' down on the memory of her lips on mine. I wanted to kiss her again, but it was next to impossible with both of us on horseback.

My gaze held hers, knowin' my ears were red, wishin' she saw herself as I saw her, somethin' fine and precious, worth more than a gold mine. Her eyes searched mine before they lit with pleasure, cheeks pinked, before they dropped again.

I watched her, this beautiful woman, the flush spreadin'. Hammer nibbled at Bella, both the horses shiftin'. I pulled on his reins, distractin' him from the mare.

When she spoke next, it was a tear-filled whisper, pained and afraid, uncharacteristic of such a bold woman. "And I-I hhate my ssstutter."

I leaned down, tried to get her to look at me, see I meant what I said. "Aww, sweetheart, it just makes me listen closer."

She wiped quickly at her eyes before smilin' up at me. "Y-you're a poet at heart, Eli."

"Nah," I mumbled, "It's just the truth."

We continued our way through the landscape, the sun beatin' down on my neck. The weight of my past, once an anvil on my shoulders, was fallin' off, bit by bit. I looked again at Emma, knowin' I'd do anythin' for her.

I didn't understand why she believed in me, but I was glad for it, determined to be the man she thought I was. Maybe there was trouble on down the trail, but I figgered with a woman like her fightin' for me, I could take just about anythin' on.

"I been feelin' out of place," I finally admitted, the words tumblin' out like water out of a pitcher. "I ain't like nobody here, you know that. And sometimes, I feel that dark risin' up in me…"

She reached out to put her hand on my arm, her touch like cool water to a thirstin' man. "You are a good man, regardless of what you did in that previous life. I see your heart, the goodness in it. I believe in you."

I blinked rapidly as her words fell over me like a cleansing rain. I didn't know why she thought so good of me, but I needed it like a horse needs water. Even so, I still feared I'd be her downfall.

"But what if I bring bad things to you, Emma?" I whispered, my heart in a vice. "What if my past catches up to me, and you get caught in the crossfire?"

She shook her head, her eyes blazing with determination. "I won't let that happen, Eli. We'll face whatever comes our way together, as a team. I believe in us."

Her words hit me square in the chest, but instead of a mule kick, it was like I was filled with somethin' light, and sweet, and good, like the fluffy white dressin' on a pie. Everythin' rang true as a church bell. Like for the first time in my miserable life, someone truly recognized me and accepted, no, maybe even loved me. I was determined to be that man.

30

Montalvo's Comin'

The day was blistering hot, the sun beating down as I gave the porch new paint. I looked up to see Sheriff Alvarez walkin' to me. His gaze was as steely as ever, the brim of his hat casting a shadow over his weathered face as he regarded me with a dark look that spoke volumes.

"Eli," he began, his voice gruff but tinged with an undercurrent of concern, "I reckon it's time we had ourselves a little talk."

I nodded, a knot of apprehension forming in the pit of my stomach as I braced myself for whatever news he had to deliver. "What's on your mind, Sheriff?" I asked, trying to keep my tone casual despite the unease that gnawed at me like a hungry coyote.

Sheriff Alvarez took a moment to gather his thoughts, his gaze fixed on the horizon as if searching for storm clouds. "I wanted to warn you," he said at last, his voice low and measured, "that I've been told a bounty chaser's headin' for town. Goes by the name of Montalvo. He's a days ride off, in Clintonville."

My blood ran cold at the mention of the name. Montalvo had taken me in, that cold-eyed bounty hunter that'd held a shotgun to my gut. The hairs on the back of my neck stood on end, shivers runnin' down my spine like a knife's edge on stone. Was that flicker of light I'd seen, while ridin' with Emma, the reflection of a spyglass, the glint of a rifle? My mind began to spin, my gut churnin'. Had Emma been in danger?

"What's he want?" I faltered.

His jaw clenched tight as he regarded me with a solemn intensity. "He's lookin' for you, Eli," he said, his words ringin' with truth. "And from what I hear, he ain't plannin' on takin' no for an answer. No matter Clintonville showed him the telegraph inquiry on Will Carter's hangin.'"

I swallowed hard, the lump that formed threatening to choke me as my mind spun. Montalvo was lethal as a snakebite, and if he was looking for me, it could only mean trouble.

"He'll recognize me, Sheriff. He's the one brung me in. What do I do?" I asked, momentarily frozen with uncertainty.

I knew how I would have handled it, before. A few hours wait, a shot from the side of the road, and the trouble would be over. I knew better than to hint that to the law. And somethin' in me pulled away, an unpleasant taste at the thought of takin' that action.

"Maybe I should head out for a while," I offered, squintin' down the street. "Draw him away from town."

Sheriff Alvarez fixed me with a steady gaze, his eyes hard as flint as he met my gaze brookin' no argument. "You aren't goin' nowhere. We'll handle it," he assured me. "I'm not about to let some two-bit drifter take out one of our own. But you best keep your wits about you, Eli. Montalvo's a snake in the grass, and he won't hesitate to strike if given the chance."

I nodded, a sense of grim determination settling over me like a heavy blanket as I braced myself for the storm that was sure to come. Montalvo was trouble, but I wouldn't let him hurt these people. I'd give myself to him all over again to keep them safe.

"Thanks, Sheriff," I croaked. "I appreciate the warning."

Sheriff Alvarez nodded, a hint of a grim smile tugging at the corners of his lips as he clapped me on the shoulder with a reassuring squeeze. "You're a good man, Eli," he said, his voice gruff but genuine. "This town needs you. And don't you forget it."

With those words echoing in my ears, I squared my shoulders. Montalvo might be on the hunt, but I wasn't about to go down without a fight. I just needed to keep Emma away from him. I walked inside, diggin' into my things for my Colt. My knife was always on me, but now I'd have them both.

I spent the mornin' looking over my shoulder, scannin' the streets, my hand frequently straying to the revolver holstered at my hip, a comforting weight against my side. I knew the Senator should know, so we could put everyone's guard up, but I dreaded bringin' that shadow to this idyllic life. So I didn't say anythin', just kept my watch.

I tossed idea after idea, like a juggler's balls, finally lightin' on the only one that made sense, the one I'd already failed. No matter what the sheriff said, I had to leave, draw Montalvo away from this perfect place. The thought left a hole in my heart, as real as any bullet, but it had to be done.

Beside me, Feather lounged in the shade, his tongue lolling out as he surveyed the scene with lazy indifference. Wished I could be as carefree as the fool dog. But I knew better than to let my guard down, especially with someone like Montalvo on the loose.

At dinner, I pushed my food around on my plate, a gnawin' in my gut killin' my appetite I had to tell them, but I dreaded the conversation. Waitin' only put them in danger. I kept glancin' around the table, lookin' at these faces that thought me better than I was. Well, I was about to turn things on their side.

I waited 'till the kids was gone, that knee of mine so jittery it rattled the china in the sideboard

"Are you all right, Eli?" Emma asked as she took my plate, her forehead creased with worry, putting the back of her cool hand on my forehead.

I leaned back, lookin' the Senator in the eye. It was time to bite the bullet. I took a deep breath, fortifyin' myself. "I reckon I ought to tell ya about somethin' that happened today."

The Senator's eyes sharpened, and I knew he could hear the danger in my voice. "What's that, Eli?"

"Well, Sheriff Alvarez came by. He warned me 'bout a fella named Montalvo who's comin' to town. Says he's lookin' for Will Carter."

Emma whispered the question, but I could tell she knew the answer. "Who's W-will Carter?"

I took a deep breathe, wishin' for all the world I didn't wear this noose around my neck.'"That's…" my voice cracks. "that's me, Emma. It's my old name. I'm sorry I brought this to you."

Emma's eyes widen in alarm, and she reaches out to take my hand with her tremblin' fingers. "D-didn't anyone t-tell this Montalvo you aren't him?"

"Yep, they showed him the telegraph telling I…Will Carter was hung and everythin'. Montalvo don't care. He's ridin' for money, and he's a coyote."

The Senator's jaw clenched, and his eyes flashed with anger. "We won't let that happen, Eli," he growled.

"I appreciate that, Senator," I nodded, grateful for his unwavering support. "But I reckon I oughta just ride outta here. He'll know it's me, if he sees me. I gotta keep Montalvo away from you."

Emma tightened her grip on my hand as her eyes filled with tears. "No, Eli, y-you can't leave. We won't let you face this alone."

"Emma, darlin'," my voice grew rough as I struggled. "I can't risk puttin' you or the Senator in harm's way."

The Senator had risen, and I saw him as he'd surely been as a young man, commanding and determined, as he laid a reassuring hand on my shoulder. "Nonsense, Eli. You're family now, and family sticks together. We'll face this fella Montalvo together."

I was gobsmacked at their loyalty to me, a broken down orphan boy, a murderer.

"But, sir, Montalvo's dangerous. I…"

"Listen to me, son," his eyes bore into mine. "You might have had to face things alone in the past. But we are stronger together. You'll stay."

I didn't really want to leave, and I allowed them to convince me, against my better judgment.

"Alright, Senator," I conceded, turning to Emma, whose eyes were frightened but determined. "But Emma, promise me you'll stay inside until Montalvo is gone. I can't bear the thought of anythin' happenin' to you."

The Senator marched into his library, opened up a box, takin' out a belt and a pair of revolvers and slinging it around his hips. "I see you are armed, Eli. Do you want anything else?" He placed a knife in his boot.

"No sir," I respond, seeing quite a different man than the refined statesman

I thought I knew. This was the commander of soldiers, the defender of his home.

"Emma, you'll carry your pistol and your knife at all times," he instructed, and she nodded, her face pale but resolute as she rushed up the stairs to her room.

My eyes followed her as she went, then I looked back to the Senator, held his eyes. "I could go after him. Cut the head off the snake before it strikes." Odd, but the thought made my guts tighten like I was gonna be sick.

He shook his head. "Don't go dirtying your hands, Eli. There's other ways to handle coyotes. You aren't alone, you hear me, boy?"

"Yessir," I nodded, in full agreement.

"Our Apaches will watch the children, but you know they won't be allowed weapons. If the Colonel heard of us arming them…"

"Understood." I hesitated. "When Montalvo shows up…"

"I'll handle it," he insisted. But I had a bad feelin' snakin' through my belly.

31

The Waitin'

We all waited as the hours ticked past, all of us feelin' the impending trouble. The wind began to kick up to a howl outside, rattling the rafters of the Senator's house and kickin' sand against the windows, as I second-guessed my decision to stay. But seeing the determination in their eyes as they stood by my side, ready to face whatever came our way, gave me a peek at hope in the darkness.

"Emma," I tried again, my voice rough with emotion, "I can't let you face this danger on account of me. Mebbe if you and the Senator got outta here, he'd let you go to come after me."

Emma's eyes flashed with defiance, her grip on my hand tightenin'. "W-we already said, we aren't leaving you, Eli," she declared, her voice steady despite the fear pinchin' her eyes. "We're in this together, come what may."

The Senator nodded in agreement, his expression resolute. "We made a pact, Eli. We're family now, and family sticks together through thick and thin."

Their unwaverin' loyalty touched something deep within me, stirring a sense of determination that I hadn't come on so strong in years. Fillin' my lungs, I squared my shoulders and met their gaze with a newfound resolve.

As the afternoon wore on, tension hung thick in the air like the smoke from a campfire on a still evenin'. We gathered in the parlor of the Senator's house, dark with the curtains drawn, the soft glow of the oil lamps casting flickerin' shadows on the walls. Emma sat beside me, her fingers clenched around the handle of her pistol as it lay in her lap. Her eyes darted to the windows with every gust of wind.

The Senator stood by the window, a shotgun leaned ready against the frame. His stance was firm and unwaverin', his gaze fixed on the darkness outside like a sentry watchin' for signs of trouble. Feather lay at our feet, his ears perked up and his gaze sharp, as if he sensed the danger lurkin' just beyond the safety of our walls.

For hours, we waited in silence, the only sound the rhythmic tickin' of the clock on the mantel and the distant howl of the wind. Each minute passed as an eternity, the anticipation gnawin' at my insides like a hungry coyote. But despite the fear churnin' inside, I couldn't help but feel a sense of gratitude for the company of my newfound kin.

Even so, my mind continued to search for the better path, the one that didn't put my people at risk. I'd started to pick at my fingernails, my heel beatin' a rapid rhythm on the floorboards. I hated this. Sure, I'd done my fair share of waitin', but I'd been watchin' my prey, lookin' for the perfect time to jump. This…this infernal sittin' and lettin' him come to us, like rabbits in a burrow, it just didn't cut it.

Emma glanced at me from the corner of her eye, her expression tense but determined. "Do you think he'll come tonight?" she whispered.

I shook my head, my jaw clenched tight with apprehension. "Can't say for sure, Emma. But best to be ready for anythin'."

The Senator nodded in agreement, his hand driftin' to the grip of his gun. "We'll be ready," he declared, his voice steady but tight with an underlying tension.

As the evenin' dragged on, the wind outside picked up, howlin' like a pack of wolves as it whipped through the trees. The dust kicked against the windowpanes like a relentless drummer settin' the tempo for a battle march. But still, there was no sign of Montalvo.

Just as I began to wonder if perhaps Sheriff Alvarez's warnin' had been nothin' more than a false alarm, a sudden knock at the door shattered the silence like a crack of thunder. We exchanged wary glances, our hearts flutterin' in our chests like trapped birds.

The Senator stepped forward, his hand hoverin' near the hilt of his pistol as he cautiously approached the door. With a steadyin' breath, he swung it open, revealin' Sheriff Alvarez standin' on the threshold, his expression grave.

"Sheriff," the Senator greeted, his voice tense but polite as he stepped aside to let the sheriff in. "What brings you out on a night like this?"

Sheriff Alvarez stepped inside after dustin' himself off. "Sorry to intrude, Senator," he said, his tone serious. "But I thought you ought to know, Montalvo's been spotted in town, headin' this way."

My veins froze at the mention of Montalvo's name. Emma's grip tightened on her pistol, her knuckles white as she braced herself for the inevitable confrontation.

The Senator's jaw tightened, his eyes narrowin' with determination. "How many men does he have with him?" he asked, his voice hushed and measured, his military background apparent.

Sheriff Alvarez glanced over his shoulder, his expression grim. "There's two others, look to be mean hombres. They're armed to the teeth and lookin' for trouble."

A heavy silence fell over the room, the gravity of the situation weighin' down on us like a leaden cloak. Montalvo was no ordinary outlaw; he was a ruthless killer with a score to settle, and he wouldn't stop until he had me in his sights.

Emma's voice broke through the silence, her tone firm and resolute. "We'll make our stand right here," she announced, her voice cuttin' through the silence like a blade. "We'll show Montalvo we aren't afraid to defend what's ours."

With a nod of acknowledgment, I turned to Emma, a silent promise passin' between us like a secret shared between confidants. "You stay close to your father, Emma," I murmured, wantin' her out of the line of fire.

"And you stay out of sight, Eli. We don't want him seeing you," she snapped back.

With that, we took our positions, waitin' in tense anticipation for the inevitable confrontation. The night stretched on, the wind sendin' the house creakin', but still, there was no sign of Montalvo or his men.

Perched on our toes, we waited, the tension mountin' with each passin' moment. But just as I began to fear that perhaps Montalvo had slipped through our fingers, a shadow emerged from the darkness, movin' towards us like a ghost in the night.

With a heavy heart and a sense of determination burning in my chest, I rose from my seat and made my way to the window. Memories of my past as Will Carter, bodies covered with blood, flooded my mind, a reminder of the darkness that still lurked within me.

I could spend years tryin' to leave that life behind, to atone for my sins and seek redemption in the eyes of God. But now, faced with the prospect of confrontin' my past head-on, I couldn't help but wonder if I was truly worthy of the second chance I had been given.

32

The Bounty Hunter

Emma jumped on the settee beside me as a pounding on the front door sounded like a death knell through the still house, a gasp escaping as she put a hand to her throat.

"Will Carter," a voice thundered, slicin' through the thick wood. "I reckon you're hunkered down in there, and I aim to collect what's owed. Step out, hands high, and we might spare these folks any further hassle."

My heart skipped a beat at the sound of my old moniker, Will Carter, a name I'd fought hard to bury. I wasn't that man anymore. I'd changed, was a new man. But I knew Montalvo would never be convinced of that, if he even cared. He was focused on the reward.

I tightened my grip on my pistol, the cold weight of it reassuring me. My heart pounded, nearly leapin' out of my chest with its ferocity. This was it, the moment we'd been dreadin', the moment when our fate would be decided at the barrel of a gun. But as I met Emma's gaze with steely determination, I knew that no matter what happened, I wouldn't back down without a fight. Not with everythin' on the line that mattered to me.

"Eli, stay put," the Senator commanded, his voice firm but edged with concern. I called myself a coward for lettin' him go to the door, but I stuck with the plan. Montalvo would be in a passel of trouble if he opened fire on the Senator, especially with the Sheriff around. It was the only thing that kept me from jumpin' in front of him.

With a swift motion, the Senator swung the door open, shotgun at the ready. "There is no Will Carter here," he stated firmly. "I believe you've already been informed of your misinformation."

I breathed a sigh of relief as Sheriff Alvarez followed him outside. More protection for our side.

"What's the play here, Montalvo?" the Sheriff's voice sounded sharp like a whip crack. "You know as well as I do that Will Carter's six feet under. I know you been told he's hung and buried."

Montalvo's voice dripped with menace as he faced off with the lawman. "Don't try to play me, Alvarez. I've seen him around, the same face I brought in a year ago. I know he's holed up here, and I'm aimin' to drag him out, whether he's breathin' or not. Anyone gets between me and him, well, I ain't responsible for that."

He'd shoot up the house, given half the chance. I knew that sure as the sun shines. He could hurt Emma. I couldn't let anyone suffer for my past mistakes.

I swallowed hard, the lump in my throat becoming solid as I stepped into view, meetin' Montalvo's glare with one of my own, his eyes flarin' with recognition. Fear grew in me, threatenin' to burst out, but I couldn't let him cow me, not when the safety of my loved ones hung in the balance.

Behind me, I heard the window throw open, and guessed Emma'd stuck a shotgun through. Fool woman just had to stick her nose in, no matter what we'd told her. My heart beat harder, in fear for her.

"My name's Eli Colton, mister. Will Carter ain't here, just as these good men have told you," I called out, my voice surprisingly steady. "Why don't you skedaddle back to whatever rock you crawled out from?"

Montalvo's eyes narrowed, a dangerous glint flickerin' in their depths as his hand drifted to his holster. "I know who you are. You should be dead, Carter," he snarled, his words finding their mark. "I don't know how you escaped prison, but it don't much matter. I'll just get my bounty twice. Make no mistake, I'll be watchin', and when I catch up to you, there'll be hell to pay."

Before I could retort, Sheriff Alvarez stepped forward, his stance unwaverin' as he faced down Montalvo. "This young man is not who you think he is. He's an upstandin' citizen of this town. Like you been told, Will Carter's met his maker, Montalvo," he growled, his gaze unyieldin'. "You've got no claim here."

The bounty hunter laughed, a short, cruel bark that sent shivers down my spine. He nodded in my direction. "He's standin' right there, Sheriff, the spittin' image of that wanted poster. Don't know how he got out, but I'll take him back in. No outlaw goes free while I'm ridin' after him."

"You do that, Montalvo, I'll bring you in for assaulting a law-abiding member of our community. Anythin' happens to the folk of this town, I'll know who to send the posse after."

For a moment, the tension hung thick in the air, broken only by our ragged breaths and the distant whinny of a horse. Then, with a muttered oath, Montalvo wheeled around and mounted his buckskin, disappearin' into the swirlin' dust. His compadres, who'd been silently witnessin', followed.

As Montalvo's shadow vanished into the distance, I let loose a heavy sigh, feelin' the tension drain out of me like water from a busted barrel. Beside me, Feather whined, his eyes filled with worry as he leaned against my leg, offerin' silent comfort.

"That was too close for comfort," Alvarez leaned against the porch rail. "You best keep your eyes peeled, Eli. Montalvo's as persistent as a tumbleweed in a dust storm."

"We'll be waiting for him," the Senator affirmed.

Emma appeared beside me, grabbin' hold of my arm. I could feel her fear through her tremblin' fingers. I couldn't take it no longer, couldn't bear to watch her fret. The war inside me battled on, fightin' against my love for these people and my fear of Montalvo. And truly, it wasn't fear for myself as much as it was fear that she'd be left without me to protect her.

Tension ate at me, nibblin' at my nerves. I wanted to go after Montalvo, to end his threat to these people who'd become so important to me. The itch raged beneath the surface, a palpable force. I could only think of one thing to to push that itch back down.

I grabbed my hat and mumbled a goodbye to Emma and the Senator, their worried hands falling away from my arms. Stepping out, the dusty sun had disappeared like the ease my life had been here, leavin' a cold moon in its place. The primal itch had turned my blood to fire, the feeling of fire ants sparkin' under my skin.

A hot wave of stale sweat and cheap booze slammed into me as I pushed the saloon doors open. Raucous laughter filled the air, the sound of a saloon night still young. I settled onto a creaky stool, keeping the corner of my eye on the single door. My thoughts raced, fillin' my head so that I barely registered the bartender's gravel voice.

"Whiskey," I rasped, downing the amber liquid in a burning gulp, feelin' the burn trace down into my churnin' belly. It did little to ease the phantom itch, the gnawing fear.

Drowning my sorrows felt pathetic, but facing Montalvo and the darkness within me was a terrifying prospect. Glancing around, my gaze lingered on the men – soldiers, ranchers, drifters – all potential prey for someone like my former self. A pang of yearning stabbed at me, a hunger for the freedom of the wild edge.

Suddenly, Alvarez materialized beside me, turnin' his back to the bar to watch the door, not lookin' me in the eyes. "Taking a big chance leavin' the house, Eli," he muttered, his voice laced with concern.

I nodded, guilt layin' on me like scum on a pond. "Just needed a breather."

"Montalvo's a snake. Keep your guard up."

"Don't plan on letting him get the drop on me," I vowed. Alvarez's dark gaze held mine, sharp as a sharpshooter's aim, studyin' me a moment before noddin' and meltin' back into the shadows like a phantom on a mission. With a grateful nod, I drained my glass and left the stifling saloon. Feather met me at the door, a comforting presence at my side. He whined softly.

"You feel it too, boy, don't you?" I confided, scratching his fur. "The storm brewin'. He ain't gone, he's just bidin' his time."

Feather's eyes mirrored my unease. He was more than a dog; he was my anchor in this storm, a beacon against the encroaching darkness.

I straightened my resolve with a deep breath. I'd come too far to let the darkness win. For Emma, for the children, for my own soul, I would fight.

With newfound purpose, I set off down the dusty street, Feather trotting at my side.

33

A Nightmare

I bolted upright in bed, gaspin' for air. The echoes of my nightmare still rattled 'round the room, clingin' to the walls like the stench of gunsmoke after a shootout. My heart beat like a runaway horse, gallopin' blindly toward a cliff.

The terror of the dream, the same bloody acts that had been plaguin' me for weeks, stuck to me like a leech, drainin' me of fight. I trembled, my shirt wrapped tight around me from my tossin' in bed. Beside me, Feather whined.

I stumbled toward the window. The wind gusted, rattlin' the panes, the moon castin' a ghostly glow over the landscape. Phantom clouds passed over it, glowin' with an eerie light.

Coyotes gathered somewhere nearby, their song off key and badly timed. But in my mind's eye, I could still see the blood-soaked earth, the lifeless bodies I'd left strewn about like discarded playthings, broken and forgotten. Emma's terrified screams rang in my ears, hauntin' me, freezin' my blood.

I yanked on my trousers and boots, the urgency of the tempest brewin' outside matchin' the turmoil roilin' within me. I needed air, needed to get out of these walls that were closin' in on me like that cell I rotted in for months. With a heavy sigh, I stepped out into the night, wind whippin' around me like fire lickin' at the wood.

I lowered myself to a weathered stump set just outside the back door, tremblin' and weak. I buried my face in my calloused hands, the guilt pressin' down on me like a ton of bricks. I'd brought this danger to town, to Emma. If I'd been the man she deserved, Montalvo and I would have never crossed paths. Feather's warmth beside me offered silent solace, his eyes speakin' volumes as if he could feel the storm ragin' in my soul.

Emma's safety worried me, her vulnerability to the shadows of my past eatin' at me. She was a spitfire, sure, but she'd jump into danger with both feet and never look twice. My nightmares reminded me just how fragile a woman like her could be. With a heavy heart, I knew I couldn't ignore the danger lurkin' any longer. I'd have to go after Montalvo, settle things one way or another.

With a heavy sigh, I rose from my makeshift seat, the cold ground clingin' to my boots like a reluctant lover. Lost in the whirlwind of my thoughts, I scarcely noticed the figure emergin' from the darkness, Montalvo flanked by two shadowy enforcers. My hand instinctively went for the iron strapped to my hip, only to come up empty. I hadn't thought to strap it on after wakin' from that cursed dream.

I cursed him, cursed myself. I was caught now. I was thankful that at least I hadn't brought anyone else down with me.

He approached with the grace of a prowlin' mountain cat, his movements fluid and sinuous, every step calculated to unnerve. My heart quickened its pace, hammerin' against my ribs like a prisoner beatin' against his cell door.

A chill crept over me as he closed the gap, his eyes sharp as a gambler's blade cuttin' through the night. "Well, well, well," he drawled menacingly. "Ain't this a surprise? The notorious outlaw himself takin' a moonlit stroll."

My fists clenched tight, a stampede of wild horses in my chest. "I ain't Will Carter," I spat the lie, the truth, fear scratchin' at my throat like a dog after a bone. "The sheriff made that clear to ya."

He sneered, teeth flashin' yellow in the dim light, the moon catchin' in his cruel eyes. "Oh, I heard," he mocked, "But that bounty's still hangin' over your head, as far as I'm concerned. Long as the poster's out, I aim to collect."

The sound of the backdoor creaking open sent a fresh wave of terror through me. Emma stood there, like a rabbit caught in a clearin', her eyes wide. I cursed. Instinct drove me to shield her, but before I could react, Montalvo's gun clicked. His cronies emerged from the shadows, reachin' for Emma with rough hands. She fought them, of course she did.

Rage surged through me, a prairie wildfire threatenin' to consume me whole, as she struggled against them, goin' so far as to stomp her tiny boot on one of their large feet, causin' the outlaw to grunt in pain. "Let her go!" I roared, my voice cuttin' through the night like a shotgun blast, as I forced myself to stay in my spot. Montalvo was too close to miss, too far away to give me hope I'd foul his aim. "She's got no part in this."

The headhunter's laughter echoed, mockin' and cruel as Emma was brought to him. They only handled her rougher for her struggles, but the woman didn't know to quit. I had a moment to be grateful she'd dressed before comin' out, afraid she'd be in more danger if she was only in her nightgown.

"Let her go? Well, now, ain't that just precious," he scoffed, his voice laced with contempt. "What's it to you, Carter? She's worth more to me than a sack of gold. Why'd I let go of a prize like her? You'd best keep your yap shut, or things could get messy."

His words sliced into my heart, my muscles tensed for a fight. Feather nudged my leg, a silent plea for patience. I had to hold back, thinkin' before actin', or I'd be riskin' Emma's safety.

Takin' a deep breath, I met Emma's gaze, a silent promise passin' between us. We'd weather this storm together, come hell or high water. I'd be ready when the moment came, and fight tooth and nail to keep her safe.

With determination steelin' my soul, I calmed the turmoil within me, plannin' my next move carefully. If I aimed to keep Emma safe from these varmints, I had to be smart and swift, puttin' her well-being above all else. I didn't cause trouble when Montalvo wrapped my wrists with rope, just clenched my teeth, knowin' each step I had to bide my time, that justice would come.

The wind was a devil's whip as Montalvo and his band dragged us away from the shelter of the town and into the barren stretch of the wild frontier. Emma's face was drained of color, her eyes wide as saucers, fear clingin' to her like a shadow. I couldn't blame her – Montalvo was trouble, the kind that could carve our lives in two. But her grit showed in the thin press of her lips, and I knew she'd be ready when it was time.

The trek to their hideout was like a march to the gallows, each step leadin' us deeper into the jaws of danger. But this time I had somethin' to lose, somethin' tying me to this earthly plane.

The night air was heavy with the scent of sage and pine, the wind kickin' up dust clouds and sendin' tumbleweeds dancin' in the breeze like phantoms playin' ball. Emma rode stiffly in Montalvo's arms, her face a mask of pale defiance. I was left to trail behind on a rope like a dog, fightin' to keep up as they pushed their horses to a brisk trot out of town.

My jaw ached from clenchin' my teeth, cursin' myself for my stupidity, battling with the gnawing worry for Emma's safety. Every once in a while she'd scuffle with him, and my gut churned knowin' the indignities she was likely subjected to. Montalvo and his gang kept us under their hawk-eyed watch, their movements as smooth as snakes slitherin' through the brush. They knew these lands like the back of their hand, navigatin' the rugged terrain with the ease of seasoned outlaws. And I was not the first man they'd taken in.

We'd been on the trail close to an hour when my left boot began to bust open at the toe, each step expandin' the opening until I was limpin' along. The worn leather, soft but thin, couldn't hold any longer. The outlaws looked back at my predicament and laughed, their jeers like vultures circling a carcass. Kept yankin' the rope to send me off balance, revelin' in my humiliation.

Finally, I managed to hop on one leg long enough to pull the fool thing off, the ragged leather offering no further protection. Then I was barefoot and lopsided, the sharp rocks diggin' into my sole, soon leavin' a bloody trail, a constant reminder of my vulnerability, my failure to protect Emma.

I felt like that old boot - worn and bustin' apart under the strain of this ordeal. But defiance still sparked within me. I wouldn't break. Not yet. My sole purpose, my entire being, was put in place to save Emma.

They musta got tired of my laggin' behind, because soon after they paused.

The two followin' Montalvo doubled up while they gave me a horse, tying me to the saddle and leadin' me on like a kiddie who'd never rode a horse. Feather had disappeared quietly, but I could feel his presence lurkin' in the shadows, a silent sentinel keepin' watch over us from afar. His absence only added to my sense of forebodin', my instincts echoin' through my mind like a mournful dirge.

Lightnin' cracked overhead, castin' twisted shadows across the land. It musta been close to dawn as we neared the dilapidated shack that must serve as Montalvo's lair. Its weathered walls loomed ominously in the night, a silent sentinel guardin' the secrets hid within.

As we approached, thunder rumbled in the distance, settin' my nerves on edge. A sense of dread coiled inside, weighin' me down like a millstone. I searched for a way, any way, to keep us out of that shack. I knew our chances to escape unscathed went down once we were inside. Emma shot me a worried look, her eyes mirrorin' the fear chokin' me from within. I wished I had somethin' to offer her. The best I could do now was shield her with my body.

Montalvo turned to us with a cruel grin, his eyes flashin' with malice. "Welcome to your new digs, folks," he spat, gesturin' towards the shadowy doorway.

I shared a glance with Emma, her face etched with apprehension. We'd wandered right into the lion's den, and who knew what awaited us inside. The rain started to fall, heavy and relentless, soakin' us in seconds. Montalvo lowered Emma to his dark haired assistance while the blonde one untied me from the horse and shoved me over the side.

Emma was already inside before I made it to my feet. My heart was poundin', chanting "Go, Go, Go." I couldn't tell if it wanted me to run away or run to Emma, but there was only one way I'd go. I followed her inside.

34

Danger

As the man pushed me into the cabin, the air hung heavy with the stench of sweat and fear. Montalvo's henchmen leered at us from the shadows, their faces twisted in cruel anticipation. A surge of anger rose within me, but I forced it down, knowing that any rash action could spell disaster for Emma and me.

I had to keep my wits about me, ready for action when there was opportunity. I rushed to her side, where she'd crouched against the wall, placin' myself in front of her, tryin' to protect her from their cruel eyes. The three men moved around, lightin' the fire and makin' themselves at home.

I turned to Emma, takin' her hands in my bound ones. "You okay?" I whispered, mouthin' the words with less air than a gnat's wings. She nodded, face drawn up tight like a mask, her eyes beginnin' to tear up. It cut through me, seein' her like this.

We had Montalvo's full attention, his eyes predatory as he measured us, his tongue comin' out to moisten his lower lip. He rested on one leg, a satisfied air causin' a cruel tilt to his lips. His voice was salt on the wound in my soul, his words dripping with malice as he addressed Emma directly.

"Now, darlin'," he drawled, "I hope you understand the predicament you're in. You see, your little beau here is gonna bring me a reward, and I aim to collect. But I aim to collect a little somethin' from you too."

Emma's eyes widened in terror, her gaze darting between Montalvo and me, a silent plea for reassurance. I squeezed her tremblin' hand tightly, my heart aching at the sight of her fear. But I couldn't let Montalvo know how much his words affected me, couldn't let him revel in our weakness.

I heard coyotes howl in the distance, reminding me I had to be sly and patient, that we had to wait for the right moment to make our escape. But as Montalvo's grinning face drew closer, his fingers trailing along Emma's cheek with sickening familiarity, rage boiled in my veins like molten lava.

"Let her go, Montalvo," I growled, pushin' myself to my knees in front of her, my voice low and steady. "I'll go with you easy as you please, if you let her go."

Montalvo's grin widened, his eyes glintin' with dark amusement as he stepped closer to her. He pushed me away with a foot. I fell to my rear, bruisin' the tailbone, while he bent until he was only a foot from Emma's face.

"Oh, just a little favor, Billy," he taunted in a sing-song voice. "Your pretty girl here is quite the feisty one, just how I like 'em."

My muscles tensed with the checked urge to lash out, knowing that any show of resistance would only make matters worse. *Play it smart, Eli,* I reminded myself.

"I don't want to kill you, Montalvo," I gritted out. "Leave her be."

He threw back his head and roared with laughter. "Oooh, Billy boy, you ain't got a leg to stand on. I'll do whatever I please. She wants to live through this, she knows what she's gonna need to do."

Montalvo laughed as he turned to pick up the bottle on the small table. He took a large swig, wipin' his mouth with the back of his hand and sighin' with satisfaction.

Emma's fearful eyes met mine, and I hoped she gained strength from my own. I forced myself to remain calm, to focus on the task at hand. We had to bide our time, to wait for the opportune moment to strike.

I nodded imperceptibly, my eyes flickin' toward her boot where I knew she kept her hidden blade, glad she'd bothered to put the boots on in the night. She caught my meaning with a steely determination, her jaw set . She adjusted her position, puttin' her ankle behind me, where my hands were tied.

With a wary eye on the bounty hunter, I slipped my hand beneath Emma's skirts, feelin' for the hilt of the knife. Only a fleetin' thought that I'd hoped for a brighter time to be gettin' this close to her. My stomach twisted further, the knot a livin', writhin' thing inside.

My fingers closed around the cool metal, and I carefully began tryin' to get at the rope around my wrists, careful to keep it out of sight of Montalvo's watchful eyes. It might not be much against their guns, but it was better than nothin' at all.

Montalvo wiped his mouth again, glanced at his compadres. "We'll all have a chance see what that kitten can do, won't we boys?"

She shuddered, leanin' into me as I shoved myself back to my knees in front of her.

"I'm warnin' you, Montalvo…"

He spun, backhandin' me hard enough to rock me into Emma, who cried out. I managed to keep the knife behind me, my hands frozen behind my back. An iron taste filled my mouth, I noted a tooth loosened before I spat back at the bounty hunter.

Hate filled his eyes. "I think we might just have to teach both of you a lesson." He grabbed for Emma's arm, jerkin' her to her feet and pullin' her into him. Tears ran down her cheeks, but her eyes burned with fear-filled rage.

I slid the knife into my sleeve as I thrashed to my knees, earnin' a boot to the gut that sent me back to my side.

Each moment stretched on like an eternity as I waited for the perfect moment to make my move. I watched them, muscles tense. Montalvo's grip tightened on Emma's arm, his grin twistin' into a cruel smirk, I knew that our moment of reckoning was fast approachin', that all things would soon come to a head, for better or worse. That didn't make it any easier to see him stroke the side of Emma's cheek.

She turned her head and snapped at his fingers with an audible click, her eyes flashing, burnin' through her fear. "Don't touch me!" she hissed. Panic hit me as the raucous laughter of Montalvo's men echoed through the cabin.

Men like this enjoyed the violence she offered. I grit my teeth, my muscles coilin' as I readied for the fight.

"Oh, kitten's got claws!" the blonde one exclaimed. "C'mon baby, I like it a little rough."

"Let her go!" I shouted again, flippin' myself over to struggle once again to my knees.

Emma met my gaze, her eyes hard with determination, the apology in them tellin' me I wasn't gonna like what she did next.

"I-I nnneed to…to freshen up."

Emma's sudden declaration dropped the bottom out of my stomach. I panicked at the thought of them takin' her outside without me.

"Emma, no," I breathed, unbelievin' that she'd put herself at risk like this.

That fool woman, once again jumpin' feet first into trouble. Why would she separate us like that? I couldn't protect her if I wasn't next to her.

But she met the outlaws' leering gazes with a steely resolve, her spine straight as a ramrod. Crude laughter erupted from the three of them, their vulgar jests and lingerin' looks makin' my blood boil with impotent rage.

I thought fast through my choices, tryin' to somehow change the events that were unfoldin' like a bad hand. I still had my hands tied, only able to get the knife edge against the rope with the tips of my fingers.

"Let me go to," I begged. "Montalvo, have some honor!"

I couldn't protect her if she was separated from me. But my words fell on deaf ears as they all chuckled darkly. The blond outlaw roughly seized her arm and dragged her toward the door, their boots scufflin' on the floor, raisin' the dust.

"You want me, not her!" I shouted once again.

I sawed frantically at my wrists, not carin' how much I nicked myself. The knife handle became slippery with my blood as the ropes began to give. He laughed, lickin' his lips, watchin' them walk out.

"Don't worry yerself, Billy boy, he'll break that filly in nice and easy for us. Reckon it won't take too long, not the way he rides 'em."

As the door slammed shut behind Emma, a cold dread settled over me like a suffocatin' blanket, my mind racin' with a thousand fears for her safety. I cursed myself for lettin' her out of my sight, for failin' to protect her as I had promised. The rope came apart just as Feather's low growl reached my ears, a sense of urgency swept through me like a desert wind, drivin' me to action.

With a silent prayer on my lips, I braced myself for what was to come, my hand adjustin' my hold on the hilt of the hidden blade. Feather's snarl ended with a pained human yelp, cuttin' through the tense silence. A shout and the sound of leather on rock indicated a scuffle, a signal that our moment of reckoning had arrived. It was now or never.

Montalvo turned toward the sound, his dark haired companion peerin' out the window of the cabin. Seizing the opportunity, I sprang into action, lunging at Montalvo and the remainin' henchman with a speed and ferocity born of desperation. I knew the odds were stacked against me, but anyone I took out of the fight was one less for Emma to deal with.

I knocked them both down with me, crawlin' on top, my fist makin' a dull crack as I hit Montalvo in the jaw, stunnin' him. A new reluctance to kill forced me to fight different than I'd ever done, usin' Emma's blade as defense more than attack. It put me at a disadvantage as openings for fatal strikes passed by.

Gruntin' with effort, I rose with the other man, swingin' the blade at him. The metallic tang of blood filled the air as I sliced through his arm with a satisfyin' squelch, the resistance of muscle draggin' on the blade. He yelped but didn't back off. I fought back, desperate, my every movement fueled by the knowledge that Emma's life hung in the balance.

As I grappled with the henchman closest to me, I caught sight of Montalvo advancing towards us, a malevolent gleam in his eyes. His lips curled into a cruel smirk as he raised his gun, aiming it straight at my chest.

Instinctively, with a swift motion, I slashed out at my attacker, the blade biting deep into the flesh of his shoulder with a sickening crunch. The henchman let out a cry of pain, and I pulled him in front of me.

Montalvo had held his fire, reluctant to hit his compadre, but he kept his gun trained on me with deadly accuracy. "Give up, Montalvo. No one has to die today," I shouted at him, urgin' him to back out, let us go.

"You're gonna die for this, Carter," he growled as he began to squeeze the trigger, choosin' to sacrifice his man to get me.

With a surge of energy, I threw the groanin' man to the side as I ducked and dodged, narrowly avoiding the bullet that whizzed past my head. In one swift motion, I lunged at Montalvo, the knife gleaming in the dim light of the shack. The blade cut through the air with deadly precision, finding its mark in his gun hand with a sickening thud. Montalvo's eyes widened in shock as he stumbled backwards, droppin' his revolver as he clutched his ruined hand, the blade stickin' clean through.

I picked his gun off the floor, stupidly takin' my eyes off him because when I stood up, he had a peashooter trained on my heart. With only a few feet between us, even that tiny thing could end me.

I mighta been okay with that, if I didn't know he'd immediately go after Emma. "Call your man off the girl," I said, hangin' the revolver loosely with one finger in the trigger guard, strainin' to hear what was happening outside. "I'll drop the gun, you can take me in once she goes free."

Montalvo snickered, his cruel lips twistin' with evil intent. "You've got a foul hand, Carter. You better fold, or I'll kill you and still have the girl."

For the first time, sadness met me as the darkness raised its head, foreseein' the bloody outcome I dreaded. I wouldn't let him have Emma.

"I'll shoot you before I die," I threatened, knowin' it wouldn't stop him. I'd ridden the same evil horse he sat on. Maybe he'd get a chance, like I'd had. But it wasn't my responsibility. He'd made his choices.

Emma shouted from outside, something unintelligible, catchin' Montalvo's interest for the second I needed to flip the pistol in my hand and pull the trigger. My aim, as always, was true, catching him in the chest, blood blossoming where his heart should have been. His eyes widened as he found himself on the ground, blood soaking through his fingers, before they began their journey to death.

Even as I watched him fall, a surge of conflicting emotions flooded through me – relief at having beaten our enemy, and a sickening guilt at the violence that had brought us to this point. I had wanted to end the bloodshed, to change my ways. But in the unforgivin' land of the Old West, sometimes there was no other choice.

As Montalvo's lifeblood stained the floor, my throat tightened, and bitter taste rose up from my gullet. The metallic tang of blood hung heavy in the air, a gruesome reminder of the price of survival.

35

Resolution

Pressed to get outside, to help Emma, I aimed the gun at the remainin' outlaw. He let out a defeated sigh as he clutched at his shoulder wound, a balled-up bandanna quickly soakin' through.

"'M throwin' in my hand," he grunted, scootin' back from Montalvo's corpse, free hand high. "Won't give you no more trouble."

Momentarily relieved, I took his gun and risked turnin' my back on him, driven beyond reason to check on Emma. My ears were ringin' from the gunfire in the small cabin, the smell of gunsmoke thick enough to choke on. My bare foot stung somethin' fierce, but I opened up the door with a creak, ready to do battle.

Outside, the early mornin' sun cast pale light over the clearing. I scanned the area hastily, searchin' for Emma. When I found her, a gust of air left my lips.

She stood a few paces away, shakily hoverin' over the remaining outlaw as he clutched at his torn leg, blood from a scalp wound tricklin' nearly into his eye. She still held the bloody rock, half-raised and ready to go.

I read the scene quickly. Her russet hair was tousled, strands flyin' every which way. Her clothes were stained with blood and dirt, but it wasn't hers. She was unharmed, I thanked God. Feather sat at her feet, his dark eyes fixed on me, lickin' red stains off his muzzle, his ear notched and bloody from the fight.

I scanned the area for any signs of movement before I limped toward them. My foot was throbbin', my heart still racing from the fight. Emma looked up as I drew near, her eyes wild. She looked back to the outlaw moanin' on the ground, starin' for a long moment. She turned to me, blank and wide-eyed, rock still held high. I shuffled closer, hands out toward her like I'd approach a spooked horse.

"It's okay, darlin'," I cajoled. "He's down. You can let go that rock."

A long moment passed, 'till I was right in front of her, her eyes jerkin' wildly between me and the outlaw. Her eyes were so big I could see the whites all the way around, but she didn't seem to see much. I never wanted to see that empty look in them again.

"Shhhh, darlin'," I put my hand over hers, causin' her to jerk with a sudden intake of breath. Her fingers tightened on the rock, pullin' away from me. "Let it go. It's over."

I held her hands in mine for a few breaths before she let out a breath, her body softening, and opened her fingers. The rock made a heavy thump as it hit the ground. She still didn't move, a ghost caught out in the sunlight, as the seconds ticked by. The birds had picked their singin' back up, and a light breeze lifted copper tendrils of her hair.

"E-E-Eli?" she stammered, voice tremblin' and weak, finally raisin' her shadowed eyes to meet mine. Her face was pale, the bruised skin under her eyes a stark contrast. Tears began to well in her wide eyes, the honey of her eyes barely visible around the black.

I nodded, unable to speak. "I'm fine," I managed to say, hoarse and shaky myself. "You okay?"

Sobbing, Emma threw herself at me, embracin' me tightly, her touch keepin' my thoughts to the present. I held her soft body for a minute, her hair ticklin' my nose, relishin' the joy that she was alive. I patted her back, just tryin' to reassure her, for a long while as her body shook. I pushed my face into her hair. She smelled like home.

When she calmed and drew back a little, her gaze was steadier as she met my own. She delicately wiped her tears with the backs of her knuckles, glanced around.

"Mmontalvo?" she whispered.

"Dead," I acknowledged reluctantly, torn between my emotions. I'd tried to get him to make the right choice, tried to keep from killin' him. But I wouldn't let him hurt Emma. What that meant for my soul, I didn't know.

She nodded, her eyes still roamin' over it all, lettin' it all sink in. I watched her carefully, afraid it had been too much for her. Instead, before my eyes she pulled herself back together, her chin tiltin' to that familiar angle as she straightened her shoulders.

"W-we make a good team, don't we?" she declared, a tiny sparkle of mischief hittin' her red-rimmed eyes. I knew then she'd be alright, maybe we'd both be alright, eventually.

I couldn't help but chuckle at her words, despite the heaviness that still lingered in my heart. "We sure do," I replied, a smile tugging at the corners of my mouth.

Feather let out a low bark of agreement, his tail wagging happily as he nuzzled against Emma's leg. It was as if he could sense the relief and gratitude that filled the air, his presence a comforting reminder that we were not alone in this world. He was tellin' me what I'd done was okay. I couldn't fully believe that, though.

As I looked down at the outlaw lying on the ground, his pained moans a stark reminder of the violence that had transpired, a pang of regret pierced my heart. I had killed a man, even if it had been in self-defense, in defense of Emma. Even though I'd had no other choice, the weight of that act hung heavy on my newfound conscience.

I turned away from the scene, unable to bear the sight any longer. "We should head back to town," I said, my voice somber. "We can't stay here."

Emma nodded in agreement, her expression mirroring my own solemnity. Together, we tied the criminals up tight so they had no chance of escape. They were injured, but not worryingly so.

One had dog bites and a few bumps on his head that had almost stopped bleeding, though they'd probably scar pretty good. The other had a couple of deep knife wounds, but nothin' that'd kill him outright. They'd be all right for a few hours.

"We'll leave them here for the sheriff to sort out," I decided. I didn't want to risk them turning against us on the way.

I looked down at Montalvo's corpse, but there was no triumph in his defeat, no satisfaction in his demise. The teeth of remorse bit me – remorse for the life that had been lost, for the violence that had consumed us all.

We tied them, feet and hands, leaving them in that shack.

We took their horses back, the weight of our actions, of the unspeakable horrors that could have been, hanging heavy in the air. But as we walked, a sense of peace began to settle over me, knowing that Emma was safe by my side.

We hadn't gone far when we were met by a posse led by Sheriff Alvarez and the Senator, with Nantan at their side. Their expressions were a hodge podge of relief and concern as they took us in, battered and weary but alive.

"Are you alright?" the Senator asked, full of paternal concern, his eyes flittin' between us, likely seeing the blood we both wore.

I nodded, unable to find the words to express the tumult of emotions that churned within me. "We're fine," I murmured, watchin' Emma carefully. She was notably silent, her gaze faraway and thought-filled.

The Senator nodded, his gaze lingering on Emma for a moment, searchin' for reassurance that she was unharmed.

"Emma, honey?" he asked.

She blinked, gave her father a weak tear-filled smile.

"I-I'm fine, Daddy. It was j-just…a long night."

His eyes rested on her a touch longer, brows knit, before he turned back to me.

"We were lucky, sir. Just some bumps and scrapes."

He tilted his head, acknowledgin' what I was tellin' him.

"Are any of them still alive?" Alvarez asked, his tone grave.

I glanced back toward the shack wearily. "Montalvo's dead. We left the other two there, and a horse. They're hurt, but they'll be fine for a few hours."

"What happened?" he dug.

I breathed deep, shuttin' out the memories that threatened to overwhelm me. "I'd gone out for a breath of air. Montalvo ambushed me, then Emma stepped out into the mess," I explained, my voice steady despite the turmoil that churned within me. "But we managed to fight them off and make it back here."

I glanced at the senator, his expression grim as he listened to our tale. He clenched his jaw, eyes narrowin' with channeled anger. "We'll make sure they face justice for what they've done."

I nodded in agreement, grateful for the support of the senator and the sheriff. But even as I spoke the words, I couldn't shake the sense of unease that gnawed at my insides.

"Look, Sheriff," I began.

His gaze swung to mine. "I know all about Will Carter and his hangin'," he said. "You've got nothin' to fear from him, or me. Ya'll done what you needed to in self-defense."

His eyes bore into mine, filled with knowledge and understandin'. I hesitated, still uncertain.

"I'll handle these two," the Sheriff jerked his horse toward the shack that held the outlaws. "You get your girl home."

Emma looked my way, cheeks pink, her sniffles mingled with a choked laugh. I was mightily relieved that she had revived. A quiet Emma was worrisome. The Senator's laugh boomed through the dusty brush.

"Let's go home," he said, turnin' his horse back to town. We continued on our journey, all of us quiet, leaving the outlaw's hideout behind us as we made our way back to the safety of town. And as we rode, I couldn't help but feel a sense of gratitude for the outcome, and I sent up another prayer.

Nantan rode up beside me. "You blessed by Great Spirit," he said suddenly, breaking the silence that had settled over us like a heavy blanket. "He send Feather."

I glanced over at him, raising an eyebrow in curiosity. "Feather? What about him?"

Nantan hesitated for a moment, as if unsure how to voice his thoughts. "The elders speak of spirit animals," he began slowly. "Animals that come in times of great need. Like Feather."

I furrowed my brow in confusion, unsure of what he was getting at. "What do you mean?" I asked, my voice tinged with skepticism.

Nantan shifted uncomfortably. "Feather, he seem more than a dog," he said quietly. "He help you make new man."

I felt a chill run through me at his words, the hairs on the back of my neck standing on end. A spirit animal? It seemed far-fetched, but then again, so did waking up in a grave after being hanged. So did a serial killer like Will Carter becoming a man regretful of killin'.

I glanced over at Feather, studying him intently as if seeing him for the first time. He had been there for me through thick and thin, a constant presence by my side. And now, as I considered Nantan's words, it was almost plausible that there was more to him than met the eye.

With a sigh, I shook my head, pushing aside the thoughts that threatened to overwhelm me. "I don't know, Nantan," I said finally, my voice tinged with uncertainty. "It's a lot to take in."

Emma hummed thoughtfully. "It is hard to believe," she said. "But sometimes, the things we can't see are the things that matter most."

I mulled over his words in silence as we rode on, the rhythmic sound of hoofbeats filling the air. The idea of Feather being a spirit animal was strange and unsettling, but at the same time, it offered a glimmer of hope in the darkness that threatened to engulf me.

As for me…I still didn't know where I stood, one foot in the grave or not. Maybe I'd never die, as fanciful as that seemed, or maybe the next time I slept I'd never wake. But that question didn't seem so important anymore. I would live what life I had beside this incredible woman, thankful for whatever time I had.

The sun had broken through the clouds as we made our way back to town. Feather trotted ahead, his tail wagging happily as he sniffed at the familiar scents that filled the air. It was as if he could sense the weight that had been lifted from our shoulders, his spirit buoyed by the knowledge that we had emerged from the darkness stronger than before.

I couldn't help but feel a sense of relief wash over me. We had made it home, safe and sound, and now it was time to face the aftermath of our ordeal.

36

A Gift

The streets were quiet as we walked our horses through town, the early morning hour finding most folks still abed. But as we dismounted at home, I knew that the calm would not last for long. Emma held onto my arm, silently supporting me, as if she could feel the storm inside me. She pulled me away, to the alcove behind the house. The senator smiled slightly as we left, approval in his eyes, but I shifted away from his gaze, uncomfortable.

Emma pulled me back to the stump, where our ordeal had started, and sat beside me, leanin' her head on my shoulder. I wrapped my arms around her, my nose in her chestnut hair, glad to have her, glad we made it through in one piece. Feather sat on my feet, leanin' against my leg. We sat in silence for a long while, before Emma sighed and looked up at me, her eyes filled with concern.

"Y-you need to talk about what happened," she said softly, half a question and half a demand.

I nodded, my throat tight with emotion as I struggled to find the words to express the turmoil that churned within me. "I know," I replied, my voice barely above a whisper. "I just… I don't know how to feel about it all."

Emma squeezed my hand reassuringly, her touch a comfort amidst the storm that raged within me.

"We did what we had to do to protect ourselves," she said, her voice steady despite the tremor of uncertainty that lingered in the air.

I imagined she was talkin' to her own conscience as much as she was mine. She didn't have a violent bone in her body, and she'd taken that rock for a weapon like a savage.

"You saved my life, Eli. And I'll never forget that."

I looked into her eyes, searching for any sign of doubt or hesitation, but all I found was unwavering love and support.

"I killed a man, Emma," I said, the words heavy on my tongue. "I took another life, just like I used to do back in my outlaw days. I was tryin' so hard…what if it comes back, the itch?"

Emma nodded, her expression sympathetic as she reached out to stroke Feather's fur.

"I know it's not easy, Eli," she said softly. "But you're not that man anymore. You've changed, and you're trying to do the right thing now. That's what matters."

I sighed, her words settlin' over me like a blanket of peace.

"I just don't know if I can ever make up for what I've done," I admitted, my voice raw with emotion.

Feather whined softly, his gaze fixed on mine as if he could sense the turmoil that raged within me. I reached out to ruffle his fur, grateful for the silent comfort he offered.

"You did what you had to do, Eli," Emma said firmly, her hand coming up to my cheek. "You protected the ones you love. And that's all that matters."

Emma smiled, her eyes shining with affection as she leaned in to kiss my cheek.

"We're in this together, Eli," she said, her voice soft but determined. "No matter what happens, I'll always be by your side."

A surge of warmth flooded through me at her words, a sense of peace settling over me like the first light of dawn breaking through the darkness.

"Thank you, Emma," I said, my voice filled with gratitude. "I don't know what I'd do without you. I…I don't really know what love is, but I think it might be what I feel for you."

Her face lit up, and she took my breath away. "I love you too, Eli."

We sat there in silence for a moment, the only sound the soft rustle of the wind through the trees and the steady rhythm of our breathing. Eventually, she filled a basin with water and tended to my foot, brought me a pair of her father's boots.

They were about the right size, but felt off, stiff and curved in all the wrong places, like wearin' angry armadillos on my feet. They pinched my already sore feet so's I nearly just did without. But hobblin' around tender-footed, like I'd done when I crawled outta that grave, like I'd done on that terrible trek to the outlaws' cabin, wasn't somethin' I wanted to do again. I gritted my teeth and slipped them on.

The sun hung low in the sky as Sheriff Alvarez led the two outlaws we had left tied in the shack down the dusty main street of our frontier town, causin' a ruckus as folks took notice. They'd be around to ask me about, it, I knew. People talked, and the news would make its way around town soon enough. I wondered what they would say about me, when the story come out.

Nevertheless, as I watched from the porch of the Senator's house, a knot of tension loosened in my chest as he led them away. Sheriff Alvarez had assured me that justice would be served, that these men would pay for their crimes. I knew that debt showed as paid, and I hoped no others got the same idea as Montalvo'd had.

Feather sat at my feet, his golden fur glinting in the fading light. He nuzzled against my leg, a silent reminder of the support he had offered me throughout this ordeal. With a heavy sigh, I reached down to scratch behind his ears, grateful for his comforting presence.

Emma stepped out onto the porch beside me, her eyes filled with concern.

"Are you alright, Eli?" she asked, her voice soft with worry.

I offered her a weary smile, grateful for her unwavering support.

"I reckon I'll be alright, Emma," I replied, my voice tinged with exhaustion. "Just glad that those outlaws got taken in without anyone getting hurt."

Emma nodded in understanding, her hand coming to rest on my shoulder in a gesture of solidarity. A wave of gratitude for her washed over me, as I pulled her closer.

* * *

The sun was just startin' to peek over the horizon when I stepped out onto the dusty streets of our little town. The air was crisp with the promise of a new day, and I breathed deep, lettin' it fill my lungs as I set off toward Clara Sinclair's general store. Today, I wasn't there for just any usual purchases, but with a purpose that made my heart beat a little faster.

Mrs. Sinclair was standin' behind the counter when I walked in, her face lit up with a warm smile as she greeted me.

"Well, if it ain't Eli, the hero of our little town," she chirped.

I chuckled, a flush of embarrassment risin' at her words. A touch of unease unsettled me. All I'd wanted was to not be guilty - hero wasn't a word I was comfortable with.

"Now, Mrs. Sinclair, you know I ain't no hero," I managed to gruff out.

She waved off my protests with a dismissive wave of her hand.

"Nonsense," she said firmly. "You saved us all from that no-good Montalvo, and we're mighty grateful for it."

I couldn't help but smile at her words, feelin' a swell of pride run through me at the thought of bein' able to help my fellow townsfolk, even as I struggled with the unfamiliar praise.

"Well, I reckon I just did what needed doin'," I said modestly, shufflin' my feet awkwardly, hidin' the wince of pain it brought.

Mrs. Sinclair gave me a knowing look, her eyes twinkling with mischief.

"Modest as ever, I see," she teased, reaching beneath the counter and emerging with a pair of boots in her hand. The leather gleamed richly in the morning light. "But I ain't gonna let you off the hook that easily. Got a little somethin' for you as a token of our appreciation."

The boots weighed strangely heavy in my hands, the weight foreign to anything I'd ever held as a gift. A gift? For me? I'd never had nothin' to do with gifts, not the givin' nor the receivin'. The words echoed in my head, nonsensical against the backdrop of my life. My fingers trembled ever so slightly as I hesitantly reached for them, the anticipation a tight knot in my stomach.

With a reverence I didn't know I possessed, I turned them over in my hands. The rich scent of fine leather hit me first, a luxurious counterpoint to the rough callouses on my hands. The boots gleamed like polished obsidian in the morning light.

A choked sound escaped my throat, a sound that was somewhere between a laugh and a sob.

"I…I never had anything like this before, Mrs. Sinclair," I stammered, my voice thick with emotion.

Mrs. Sinclair beamed at my reaction, her eyes crinklin' at the corners with mirth.

"Glad you like 'em, Eli," she said, her voice warm with affection. "You've earned 'em. Ain't nobody in this town deserves 'em more than you."

I slipped them on right quick, the surge of relief as the fine leather cradled my sore feet, a sight better than the ill-fittin' borrowed boots. It was like they'd been bespoke for me, snug in all the right places, like a second skin.

"They're perfect," I whispered, my voice filled with gratitude.

I thanked her profusely, my chest warmin' at her kindness.

"I'll wear 'em with pride," I promised.

But my mission wasn't over yet. Casually, I cleared my throat and shuffled my feet again, heart thuddin' against my ribs.

"Mrs. Sinclair," I began, hesitantly. "By any chance, do you have any… well, anything a fella might need to impress a special lady?"

Mrs. Sinclair's smile widened even further, if that were possible. My cheeks were lit on fire.

"Ah, love is in the air, is it?" she chuckled. "Well, come on over here, then. Let's see what we can find to win that lady's heart."

With a grin spreading across my face, I followed Mrs. Sinclair deeper into the store, my heart filled with a nervous anticipation. Today, I wouldn't just be leaving with a thank you gift, but hopefully, with something that would mark the beginning of a new life with Emma.

She bustled around the back of the store, returning with a velvet box. Inside, nestled on a bed of white satin, lay an engraved gold band adorned with an oval purple stone. It wasn't flashy, but it radiated a quiet elegance that resonated with me, the deep purple color remindin' me of the fancy dress Emma'd worn to the church social.

"This here," Mrs. Sinclair declared, her voice filled with pride, "is one of a kind. Found it amongst some old stock. Real high quality gold, with an amethyst."

I picked it up, the cool metal smooth against my fingertips. It felt perfect.

"This is it, Mrs. Sinclair," I said, a grin spreading across my face. "This is the one."

Mrs. Sinclair beamed as I counted out the bills. "It catches the light real nice. I always thought it was a beautiful piece," she commented. "Somethin' special for somebody special."

She put it back in the box and wrapped it all up in fancy paper for me. I put it gently in my pocket, trying not to disturb the pretty paper.

"You go bring a smile to that girl's face," she ordered.

"Yes, ma'am," I nodded at her, with a grin, as I stepped outside.

The townsfolk greeted me with nods and smiles as I made my way through town, their words of thanks and praise soundin' like a sweet melody. I was proud to be a part of somethin' bigger than myself, to know that others saw good in me.

As I passed by the orphanage, Emma was playin' with the children in the yard, her laughter fillin' the air like music. My heart swelled with affection at the sight of her, knowin' that she was safe and happy under my watchful eye.

"Morning, Eli," she called out, her voice bright with cheer as she waved me over.

"Mornin', Emma," I replied, a smile playin' at the corners of my mouth as I joined her in the yard.

We spent the rest of the mornin' under the cottonwoods, playin' with the children. Their laughter filled the air like birdsong, and a smile I couldn't quite tame stretched my mouth wide.

I was amazed to be surrounded by such warmth and love, to know that I had found a place where I belonged. When it was time to head into the cool of the schoolroom, I followed Emma like a colt after its mama. Couldn't help it. My eyes kept driftin' back to her as she paused by each child, the low murmur of her voice soothin'. A warmth began to spread through me, like a fire through a bucket of kindlin'.

I helped her peel potatoes for dinner, marvelin' at the way she managed all the different foods at once. Mashin', stirrin', choppin' - she did it all at once, like a whirlwind. The aroma of it all had my mouth waterin' long before she divvied everythin' up and brought it out to the dinner table.

We told stories in the parlor after dinner, each one relatin' what they wanted, the kids with their simple stories. Nantan and the other adults pitched in, relayin' tales from their lives, their history.

I looked around, at the people who made my new life, awe and fear and joy mixin' into somethin' indescribable, almost like I'd guzzled too much ginger ale. As the sun began to sink low in the sky, castin' long shadows across the town, Emma and I bid the children farewell, promisin' to return the next day for more fun and games.

Goyan ran to me for one last hug, and I clutched her to me, revellin' in her simple love. Something rushed up, from deep inside, not a darkness for once, but pure light. I thought beyond just the need to protect her, but a desire to grow, to nurture. I wanted to give her what had been taken from her, a ma and a pa that cherished her.

37

The Man She Deserved

I knew somethin' had changed inside me as I sat outside on that old stump, thinkin' on it. The town was quietin' down for the evenin', the last traces of daylight fadin' away as lanterns flickered to life outside the saloons and general store. The cicadas were pickin' up their banshee hum.

I glanced down at Feather, his dark fur glintin' in the dim light, and couldn't help but feel a swell of gratitude for his constant presence by my side. I figured Nantan had been right, he was somethin' more than an ordinary dog. The best changes in my life had been with him as my partner.

"You got somethin' on your mind, boy?"

Feather let out a low whine, as his ears perked, his tail waggin' in response to my touch. But there was somethin' in his eyes, a trace of somethin' like concern.

"What is it, boy?" I asked, furrowin' my brow in confusion. "You tryin' to tell me somethin'?"

Feather tilted his head to the side, his eyes lockin' onto mine with an intensity that sent a shiver down my spine. It was as if he could sense the turmoil ragin' within me, the questions that had been weighin' heavy on my mind ever since that fateful night. I touched the box still in my pocket.

Lost in thought, I scarcely noticed the figure emergin' from the darkness, Sheriff Alvarez. The man was a shadow. I tensed as I wondered what he'd come to tell me. He'd assured me things were clear, but I still worried.

"Evenin', Eli," he greeted me, his voice gruff but not unkind.

I tipped my hat in return, my eyes meetin' his with both respect and apprehension.

"Evenin', Sheriff," I replied, tryin' to keep my voice steady despite the nerves that churned within me.

Sheriff Alvarez glanced down at Feather, a small smile playin' at the corners of his lips.

"Still stickin' by your side, huh?" he remarked, reachin' out to give Feather a friendly pat.

Feather let out a happy bark, his tail waggin' furiously as he soaked up the attention. I couldn't help but chuckle at the sight, feelin' a swell of affection for my odd companion.

But Sheriff Alvarez's expression grew serious as he turned his attention back to me.

"You're lookin' mighty thoughtful lately," he said, his voice low and measured. "I thought maybe it had somethin' to do with that bounty hunter."

I felt a knot form in my stomach at his words, the memories of my past misdeeds loomin' large in my mind. I decided then I'd go for full honesty, my fingers runnin' over the soft velvet of that ever present box in my pocket.

"I've been feelin' changed since then, Sheriff," I replied, my voice laced with sincerity as I realized what had happened inside me. "I've got regrets, but that life don't hold a lasso on me no more."

Sheriff Alvarez studied me for a moment, his gaze piercin' through me like a knife. But then he nodded, his expression softenin' with understanding.

"We all got things best left dead and buried, Eli," he said quietly. "But what matters is what you do today, and then again tomorrow, and again the next day."

I let out a breath I hadn't realized I was holdin', feelin' a swell of relief wash over me at his words.

"Thank you, Sheriff," I said gratefully, my voice tinged with emotion.

Sheriff Alvarez gave me a nod of acknowledgement before turnin' to leave. As he disappeared into the fadin' light, I couldn't help but feel a sense of gratitude for the second chance I had been given – and a renewed determination to make the most of it.

As I sat there, my thoughts turned to Emma, her smile and laughter fillin' my mind with warmth and light. She had become my anchor in this whirlwind of a world, her presence a constant source of comfort and joy. But she deserved a man with a clean slate, someone worthy of her. I thought, maybe, I could be that man, and maybe, I wouldn't have to do it alone.

I touched the box again, and I knew it was time to seek the counsel of Emma's father, the Senator. He had taken me under his wing since the day I arrived in town, treatin' me like a son despite my troubled past. I found him sittin' on the porch, a glass of whiskey in hand as he watched the sun set in the distance.

"Evenin', Senator," I greeted him, my voice tinged with nervousness as I approached.

He turned to me with a warm smile, his eyes crinklin' at the corners with affection.

"Evenin', Eli," he replied, gesturin' for me to take a seat beside him. "It's a right pretty sunset, isn't it?"

"Yessir," I answered, barely glancing toward the horizon.

I took a deep breath, tensin' for the conversation ahead.

"I wanted to talk to you about Emma."

I managed to keep my voice steady despite the flutter of nerves. The Senator raised an eyebrow in interest, settin' down his glass of whiskey as he turned to face me fully.

"Go on," he prompted, his tone filled with curiosity.

I took a moment to gather my thoughts before continuin', my words spillin' out in a rush.

"I love her, Senator," I said earnestly, meetin' his gaze and hopin' my determination was clear. "And I want to ask for her hand in marriage."

The Senator's eyes widened in surprise, but then a smile spread across his face, his eyes twinklin' with pride.

"Well, I'll be snickered," he laughed, a deep, happy sound. "I thought it'd be months before you'd get the wherewithal to come askin'."

I chuckled nervously at his words, feelin' a swell of relief wash over me that he hadn't outright rejected me. But that was a lot different than acceptin' me. A dead outlaw for a Senator's son-in-law.

"I know I ain't got much to offer her in the way of material wealth," I said, my voice tinged with self-doubt. "And I got a lot of things I could do better. But I promise to love her with all my heart, to protect her and cherish her for the rest of my days."

The Senator placed a hand on my shoulder, his touch warm and reassuring.

"That's all any father could ask for, Eli," he said softly. "Emma's a lucky girl to have found someone like you."

With the Senator's nod of approval tucked into my pocket, I hurried off to find Emma, my boots kickin' up dust as I hurried along, heart poundin' like a stagecoach team.

Feather and I found her in the parlor, bathed in the soft glow of the settin' sun, her nose buried in a book, her dark hair shimmerin' with copper in the light. My chest swelled with excitement and nerves, but I plastered on a grin as wide as the Rio Grande and plopped down beside her, earnin' a surprised gasp as the settee groaned under our combined weight.

"Well, look who it is," she said, her voice as sweet as molasses. "To what do I owe the pleasure of your company, Eli?"

I chuckled, feelin' lighter than a feather in the wind.

"Just thought I'd come by and shoot the breeze with the most beautiful gal in town," I sang, givin' her a playful nudge with my elbow.

She pinked up, eyes twinklin' with pleasure.

"Most beautiful gal in town?" she humphed playfully. "You been looking at all the other girls, Eli?"

My face heated. "Naw, Emma, I wouldn't…"

She laughed, tuckin' a wayward strand of hair behind her ear. My lands, she was angelic. The box in my pocket grew hot and heavy, fillin' my awareness with the desire to time it right.

"Then how do you know I'm the most beautiful? Maybe Helen Humphreys is more beautiful, but you just haven't seen her yet?"

I caught on to her game and grinned wide. "Helen Humphreys, huh?

Where's she live, maybe I'll just go…" I made as if to rise.

"Eli Colton," she scolded, yankin' on my arm to pull me back down. "Don't you dare!"

I laughed, pulled her in to kiss her forehead as if it was a natural thing, for me to have a girl like her to shower affection on.

"Never," I reassured her. "I'll never find someone as beautiful as you, even if I searched the rest of my days."

She blinked up at me, eyes waterin', and I began to backpedal, not knowin' where I stepped wrong.

"I mean…"

She put her finger on my lips.

"No," she breathed. "Don't take it back. It's poetry, is what it is."

I froze, my focus on that single finger, the nearness of her. She studied me for a moment, then smirked.

"Don't worry, I won't tell anyone that tough Eli Colton is a poet at heart."

The air sucked out of my lungs, like I'd been thrown off a bronc.

"I gotta tell you somethin'," I gasped, my hands startin' to shake.

Her eyes widened, mischief quirkin' her mouth.

"Do you, now? What's so important, then?"

"And maybe talk about our future."

I quickfired my words, hopin' to get them out before I lost my nerve. Emma's eyes sparkled with curiosity, her lips quirkin' up into a mischievous grin.

"Our future, huh?" she echoed, settin' her book aside and turnin' to face me fully. "Sounds mighty interestin'. What's on your mind?"

I wrapped every kind word she'd ever said to me, held 'em all to my heart, to fortify myself for what was about to come. I thought she'd agree, but maybe I was mistaken. Maybe she was just bein' kind.

"Well, darlin'," I began, my words slow and deliberate, "I've been thinkin' a lot lately about where I'm headed. And, truth be told, I can't imagine spendin' the rest of my days with anyone else but you."

A blush crept up Emma's cheeks, her eyes widenin' with surprise.

"Eli," she whispered, her voice risin' at the end. "Are y-you saying what I think you're saying?"

I nodded, my heart thuddin' like a herd of cattle on the stampede.

"I reckon I am," I admitted, a nervous grin playin' on my lips. "Emma, I wanna marry you."

A gasp escaped Emma's lips, her hands flyin' to cover her mouth as tears welled up in her eyes. I only had a moment to panic before she threw her arms around me in a fierce hug.

"I've b-been w-waiting for you to say that."

I held her close, breathin' in the scent of her hair, feelin' like the luckiest man alive. Then I realized she hadn't actually said yes.

"So that's a yes?" I asked like an idiot.

She giggled as she sat back to look at me from under her lashes.

"I don't remember you actually askin'."

I tensed, replayin' my words. She was right, I hadn't asked her. What a hare-brain I was becomin'. She laughed at me, her eyes sparklin'.

"Of course it's yes, silly!" she exclaimed, pressin' those soft lips to my cheek.

I noticed then how much I'd been sweatin', like I was sittin' next to a wildfire. Feather nudged at my pocket, insistent, even after I pushed him away. Then I remembered that box.

I hated havin' to push her away so I could stand to get it out of my pocket, but the way her eyes lit up when I brought it out, all wrapped in Mrs. Sinclair's fancy paper, made it worth it. Feelin' grand, I bent to one knee.

"I," I cleared my throat. "I got this for you."

She tore it open, her fingers tremblin' with excitement, carefully openin' the box and exclaimin' as she pulled it out of its silk bed, the purple gem winkin' in the light.

"Oh, Eli!" Her eyes shone brighter than the stone as she put it on, the gold band slidin' on easily, then looked at me.

"It's p-perfect! I love the amethyst!"

She looked at it in delight once more, then bent to hug me, kissin' my cheek. Feather barked in excitement, tail waggin' up a storm as he bounced around us.

My heart near burst with happiness, and I knew I'd never stop tryin' to be the man she deserved. I'd ridden a strange trail, but I'd found my redemption, and love. And as the sun dipped below the horizon, paintin' the sky in hues of pink and gold, I knew that our future was as bright as the stars twinklin' overhead.

Epilogue

The sun began its descent to the horizon of the rugged landscape of Colton, Texas, backed by the small mountain range that seemed like it had been tossed into the desert by a giant. Hues of gold and orange cast the town square in a warm light while a young man, Michael, stood in quiet reverence before a weathered bronze plaque. The inscription upon it chronicled the tale of Eli and Emma Colton, pioneers of the town and founders of the Native American College of Texas.

Its words were in the dry and abbreviated tone of a historical text, outlining the major historical events of their lives. But it lacked any real depth, any taste of the vibrant characters they surely had been. Only a list of names, places, and dates was left to mark their passing.

Michael held a bouquet of wildflowers in his hand,their vibrant colors a stark contrast to the muted tones of the plaque. Each bloom was a silent tribute to the memory of the ancestors he'd never met, but had shaped him from childhood.

His fingers gently traced the engraved words on the plaque, still hot from the afternoon sun, his mind echoing with the stories passed down through generations by his grandfather. The tales spoke of Eli Colton's secret past as an outlaw, his rise to heroism, and his enduring love for Emma, a woman who found the good buried deep in him.

Michael had always been captivated by these stories, a strange mix of pride and a nagging sense of doubt coiling in his gut. Could a man who'd lived such a lawless life truly become the beacon of hope these stories portrayed? How does a man change so completely before he'd turned thirty?

Lost in his contemplation, Michael barely noticed the approach of another visitor. A young woman with dark hair, her eyes holding a warmth that seemed to echo across time, stood beside him. She held a single, delicate white rose in her hand, a silent conversation starter. Beside her, a large, yellow dog wagged its tail enthusiastically, its fur the color of a summer sunset.

"Beautiful flowers," she said softly, her voice like wind chimes tinkling in a summer breeze. The scent of wildflowers and honeysuckle mingled in the air, a sweet counterpoint to the dusty aroma of the town square as the heat rose from the baked concrete.

Michael turned, surprised by the unexpected and attractive company. "Thank you," he replied, his voice tinged with a nervousness he couldn't quite place. "That's a lovely rose," he responded. Then remembering the manners that had been drilled into him his entire life, he quickly juggled the flowers to hold his hand out politely. "I'm Michael Colton," he laughed a little too loud to his ears. "Eli & Emma were my, let's see, three times great grandparents."

"Goyan," she returned, with her own hand soft in his, offering a smile that held a hint of familiarity. "These stories…" she trailed off, gesturing towards the plaque, "they're a big part of our family history too."

Intrigued, Michael raised an eyebrow. "Really? How so?"

Goyan's smile deepened. "My name… well, it's not exactly common. It was passed down from my great-great-grandmother, who knew Eli Colton quite well."

A jolt of recognition shot through Michael. Goyan. Eli's adopted daughter, the Native American girl he had rescued. Could this Goyan be her descendant?

And the strangest thing was, the dog's ear, nicked at some point, mirrored a detail from the stories of Eli's own dog, whose ear had also been injured during the fight to save Emma. Surely that was a coincidence, not the same dog? That was a crazy concept, right? He felt a shift inside him that had him reaching again toward the plaque, this time to steady himself.

"G-Goyan, the girl he adopted?" he stuttered, shaking his head inwardly. He rarely stuttered anymore, not since he'd become an adult.

She smiled and nodded, her dark eyes sparkling attractively.

The conversation flowed easily after that, filled with shared stories and laughter that echoed across the town square. As they talked, the weight of his family history pressed down on Michael. He shared his doubts about Eli's past, the dissonance between the outlaw and the hero. Goyan listened patiently, her hand resting on the dog's head, its tail thumping a steady rhythm against the dusty ground.

"Maybe the story isn't black and white," she offered gently. "Maybe even outlaws can change. Maybe Eli's love for Emma, his desire to do better, was the spark that redeemed him."

Michael pondered her words, a seed of hope taking root within him. If even a violent criminal like Will Carter could change into a community pillar such as Eli Colton, then perhaps he could also strive to better himself.

The future stretched before them, an open book waiting to be written. Goyan's eyes sparkled with a newfound excitement.

"You know," she said, "I have a small collection of things that belonged to Eli and Emma – letters, journals, even a few trinkets. Would you be interested in seeing them sometime?"

A thrill shot through Michael. A chance to delve deeper into his family history, perhaps even understand Eli on a more personal level? Not to mention more time with this beautiful young woman?

"Absolutely," he replied, his voice filled with enthusiasm. "Thank you, Goyan. I... I'd really like that. I have some things I could share as well. I have their wedding ring, a beautiful amethyst."

"Oh," she responded with delight. "I'd love to see that."

As they walked away from the plaque, the town square bathed in the warm glow of the setting sun, a new chapter seemed to be unfolding. The legacy of Eli and Emma lived on, not just in stone and bronze, but in the connection forged between two descendants, bound by a shared past and a future filled with possibility.

You made it to the gallows…and beyond!

If you enjoyed the story, please consider leaving a review – it means the world to indie authors like me!

Thanks for joining Eli and Emma on their wild ride! Even my parents got a kick out of the first part, published as "Lazarus Curse" (bless them!). Watching Eli's journey from darkness to light was as thrilling for me to write as it is, I hope, for you to experience.

This tale began years ago, sparked by Ambrose Bierce's "Occurrence at Owl Creek Bridge." The story wouldn't stay buried, and I loved watching Eli rise to the occasion and Emma grapple with her complexities.

This might not be the final soul's journey…

Doc's dry wit and sharp mind quickly stole a piece of my heart (and I suspect yours too!). He's a character who deserves a happy ending. In the next book brewing in my mind, he might just find himself on a dusty trail alongside Susanna, a widow with a dark secret of her own.

Stay tuned!

About the Author

By day, Christine Tellach crafts words as a speech-language pathologist, guiding young minds on their communication journeys. But when the pen takes hold, she transforms into a weaver of fantastical tales.

Christine is a storyteller who explores a variety of genres, her imagination a boundless playground fueled by a childhood spent devouring every book she could find. Currently, she's working on another thrilling gothic western, while fresh stories simmer on the back burner: a sci-fi romance ignited by a Bermuda Triangle crash and an alternate history whispering with possibility.

Life on her rural farm provides a vibrant backdrop to her creativity. Inspiration strikes Christine like a bolt of lightning – a heartwarming client moment, a hilarious encounter with her family, or simply getting lost in a captivating book. These sparks ignite her imagination, transforming into captivating tales that defy genre and expectation.

So, grab your reading compass, bookworms! Christine's world is a thrilling adventure, and she's eager to share it with you. Stay tuned for updates on upcoming releases, and follow her social media channels for a peek into her writing escapades.

You can connect with me on:

🌐 https://linktr.ee/ChristineTellach

f https://www.facebook.com/profile.php?id=61558204403047

Also by Christine Tellach

It's Just the Way I Talk: Facts About Stuttering for Kids 5-8
Children who Stutter ages 5-8 can find support and confidence in "It's Just the Way I Talk." This heartwarming book offers clear explanations, coping strategies, and a guide for parents and educators.

By Jennifer Tillock, M.S. CCC-SLP

Unspoken Volumes: Writing Characters with Communication Challenges
Write Characters Who Shine, Not Stereotypes: Tired of clichéd portrayals of communication challenges? **Unspoken Volumes** equips you to craft characters with stuttering, Apraxia, and more, who leap off the page with depth and inspire compassion. Packed with SLP insights, exercises, and practical tools, this guide helps you write authentic characters with rich inner lives who defy stereotypes.

By Jennifer Tillock, M.S. CCC-SLP

Talk It Out, Work It Out! A Safety & Self-Advocacy Workbook for Ages 8+
This engaging resource, developed by an experienced speech-language pathologist, goes beyond just scenarios. Kids ages 8-12 & 12-18 tackle real-life situations (like medical issues, bullying, and even traffic stops) through discussions and role-playing.

By Jennifer Tillock, M.S. CCC-SLP